PINK GLASS HOUSES

Go Sunset Seagulls !

Asha

PINK
GLASS
HOUSES

a novel

ASHA ELIAS

wm

WILLIAM MORROW

An Imprint of HarperCollinsPublishers

HarperCollins books may be purchased for educational, business, or sales promotional use. For information, please email the Special Markets Department at SPsales@harpercollins.com.

FIRST EDITION

Designed by Elina Cohen
Title page art courtesy of Shutterstock / Renat Murtaev

Library of Congress Cataloging-in-Publication Data

Names: Elias, Asha, author.
Title: Pink glass houses : a novel / Asha Elias.
Description: First edition. | New York, NY : William Morrow, 2024.
Identifiers: LCCN 2023009667 | ISBN 9780063312791 (hardcover) | ISBN
    9780063312814 (ebook)
Subjects: LCGFT: Thrillers (Fiction) | Novels.
Classification: LCC PS3605.L387 P56 2024 | DDC 813/.6--dc23/eng/20230606
LC record available at https://lccn.loc.gov/2023009667

ISBN 978-0-06-331279-1 (hardcover)
ISBN 978-0-06-339624-1 (international edition)

24 25 26 27 28 LBC 5 4 3 2 1

FOR INDIA AND JJ

From: Gabriela Machado
May 13, 2019
To: All Sunset Academy
Subject: A Message from the Sunset Academy PTA President

Dear Parents,

I'm writing to you as a follow-up to Principal Ileana Garcia's email. I assume you are all aware of this morning's tragic event that occurred at our neighboring school, Miami Beach Middle. We are enormously relieved that none of our precious children were harmed.

The Sunset Academy PTA wants you all to know that our thoughts and prayers are with the family of the deceased, and with our entire community, as we are all grieving.

I also want to assure you that both schools went on lockdown before the tragedy would have been visible to any students who happened to be outside. The Miami Beach Police Department arrived on the scene moments after the incident and were quick and discreet in roping off the area.

I've spoken with Principal Garcia, and our administration has arranged for grief counselors to be available to all students and faculty, beginning tomorrow morning.

It has been a dark day for our community, but together we will get through this.

In the meantime, we encourage you to speak with your children about what happened in an age-appropriate manner. We are working with the school administration, law enforcement, and several mental health professionals to come up with a toolkit for each of you to have meaningful family discussions. Some of those resources are already available in our shared Dropbox, which can be accessed here:

GriefToolkit_SunsetAcademy

Please do not hesitate to reach out to me with any questions. Be safe, be well, and Go Sunset Seagulls.

All my best,
Gabriela
Gabriela Machado
Sunset Academy PTA President

CHARLOTTE

There are three types of moms at Sunset Academy: the know-nothings, the think-they-knows, and the ones who get shit done. Me? I'm one of the rare birds that make up the latter. I mean, some of these moms don't even know their kid's teacher's name. Can you imagine? Try hitting up that kind with a contribution for the holiday gift. Scratching. My. Damn. Head. I mean, here we are at the best public elementary school in Florida, and these empty brains can't even pick their child's classroom out on a school map. How do you think Sunset became number one? I'll tell you how. It's because we have the most active fundraising machine of a PTA east of the Mississippi. But if I'm being honest, the dumb-dumbs aren't even the biggest problem. It's those god-awful think-they-knows. The "oh I'd love to be co–room mom with you, Charlotte," and then can't even design and fabricate a fucking door decoration ones. I know I sound triggered right now, but you wouldn't believe the flak I get from some of these moms, and after all the work I put into this place. But they still act like, just because my *work* isn't in an office, it must be easy? Excuse me if I don't have a W-2! And, by the way, a job isn't an excuse for not being active in your children's lives. Just saying.

I'm excited to see what this school year has in store for us, though. I have plans, plans, plans! Taking Sunset to the next level, and all that. It's my last year as VP of fundraising, and there's a lot of pressure on me to keep outdoing myself. Things are great, as I said, but there is always room for improvement. If no one gets in my way, I predict another record breaker.

Miami is competitive. Like New York competitive, but less angry and more tan. Trade black tailoring for brightly colored miniskirts, and you get the idea. So I started planning Sunset Academy's fundraising initiatives for this school year back in June. Everyone else was hopping into the D terminal at Miami International and boarding a plane to Mallorca or Capri, and I was posted up at Panther Coffee with a cold brew, my laptop, and a prospect list. Donors are hit up relentlessly from September to December, but if you catch them early enough, before the vultures start picking at the carcasses of those family foundations and grants, you can pull in so much more cash.

I wouldn't say that fundraising is my calling; my calling is motherhood. But I'm good at raising money and it gives me a platform to help with my children's education. And it's not like my family has the time to just flit away for six weeks, anyway. My husband, James, has always said, "Babe, all these people spending the whole summer away? They aren't focused on daily market volatility."

To which I say, "Fine with me! I have work to do, too." He always rolls his eyes at me when I call fundraising *work*, and isn't that just typical for a finance guy? If it doesn't inflate your own bank account, it must not be a worthy use of time!

But at least we are on the same page about getting a late start to summer vacation. The kids went to day camp for the first few weeks, and James got all those extra days in the office. A good investment banker doesn't come with a pause button, but that's probably why I married him! Well, that and because he "Miami Viced" me on our first date way back when. You know that move? It's when you're driving over the causeway in a convertible, and as you pass over the sparkling Biscayne Bay, the guy puts the top down and starts blasting Phil Collins's "In the Air Tonight." James had game.

So to kick off the summer, I closed as many deals as possible (hello

Walker Family Foundation! Check your grant request!) and *then* we peaced out on Miami until the beginning of August. A small sacrifice in service to a school that is a true gem in the community.

We spent three weeks traveling in Sardinia and Capri, sunning ourselves along the rocky beaches and eating the most incredible fresh pastas. Little Madeline got so bronzed that we all started calling her golden girl. And isn't that just fitting? Even Axel soaked up the Italian lifestyle, which is saying a lot. You know how these adolescent boys can be, and he really nails the moody, hormonal thing. I was actually so proud. He added a little color to his pastiness (that's what happens when you don't have PlayStation at the hotel). And he loved, I mean *loved*, the food. He clearly shares my enthusiasm for a good meal, though I rarely let myself indulge. But it's all so good and clean there, and Ax and I would both literally lick our pasta bowls clean after every dinner, much to the disgust of Maddy and my husband. Even James relaxed a bit. He worked for only, like, three to four hours per day. It was the perfect family vacation.

By the time we touched back down at MIA, my inbox was exploding with requests. Every family at Sunset wanted me to plan an event for their *super cool* local business in return for a meager percentage of sales back to the school. Umm, no thanks. I'm raising money for Sunset Academy, not your family's pizza restaurant. But also, my girlfriend slash PTA president, Gabriela, was begging for my Back-to-School PowerPoint slides.

Back-to-School Night is like the social kickoff to the school year, when all the students and parents get together to hear about bell schedules and fundraisers and dress codes and all that. So, that was on deck in a couple weeks and I had to be ready to present. It's not easy to step onstage in front of a thousand Miami Beach families and deliver my spiel for the year, especially when some of those families (and I mean a small minority, and I mean clearly the losers) are absolute haters. I could raise a billion dollars and have Bill Gates himself give a kindergarten commencement speech and some people would still be all "but you used plastic cups at the post–Bill Gates commencement reception and don't you know how bad that is?"

I know. Why on earth would I slog away for no money and deal with all this whining from the peanut gallery? Well, what wouldn't I do for Madeline Rose? My sugar-and-spice, cooler-than-ice, perfection-in-motion little Maddy? She's my forever "why." If that girl asked me to hang the moon over her four-poster bed, I'd call Elon Musk and say, "Get me on the next SpaceX mission pronto."

In the meantime, I'm content to bust my butt for her school with my fundraising initiatives, as their gala chair, Safety Council founding member, and, ahem, room mom of the year. My events have raised 300 percent more than what my predecessors scrounged together. And that, my friends, is how you give your daughter the best education in the U.S. of A. My efforts alone have resulted in resurfacing the entire basketball court, installing a state-of-the-art STEM lab, a daily organic salad bar in the cafeteria, cutting-edge online reading and math supplements, and completely new instruments for the music room. And now that my little angel is going into the third grade, you better believe I'm kicking things up a notch.

This is the year of statewide standardized tests! We need be up on our p's and q's. Test scores equal funding, funding supports our reputation, our reputation gets us into the best middle school, the right middle school feeds into the most competitive high schools, and before you know it . . . *boom*, Harvard. You think I'm joking, but this is very serious. Nothing is guaranteed, of course, but future success in children is dependent on taking early action and following a bulletproof plan toward advancement.

I wish my parents would have been this methodical with my own education. Sure, I was studious and hardworking and kept a breakneck extracurricular schedule, but there was no *strategy* to it all. The Ivys are looking for excellence these days, not some no-name B-rated school salutatorian from the burbs with a JV cheer career. Public schools, the *right* public schools to be exact, are very in favor right now. Yes, by high school you really need to be in an elite private, but first it's preferable to come up with the masses. The *right* masses. And that's why we're at Sunset.

Just this morning, Maddy told me, "Mommy, you're the MVP of this school and everyone knows it. You should run for president."

And you know what? She's right. Why am I slogging away making everything happen for this place when the PTA president gets all the glory? I mean, I'm doing all this work for the benefit of the kids, but come on. Even Mother Teresa got to be on the covers of magazines. They made her a saint, for Christ's sake! And I'm not going to wait until I'm dead to get what I'm due.

I told James, "I think I'm going to run to be PTA president next year. It's a two-year position and after that Maddy will be in middle school. We need to leave Sunset with a bang!"

He said, "That job is a sucker's bet. Why are you going to work like a whipped dog for no pay? And who is going to manage things here at home while you're off being the Sunset Academy Mother Teresa?"

Major eye roll, I know. I said, "Umm, the housekeeper, obviously. And don't you want me to make a difference in our daughter's school? For her education?"

But he was already back to checking his email at that point and, I swear, I could run, win, and serve as PTA president and he would not even notice.

MELODY

We were in the wrong place. We had to be. We pulled into the Sunset Academy parking lot for Back-to-School Night and I double-checked the address on Google Maps. I mean, it was the same building where we had registered Lucy just days earlier, the school name was affixed to the entrance, but this wasn't an elementary school event. It just couldn't have been. Stepping out of the rows of fancy cars were the oddest families I'd ever seen. Moms were wearing denim cutoffs—short denim cuttoffs, like, their butts were hanging out. Daisy Dukes we used to call them. These were paired with high heels and pussy bow blouses. The dads were in loud button-up shirts and used an alarming amount of hair gel. The small children kept walking into people because they (and everyone!) had their faces glued to their cell phones.

I bit my tongue but gave Greg some major side-eye. Couldn't he have gotten a promotion to relocate literally anywhere else?

It was all wildly confusing. But Back-to-School Night was our introduction to Lucy's new school, and a swan dive, as it turned out, into Miami culture. The shock was immediate. It seemed like we'd slipped into a parallel universe where moms dressed and talked like teenagers, and elementary school kids also dressed and talked like teenagers, and everyone drove Maseratis and Porsches, and had professional hair and makeup done for an event that takes place at five P.M. on a Monday.

And this is at a *public* elementary school! Miami Beach is definitely not Wichita.

Weeks earlier, we had found our new home. A charming 1930s art deco house painted cotton candy pink. It was located in Miami Beach's Pine Tree neighborhood, which several of Greg's coworkers had told us was perfect for families. With its cozy two bedrooms, the new place was much smaller than our Wichita home, but it had won us over right away with the tidy pair of sabal palm trees that flanked the front door and, the pièce de résistance, an oblong backyard pool. On moving day, Lucy ditched Greg and me with the moving van and dove into the deep end, fully clothed, staying in the water until well after the boxes had been unloaded.

The Pine Tree house, adorable and homey as it was, also came with a rent that made our Wichita mortgage look like a grocery bill. We were used to sprawling lots of land and grand homes. In Miami Beach, which is locally referred to simply as "the Beach," the houses were stacked on top of one another, even in the most desirable neighborhoods. Lot lines overlapping lot lines. Here, a three-thousand-square-foot home like the one we had in Wichita was considered almost luxurious. Sticker shock aside, Greg had received a significant pay bump with his promotion, and, as an added bonus, the house happened to be zoned for the number-one-rated public elementary school in the state of Florida, which also had a top-notch gifted program. So, it was settled. We signed the lease on the house with the pool and Lucy enrolled in the third grade at Sunset Academy.

On Back-to-School Night, Lucy tried on every piece of clothing in her closet. She settled on her favorite seersucker overalls with leather strap sandals. "It's a new chapter!" Greg teased. "I'm sure all these Miami kids are going to love meeting a down-home Kansas girl."

Greg could have eaten those words as we pulled into the Sunset parking lot. "What is this, an exotic car show?" he said as we squeezed our old Nissan SUV between a Maserati and Porsche.

"Don't say it," I warned.

"I don't think we're in Kansas anymore," he said.

He earned a serious *oh, come on* look with that one. I thumped his ribs. Lucy covered her eyes and slumped down into her seat. "Please, no Dad jokes, not today."

It got worse from there. We huddled wide-eyed in the packed auditorium for the official Back-to-School presentation, where the seats were filled with the fanciest people I'd ever seen: sequined jackets, designer sneakers, logo T-shirts, all of them entranced with their phones. And that was just the kids. It was like walking into a Las Vegas nightclub, if for some reason that nightclub allowed children.

"Welcome back, Sunset Seagulls!" a perky voice boomed from the stage. "And welcome to our new families." The speaker introduced herself as Gabriela Machado, proud fifth-grade parent and *your* PTA president.

Gabriela was a statuesque brunette, with perfectly beach-waved shoulder-length hair. She wore an army green romper that was cinched at her impossibly tiny waist and cut short to reveal a mile of tanned legs. Were jeans and a white T-shirt the wrong choice for this event? Why would I even care about how I looked at my daughter's school orientation? I felt suddenly conspicuous, like I'd stumbled into a men's bathroom and all the urinals were full.

The PTA president presented some slides introducing the board of directors, all of whom had professional headshots, and some accolades and accomplishments from the last school year. Tame, housekeeping things, and I relaxed a little. Then she faced the audience with a wide smile.

"Sunset parents!" she said. "Don't forget that this is an election year. Yes, I'll be leaving you next fall to take my Bella to Beach Middle." A weird coo of *awww* came from the first two rows. "But fear not," Gabriela continued, "because I know you will elect a replacement who will take Sunset into the next era! So tell me, which one of you is going to be our next PTA president?"

Half of the crowd erupted in cheers, while the rest sat with their arms crossed, looking bored but not as surprised as I was. Random names were called out, but none that I could catch.

It was hard to imagine that anyone would need to run an election for PTA president. At Lucy's old school, that role went to any sad sap who was unfortunate enough to say yes. It was basically an unpaid full-time job. I had always been quite active in the PTA, but president was a sucker's bet.

"And now," Gabriela announced, "make some noise for our own fundraiser extraordinaire, Charlotte Giordani!"

Make some noise?

Volunteers seemed to be de facto celebrities at Sunset Academy. Applause filled the room. That should have been the most ridiculous thing to happen all night, but the fun was just getting started.

"Hello hello, Seagulls! How are the best and most generous parents and kiddos in all of Miami doing tonight?" More applause.

Charlotte Giordani worked the stage like a professional auctioneer, her petite stature augmented with sky-high platforms. She was wearing what had to have been marketed as underwear: a lacy black camisole that not so subtly highlighted her can't-be-natural cleavage and high-waisted black shorts. Her long chestnut hair cascaded halfway down her back in a delicate sway as she turned around to point to her first slide in the Back-to-School PowerPoint. I swear, it seemed like everyone in this town was drop-dead gorgeous.

I pinched Greg on the arm, and he shot back with a boyish *I didn't say anything!* look.

This was when I started questioning why we had left a perfectly sweet, stable, and sane existence in Kansas for something utterly foreign. I couldn't picture my place in this glitzy world, and worse, couldn't imagine how my small-town Lucy would blend in. I mean, there was a girl in the front row with a Gucci phone case. It didn't seem like she would be playing Candy Land with my daughter.

Charlotte flipped to the slide outlining PTA fundraising events for the year and I settled. The events seemed familiar enough: Parents'

Night Out, Halloween Costume Parade, Fourth- and Fifth-Grade Dance. Then I stifled a laugh. "Sunset Moms' Bikini Car Wash?" I whispered under my breath.

"You're new here." A woman next to me leaned closer with a conspiratorial wink.

"Is it that obvious?" I asked. "I'm sorry but is this a joke? Bikini car wash for moms?"

"Oh, it's real, so very real. They all think they're Gisele"—she waved in the direction of the stage—"bouncing back from each pregnancy to walk the Victoria's Secret runway. And taking half-naked selfies for their Instagram pages. Don't worry. We aren't all like that."

And that's how I met Darcy.

Darcy Resnick was a Miami native, an unusual status I came to learn. Most people in town were like me, transplanted from somewhere else at some point. The difference between the other settlers and me was that they had already assimilated, or at least possessed the secret code to blending in that I hadn't yet received. Darcy, by contrast, was both local and foreign. She had been born in Miami Beach but refused to submit to its cultural stereotypes. "Stilettos at a school function make about as much sense as a thong bikini in synagogue," she said after the PTA presentation. I liked her immediately.

DARCY

It was wrong. It was terribly wrong. This was a Back-to-School Night, not a live auction at a charity gala. This was an opportunity to greet new parents at their friendly neighborhood school and welcome back returning students. Instead, Charlotte Giordani and her cronies ostracized around 95 percent of Sunset families. How many people have the money or desire to toss out tens of thousands of dollars at a *PTA meeting*? Unfortunately, most of the parents put off by this don't have the time or interest to be *that* involved and actually speak up. (Myself included.) The whole thing was just so cringe.

Gabriela, our current PTA president, teed up the circus act as if welcoming the parents into her big top of curiosities. Jumpsuit and clown makeup and a dancing "ta-da!" to introduce the queen of the inappropriate, our very own Charlotte Giordani. The self-styled fundraiser extraordinaire jumped through hoops like a trained lion to the tune of "Ten thousand! Five thousand! One thousand!" Until, triumphant, she relinquished the microphone to Principal Garcia so we could switch gears to the school dress code and how to access lunch menus. Give me a break.

Miami Beach is a microcosm of everything that is wrong with this country right now. The insane disparity between the haves and have-nots, put on display in an auditorium for our children to witness and conclude to which side of the aisle they belong. Sadly, Sunset Academy is really two schools in one. An affluent *gifted* school and a working-class *regular* school.

Did you know that 50 percent of Sunset Academy is in the gifted program? Isn't it incredible that half of the children in Miami Beach have tested into a group that statistically represents the highest 2 percent of IQs? So, essentially half of the school paid for their kids to be tested into gifted, and the other half? Well, they didn't, and their kids are in a program called *general education*. If anyone out there still believes that socioeconomic status, aka insane parental meddling and throwing money at the problem, doesn't exist in public education, I invite you to visit our gleaming white schoolhouse.

Charlotte and her PTA mafia think they are so progressive for sending their kids to public school, as though we should all bow down and thank them for lowering themselves to our level, to allow their children to be educated in the same building as ours.

When I was growing up, school was where your parents dropped you off in the morning (if you didn't ride the bus), maybe picked you up in the afternoon, and asked about your homework. That's it. They didn't march into the principal's office when little Johnny came home with a bruise on his knee from the playground or raise hell to the school board if their kid got a C in first-grade Language Arts. Did you know that Charlotte got a teacher fired last year? Well, *reassigned to another school,* after a well-placed phone call no doubt. It was because the poor teacher sent Patricia Walker's son Maddox to the principal's office . . . for throwing a book at another child's head. (My child's.)

Not only are these moms managing to helicopter their kids while in the classroom, they're also strong-arming all the parents into incessant social fundraising get-togethers. The Be a Kid Again Gala, another one of Charlotte's innovations, is a new event where parents can dress up in their sparkling finery and bid on wholesome items such as "Botox for a Year," "At-Home Exotic Dance Lessons," and "Boudoir Photo Shoots." Okay, that last one does sound like fun, but my point is, this is all insane.

At last year's gala, half the parents got so drunk that the fifth-grade bathroom sinks became clogged with vomit. Patricia slipped on a broken wineglass and writhed helplessly on the floor while her husband, Don, was engrossed in apparently the most amusing conversation ever with Charlotte. Of course, the Walkers had just committed to underwriting the entire cost of the new basketball court, which meant that Charlotte was just tickled with the man of the hour. Way to set an example.

Back-to-School Night was a reminder that it starts all over again, every year. Kicked off with a spectacle for our wealthiest parents while the rest of us waited, meek and unimportant.

After the horror show, I stayed for a little bit of the social hour. It was my opportunity to meet Jackson's new teacher, who was wonderful, by the way, a reminder of why we stay at Sunset—and I felt obliged to give a tour to a lovely new family, the Howards. It can be so intimidating for newbies to step into this world. Coming from pretty much anywhere else, Miami Beach can feel like Mars. *Literally,* as everyone is so fond of saying here. *Literally* like Mars.

The sweet new family was straight out of Kansas, not our typical New York tax escapees. They brought with them a refreshing Midwestern charm. The mom, Melody, looked like the type to bring apple pie to a new neighbor. I liked her instantly.

It turned out that her daughter was going to be in the same class as my Jackson (yes, a gifted one, and yes, that makes me sound like a hypocrite), so I showed her the classroom, a nice open first-floor location with windows that opened to the upper elementary playground, and pointed out the front office, the clinic, the library. Not that I'm the best tour guide at Sunset; truth be told, I step on campus only a handful of times a year. First day of school, a token special event or two, last day of school. I don't have the luxury of spending time at Jackson's school during the workday and have zero desire to fraternize with the parents that do. Not because they don't work, but because they're all Charlotte Giordani carbon copies, and, just, no thanks.

I pointed Sunset's notorious cast of characters out to Melody, while her husband and daughter grabbed muffins from the concession table.

"There's Charlotte over there, with her head firmly implanted inside Don and Patricia Walkers' backsides. She has the personality of a stinkbug and will probably find a way to make your life miserable."

Melody laughed, but I suspect she was surprised by my bluntness.

I continued. "Don and Patricia are very wealthy and like to make sure we all know it."

"I noticed that they made a very . . . umm . . . significant contribution to the school tonight," Melody said, between sips of lemonade.

"And they're thrilled that you've noticed," I responded. "Don't worry. I'm sure you'll get to know them well, when Don invites you to invest in his fund."

Melody kept it classy. "Well, it's very impressive to see what an active PTA the school has. At our old school, it was just a handful of us gluttons for punishment who did all the work."

"Oh, here it's a status symbol," I told her. "A stupid one, at that."

I can't say exactly why this certain group of women covet the PTA roles so fiercely. Perhaps because they lack power at home? Or just general unfulfillment? I mean, some of these women have MBAs and PhDs, yet they're staying at home all day watching *Dr. Phil* and crafting sock puppets for first-grade Social Studies lessons. I'm getting too Freudian about it. They like to act more important than the rest of us. I think it's just that. They are on a first-name basis with the principal and probably get a say on who their kid's teacher will be next year. It all just seems a little desperate to me.

CHARLOTTE

Back-to-School Night was a huge success. I know it's not technically supposed to be a fundraiser—welcome back to Sunset and all that—but let's just say I saw an opportunity. After I finished my presentation on last year's events and numbers, I challenged the parents and said, "Now who thinks we can out-raise those snooty private schools? Public does not mean cheap!" I knew that would get them going. Some of our parents are so sensitive about the public/private thing. It's about the education, people! Anyway, I said it and people went nuts. So I threw out a number. "Who here can commit twenty thousand dollars to the Sunset Academy PTA?"

Some of those dumb blank faces I could have slapped right there and then. Good old Darcy Resnick was locked into her standard resting bitch face, as if she has ever lifted a finger to try to make this a better place for our kids. Listen, not everyone has the money and I get that. But don't be offended when someone else does!

So then Patricia Walker makes eye contact and I knew it was on. Sunset Academy's very own Princess Di. I just love her. She raised her hand, and I pointed to her and said, "Ladies and gentlemen, Patricia and Don Walker are committed to your kids. Thank you, Walker family! Now, who can show how much they love Sunset Academy with a ten-thousand-dollar contribution?" And so on and so forth until I got all the way down to $100. By the end of the night, I'd collected

$77,000 in commitments. I think we can sacrifice a couple offended parents for that.

After the official program was over, I thanked the Walkers, once again, for their tremendous generosity. They've done extremely well in business and, I swear, sometimes it feels like the Giordanis are the only family in town who hasn't invested with them. But you know my husband. He wants to be the only finance genius in the room and invests where he wants. Too bad he doesn't seem to have Walker's Midas touch, though he does well enough.

Don, the husband, gave me the sweetest hug and said, "Anything for the kids, Char. If we can't give back, then what's all this even for?" He waved his hands above his glorious Ken-doll head, and I can only assume *all this* meant their jewels and fancy cars and luxury homes, and not the breezeway of the public elementary school auditorium (though they did pay for that, too). "We've been so blessed, it's our duty to help," he added.

"So blessed," Patricia agreed, and put a hand on my shoulder. Do you know how hard it is to not turn your head and stare when an eight-carat oval is right next to your head? I kept my eyes on hers.

"And we are so blessed to have your support," I said to Patricia. Wasn't that the understatement of the year? This couple is our bread and butter.

Then there were the other donors to tend to. A fundraiser's work is never done! I swear, all these people who claim to donate *for the kids* wouldn't part with a penny unless it came with effusive praise and copious ass-kissing.

I made the rounds, cheersing paper cups of lemonade with the Vogel automobile dealership couple (always good for a gala sponsorship) and passing gluten-free/sugar-free cookies to a second-grade couple, two gay dads, whom I've been cultivating for the past year. Apparently one of the dads is the heir to some kind of textile fortune.

"Where's your better half?" the textile heir asked me, cookie crumbs hanging from his five-o'clock shadow.

My husband is more or less a mythical creature at school events. Like the tooth fairy. You don't see him, but someone put the $20 bill under your pillow! But god, it's so annoying that people have to always ask about him.

"Oh, James would sooner wear a tutu to a Dolphins game than show his face at a school function," I teased.

"Now that's something I'd pay to see," the heir's husband quipped, bro-slapping his partner on the back.

And I was thinking . . . *for the right contribution . . .*

Interview Transcript with Patricia Walker

For profile in *Magic City* magazine, summer issue 2019
By Andres Castano
August 18, 2018, Session 1

INTERVIEWER: Thank you so much for sitting with me today, Patricia. *Magic City* is looking forward to spending time with you over the next nine months to discuss the impact you and Don have made on this community. This will be the key feature in our annual Philanthropic Edition. The depth and scope of the Walker Family Foundation's contributions certainly warrants special recognition. First off, do you mind if I record our interviews?

PATRICIA: Please, go ahead. Don and I are honored that you've chosen us for such a prestigious feature. Of course, the charitable work we do in the community . . . we do it because we believe in giving back. We have been so blessed in life, and it is our mission to uplift those who haven't had the same opportunities.

INTERVIEWER: Well, all of Miami owes you a debt of gratitude for your tireless service. May I ask, how did you and Don become involved in local philanthropy? Have you always seen this as your life's calling?

PATRICIA: No, no, no, quite the opposite. I came from humble beginnings and Donald was pretty much the same. Our focus in the beginning was purely to build the business and create a good life for our family. We never imagined how successful Walker Equities would become. Don and I are living examples of the American dream. If you are smart, educate yourself, and work hard, nothing will hold you back. No excuses. We quickly got to a point where we had more than we ever needed, and we looked around and said, Okay . . . it's time to pay it forward. How can we find the next Don and Patricia Walker and give them the opportunity to shine? How can we put a smile on an unhoused little girl or boy's face? And the more we gave, the more need we saw. So, we started the foundation as a vehicle to support all these worthy causes that needed our help.

INTERVIEWER: So generous. Can you name a couple of organizations that are particularly meaningful to you?

PATRICIA: Oh, that's a hard one, because we feel deeply connected to each and every charity we support. The Samson Homeless Shelter is certainly near and dear to my heart. They house a community that has nothing and helps them get back on their feet with honest employment and affordable housing. You should take a tour and see those faces. So deserving and grateful. About half of the residents are kids, which is heartbreaking. So yes, the support we give to Samson is a great source of pride.

We also give quite a bit to our boys' elementary. They are in a public school; it's one way we keep them grounded. We love to support the school however we can, and you know how it is, they really need it. Don and I want all of the children at Sunset Academy to have access to the best possible education, not just Maddox and Monrow.

INTERVIEWER: Tell me more about the boys. How hard is it to keep them grounded, as you say, when they have such accomplished parents?

PATRICIA: Oh, well, they are exposed to all types of people at Sunset. That's one way. They aren't surrounded only by privilege all day at school, which gives such great perspective. They also see how hard people have to work for a living, how it doesn't come easy. Take Lucca, for example, he's our personal trainer. Well, now he's only *Don's* personal trainer, because those two are like frat boys when they get together. Too much testosterone for my taste. Anyway, Lucca is part of the family. He comes over for dinners, events, even vacations. And the boys see that he works extremely hard. Started his own training business. It's admirable. He doesn't have what we have, but he just works so hard. Our sons understand what a special situation we are in, and how that's not easy to come by.

MELODY

Greg and I were high school sweethearts. We both grew up in Wichita, lived there our whole lives. We were the homecoming king and queen, grew up and bought a house two blocks from where my parents lived. People called us the golden couple, which was silly, but also I guess it was kind of true.

Then we left it all. We packed up and moved to Miami, where we knew no one. It will be fine, I told myself. We'll make new friends. As if making friends was ever anything I'd had to do in my whole life. The last time I made a new friend I was younger than Lucy.

"I can't believe *you* two are leaving," Gail, my childhood best friend, had said. It was one of our last weeks in Kansas, and Lucy's school was hosting an end-of-year movie night. The whole student body had gathered to watch *Moana* outside on the PE field, one last moment together before scattering to various camps and beach vacations for the summer. I felt so warm, watching Lucy and her friends chase one another in circles around the basketball court in an epic game of freeze tag, turning into sweaty statues when they got caught.

Gail and I had volunteered to serve pizza and lemonade behind the running track. The evening was that perfect Midwest moment, early summer when the sun warms your bare shoulders but the dry breeze keeps you from getting clammy. The event, Wichita Elementary's Farewell for Now, was a treasured tradition, but so bittersweet this time around since it would be our last.

"I just can't believe this is the last time she'll ever be here, and with these kids," I said, watching Lucy tackle her best friend a little too hard. The two eight-year-olds tumbled onto the asphalt. I braced for bruised knees and tears, but they popped right up, giggling in each other's arms.

"Look at them. She's been best friends with Ruthie since they were in diapers," I said, filling a batch of lemonade cups.

"You're moving to Florida, not outer space," Gail replied. "They'll always be friends! You will make sure of it. But this town is really not going to be the same without you guys."

I had plenty of friends growing up who had moved away for various reasons: divorces, new jobs, wanderlust. If they did return to visit, we never just picked up where we left off. Those people had left town, and they may as well have vanished from planet Earth.

"It kind of feels like a death," I said.

I was super conflicted about making the move. But Greg had received the promotion of his dreams, the opportunity to be the GM of the newly constructed Palm Place Hotel, in one of the hospitality centers of the country, and we decided to take the leap. My mom had taken the news in her typical theatrical fashion: clutching her pearls, and saying, *you're taking my grandchild to Miami? Where she will have no friends and family?* Even though I knew she sounded ridiculous, a mother's criticism can cut deep. Sensing my hesitance, Greg held me and promised that home was wherever the three of us were together.

I was nervous to break it to Lucy, but she was thrilled with the news. "Palm trees and beaches? You have *got* to be joking" was her reaction.

Starting a new school in a new town would be a transition, and one neither Greg nor I had experienced in our own childhoods. Would Lucy blend in? Greg was more confident than I that she would. He knew nothing about mean-girl culture, which was one of my greatest fears from the day Lucy was born. It's a wild world out there for us. Not that I was bullied as a child, per se.

There were the unfortunate nicknames in lower school—"Smelly Melody," for example—but no outright torture. If things ever got hairy with my childhood girlfriends, one mom would call another and all us girls would have a stern talking-to, and then things just sort of resolved. By high school, we were all friends again, holding hands on Homecoming Court, sneaking kegs into Greg's house while his parents were out of town.

But moving to a big city was intimidating, and Miami didn't have the most wholesome reputation, if what I garnered from watching the *Real Housewives* and *CSI: Miami* was any indication. It looked like a lot of stiletto heels and murders at nightclubs.

"You're being defeatist," Greg had said. "Kids are made of rubber, they bend. They don't break."

"What about me?" I had asked.

Maybe that's what I was more worried about.

After Back-to-School Night, I braced myself, but the first day of school at Sunset Academy put me at ease. It arrived on a beautiful Miami morning. The kind where the sun kisses your face with just the right amount of warmth, and the humidity is more comforting blanket than stifling and thick. There's a reason people always mention weather in the same breath as Miami. We all woke up before the alarm, and Lucy looked ready to take on the world in her navy-blue polo and pleated khaki skirt. She looked so similar to all her other first-day-of-school photos from Wichita—same uniform, same smile—and that comforted me.

It had been only a week since Back-to-School Night, but Lucy had made quick friends with Darcy's son, Jackson. They'd spent the bulk of the past week swimming and laughing in our backyard, with the kind of ease we were used to back in Wichita. Jackson was a very sweet boy, with a sharp sense of humor. Very much his mother's son in that last respect. Darcy and I had also fallen in easily with each other. I think she might have taken pity on me, the clueless new girl from the middle of nowhere. Regardless, she was whip-smart and so fun to talk to. I was grateful that our kids would be in class together. Their teacher—Ms. Sanchez—had a great reputation, and it was a relief that

Lucy would know someone there. Really, all you need in a new school is that one person.

Darcy was refreshingly low-key compared to the other moms I'd seen at the school. A successful lawyer and feisty as heck, but she didn't look like she spent hours on her hair and lived in the gym. She also didn't hold back when it came to the other ladies of Sunset.

"Look, at Sunset Academy there are four types: working class, wannabe rich, rich, and wealthy," Darcy said. This was when I had her over for a playdate by the pool. She and I sipped iced teas while Jackson taught Lucy the four Olympic-style swimming strokes. Her butterfly looked more like a drowning cat, but the others weren't half bad by the end of their session.

Darcy continued. "But the PTA ladies like to pretend that only the fortunate ones attend the school. Take Charlotte Giordani. She's the leader of the pack, but she's only medium rich. Her financey husband does well, she doesn't have to work. But she's not chartering planes, and she doesn't live on the water. Waterfront homes are the mark of the wealthy, like the Walkers. Meanwhile, half the school is on free lunch and couldn't dream of affording tickets to the fancy school fundraisers these ladies plan. But on that note, why would anyone want to attend those snoozefests?"

I looked around my tiny rental backyard and tried not to feel weird about it. Was I wannabe rich or not even? We were talking about a level of society I had never really thought about. Also, *money.* It felt kind of gross to be talking about other people's money. I wondered where Darcy saw herself in the mix, or if she thought she was above it all somehow.

"The Charlottes of the world have to suck up to the Walkers of the world. They say they're best friends but there is clearly a hierarchy in place." Darcy jiggled the ice at the bottom of her iced tea. "And then you've got the really sad sacks who just want to be part of the club. They'll volunteer for every PTA event and go into debt to carry a designer bag. Anything to try and fit in with the *cool* moms."

I shook my head at that one. "That's just sad," I said. "What kind of arrested development do you have to be in to need approval that desperately?"

Darcy nodded along. "'Desperate' is definitely the word for it."

If our first impression of Sunset Academy was slightly appalling, the second was a pleasant surprise. The first day of school drop-off was full of the familiar parent and child jitters, complete with long hugs goodbye and plenty of photos in front of colorfully adorned chalkboards. The classrooms were housed in a 1940s white building, an L-shaped structure with a beautifully landscaped communal courtyard in the center. Lucy and I found her classroom in the corner of the L, directly across from the more modern cafeteria building.

The classroom door was decorated like a box of crayons and read "Ms. Sanchez's New Pack." It was adorable. Jackson was seated when we arrived and waved enthusiastically for Lucy to join him at his table. My daughter gave me a quick side hug and whispered, "You don't have to stay," which is both the most comforting and heartbreaking thing your child can tell you on the first day of school.

"They're too cute, aren't they?" said a perfectly coiffed, if not overdressed, mom. She wore a cropped tweed jacket over a white silk blouse and fitted high-waisted jeans, her hair swirling around her shoulders like a Pantene commercial. I recognized her right away from Back-to-School Night. Charlotte. "Are you new here? Sorry, I just know everyone in the grade and I've never seen you before."

"Yes, we just moved from Kansas," I answered, as a steady stream of parents and students said their goodbyes by the classroom door.

"Kansas! How quaint! Miami Beach must feel like the Twilight Zone to you." She shrugged her shoulders. "It can be intimidating, but don't worry, I'll get you up to speed on everything around here. Your daughter is adorable. She must have a playdate with my Maddy. I'll set it up! I'm Charlotte Giordani, by the way, room mom and certified PTA workhorse."

It was a such a sweet gesture, and not at all what I expected after seeing her onstage at Back-to-School Night and from Darcy's harsh assessment. I extended my hand, poised to respond with my name. But before I could manage the words, Charlotte kissed me on the cheek.

I jerked back, startled.

Charlotte laughed. "Sorry! In Miami, we kiss hello. None of those germy handshakes." She winked at me and gave a half wave, disappearing back into the hallway. I hadn't even told her my name.

I spent the bulk of that day pacing, wishing I had a body cam on Lucy's uniform. But you know what? Kids *are* resilient; Greg was right about that. In one day at her new school, Lucy made two new *best friends* and joined a club. She did not sit alone at the lunch table, crying into her ham sandwich as I had feared.

"Mom, it was awesome," she told me after school. We sat together at the kitchen counter and debriefed over still-warm banana bread. "The teacher kept mixing me up with Maddy, so we decided to play a prank tomorrow and sit in each other's seats to see if Ms. Sanchez notices."

It seemed silly then, all of my parental guilt about uprooting my sweet and innocent daughter and transplanting her into a strange new world across the country. Perhaps I had been *defeatist*, as my husband had claimed. I was free to move on to the next worry. Just kidding. Kind of.

Later that same week, I ran into Charlotte again. This time it was at Publix, my new day-to-day grocery store. *Where Shopping Is a Pleasure.* I mean, how pleasurable is grocery shopping really? But it seemed like everyone I met made a point to tell me about how great it was there and how I had to try a "Publix sub." They were all so proud of it.

It was a Thursday and I'd popped in for some mid-week essentials: fresh bread, milk, some toiletries. Among the late-morning clientele, who all appeared to be either off-duty models or construction workers, I spotted the familiar chestnut ponytail. Charlotte was wearing a very flattering pair of shimmery black workout leggings with a matching sports bra, and no shirt to go over it. Maybe she'd just finished working out, I thought. And perhaps the shirt she was wearing became horribly sweaty, and really no one could blame her for not wanting to put that back on. I'd later learn that, in Miami, both shirts and turn signals were optional.

Also, she wasn't the only person in the store wearing a sports bra, so I moved on from the thought and decided to say hello. She had been friendly to me on the first day of school, and Lucy had not stopped talking about her budding friendship with Charlotte's daughter, Maddy. Lucy and Maddy were insta-friends. Bonded from the first glance, which is so easy for kids.

I ditched my cart next to a tower of yellow onions and headed to organic fruits, where Charlotte was inspecting a cantaloupe.

"Charlotte!" I said and leaned in for a Miami cheek kiss. Except it went all wrong. Upon hearing her name, Charlotte had already begun to turn her head, and by the time I made contact we were face-to-face. Lip to lip.

"Well," Charlotte answered, "next time buy me a drink first!"

I flushed and covered my face. "I am so sorry," I began.

"Oh, don't be ridiculous." She waved her hand in front of her chest. "Remind me your name again?"

I told her I was Melody Howard, the one from Kansas, Lucy's mom, and her eyes flickered with recognition.

"Yes, Melody! So good to see you. How are you settling in? We must have that playdate," she said, placing a cantaloupe into her cart, then looking me up and down. "Kansas! That is so cute. Look at you. Like a little Southern belle." I blushed and didn't want to tell her that Kansas is in the Midwest, and not the South. She was just trying to be nice.

We lingered for a bit discussing the girls, the school, the weather, and ended up exchanging phone numbers. Charlotte pleasantly surprised me. She seemed confident and unafraid to put herself out there in a way that was refreshing. I could see how it could be off-putting, too, which had been my first reaction at Back-to-School Night. But that could have been because I was a little intimidated by her. I mean, she was gorgeous, outspoken, a bold dresser. Why is it that we judge people for making choices that we are too afraid to? Maybe my first impression said more about my, I don't know, jealousy? Charlotte was clearly a leader at this school, which is exactly what I had been back home, just because I'd been there and people had known me for so long. Who knows? Maybe new people used to feel a little intimidated by me when we first met. And I'm anything but intimidating. I felt a little embarrassed for judging the proverbial book by its cover.

My new friend Darcy was very much *not a fan* of Charlotte. Which was fine. We're all adults here. Everyone can make their own decisions. As green as I was in town, I was in no position to be choosing alliances.

Interview Transcript with Donald Walker

For profile in *Magic City* magazine, summer issue 2019
By Andres Castano
August 28, 2018, Session 1

INTERVIEWER: Thanks so much for meeting with me today, Mr. Walker. I know how valuable your time is, so I'll try to be brief. I've already had the pleasure of meeting your lovely wife, Patricia, and I'll be seeing her later this morning. What a power couple you two are! *Magic City* is thrilled to be doing this piece.

DONALD: Please. Call me Don.

INTERVIEWER: All right then, Don. Just to let you know, this interview will be on the record. If you'd like to go *off* the record at any point, just let me know and I'll turn off the recording and put down my pen.

DONALD: Sounds good, Andres. I think you'll find me to be an open book. I have nothing to hide.

INTERVIEWER: Wonderful. Let's get started. I'm sure everyone asks you about your success in business, but I want to dive into your tremendous success at home. Your wife is a pillar of the philanthropic community, and your sons are straight-A students in a challenging gifted program. We've already spoken to your wife about the many hats she wears. And we know that you are a very hands-on father. I want to hear more about your parenting philosophy. What are you doing to raise your boys to be future leaders?

DONALD: We like to keep the boys *grounded,* you know. Most of these guys in my business, they send their kids to their fancy private schools with a uniformed driver. Then these shits grow up knowing only rich kids, doing only rich-kid things. Where's the value in that? Great for networking, sure. But you know half of those—well, I call them *just sons.* As in, *My dad was smart and made a fortune but I'm just his son.* Half of these *just sons* end up drug addicts by age sixteen. And the ones who actually make it lack character, in my opinion.

So I made a conscious decision to send Maddox and Monrow to public school, the best public school in the state, at that, and let them cut their teeth with normal kids. Patricia wasn't originally on board; she thought that the boys would be bullied for their privilege or that the education would be too basic or too liberal. But none of that ended up being true.

INTERVIEWER: That decision seems to be paying off for your sons.

DONALD: Yes. It's proven to be a great experience for the boys. They are thriving. Popular, excellent grades, and they know how to converse with any type of kid. Heck, it's good for me, too, to take a break from the half of a half of a half of the one percent that I deal with on a daily basis. Sunset Academy is the real world; I live in Disney World.

Take the other week, I went to some back-to-school thing for the parents. It's a quaint little event. But also, you know, I didn't come from all this wealth, so it's kind of comfortable in a way, too. Familiar. I'm sitting there with Patricia and the boys in the auditorium, which we underwrote, and next to me is a restaurant manager, next to him is a dental hygienist. Real people. Salt of the earth.

But you know it's Miami, so a lot of these people are about the flash. Spending all their money on luxury cars while they're paying rent in some walk-up apartment building. Wearing logo clothing but they've got nothing in savings. I should give these people a little free financial advice. Save your money. Park it in low-cost index funds (you know I don't have space in my fund for these little guys). Take on a moderate to low risk and diversify your holdings between cash, stocks, and bonds. These people like to look like they have money, but when it's time to pony up for the school, they are sitting on their hands.

So we're in the auditorium listening to whatever the updated bell schedule will be or whatever, and then comes the *ask*. There's always an *ask* at these things. The fundraising woman takes the stage and pleads her case for capital improvements to the school, new pencils, whatever. We know her well, Patricia and me, and I felt bad. She came out with a big number, and the audience was crickets. I gave Patricia a little nudge, and she raised her hand for a sizable contribution.

We wrote the school a big check, but man, I worry about what's going to happen when my kids age out of that place. I hope they have a plan for that, because so far we've been floating every single major project since my boys entered Sunset.

INTERVIEWER: It sounds like this school, like Miami as a whole, is very lucky to have your patronage.

DONALD: Well, we really do love to give back.

CHARLOTTE

Don't you just love the first day of school? The smell of brand-new pencils, the crisp sheets of notebook paper placed neatly into unmarked binders, the pristine backpack that has no signs of fraying and no vague cafeteria smell? It all takes me back. There's that feeling of unlimited possibility, of new friends making new memories. I loved elementary school, even if my mother didn't give a rat's tush about my education. I was there for me, to make my own way. And my girl is exactly the same (with a much better support system, that is).

Maddy was beaming in her perfectly pressed Sunset uniform: a navy Peter Pan–collared button-up shirt with khaki pleated skort (of course, I had my tailor Stefan take it up a couple inches; the Giordani ladies aren't known for long legs, and I didn't want her looking like a troll), and a matching velvet kitty-ear headband. I waved her hair for the occasion (first day of school photos last a lifetime) and I have to say, she looked like the stock photo of a perfect schoolgirl. Truly, Getty Images could do no better.

Maddy marched into Ms. Sanchez's third-grade class with such authority that even the teacher joked, "Well, good morning, Queen Bee, welcome to my class."

"Watch out, third grade!" I teased back.

Ms. Sanchez was known as the best gifted teacher in the whole school, and it was no accident that Madeline ended up in her class.

There are benefits to being very involved in the school, if you know what I mean.

After the requisite classroom hellos and "nice-to-meet-you"s, I told Ms. Sanchez that I had to duck out, but not to worry because I would be back early and often to help plan our classroom events and social strategies for the year. That day, I had to make a drop-off appearance at Miami Beach Middle with my firstborn.

If anyone needs an excuse to soak up the elementary years, visit a middle school campus for, like, five minutes. Once you get past the sea of unsmiling, hormonal, BO-reeking adolescents, you will be greeted with soul-crushing sterile classrooms and a course curriculum that is dryer than your grandma's vagina. No adorable holiday shows there!

Just a blink ago, Axel was my gorgeous blond baby boy, all dinosaur-obsessed and not able to fall asleep without plenty of bedtime cuddles. And now, oh my god. He is sticky sheets, locked bedroom door, noise music blaring, *Fortnite* obsessed, Kool-Aid dyed hair, permanent scowl, barnyard-smelling laundry bin thirteen-year-old Ax. Hold on tight to your little ones!

Funny thing is, there was a time when I thought I'd turn dizzy and blue from all the questions that came out of that boy's mouth. Every car ride, especially at the end of a long day while I'd try to zone out to the radio, he'd pepper me with questions like *Mom, did you know that there are a lot of interesting creatures in the ocean?*

ME: Yes, there sure are, honey.
AXEL: Have you ever been bitten by a crab spider?
ME: No, baby, I have not.
AXEL: Mama, are they kinda like cockroaches?
ME: No, not really, Ax. Hey, wanna play the quiet game?
AXEL: Okay . . .
AXEL: Hey, wanna see how fast I can open and close my eyes? (Blinking.)

ME: . . .
AXEL: Mama! Oh sorry, I forgot . . .

I remember feeling so distracted in those moments, wishing for silence instead of having to be "on" all the time. And isn't that the tragic thing about hindsight? These days, even one-word answers from that kid are a gift.

But even when he was at Sunset, Axel was a little different from Maddy. He's not as naturally social, wasn't involved in activities. I tried to put him in every extracurricular class under the sun, hoping that something would stick, that he would say, "Mom, I found my thing!" We tried basketball, Little League, soccer, tennis, and golf, and when it was clear that he was no athlete, we put him in piano, guitar, chess, and something called Junior Music Makers. But ugh, nothing fit.

Maddy is just a different kid. She's probably going to land one of the child roles in the Miami City Ballet *Nutcracker* this year (fingers crossed). She's also a star tennis player who plays the piano five days a week. Not that I am comparing!

Kids need two things: to be socially engaged and to be busy with productive activities. Ax wasn't having either. Ever. Unless you count video gaming, which I certainly don't. So it's not surprising that Axel has morphed into the milk carton picture of a moody teen. He needs to fill his gas tank, not that he takes my word for it.

You love your kids no matter what, though, whether they're a living American Girl doll or a step away from the FBI watchlist. I'm kidding! Ax isn't violent, he was raised right and it's not in his DNA. But Maddy sure does make things easy for me, and I can't pretend I'm not grateful.

There is an old saying about sons growing up and leaving you, while daughters take care of you until the end. I *always* wanted a daughter. When we were sitting in that ultrasound room at twenty weeks pregnant, and Dr. Cho said the most beautiful words I'd ever heard—"It's a girl!"—I turned to James and said, "You've got your boy, but this one is all mine." I couldn't wait to dress her up, strap her into a stroller, and bring her along to lunches and shopping dates. The newest, tiniest addition to my girl gang.

And I was right; she's all mine. Madeline Rose is my mini in almost every way, from her blue eyes to her positive attitude and unbridled passion to be the absolute best she can be. As I read in that *Lean In* book—don't call her bossy, she has leadership skills. That little girl has CEO written all over her. All she needs is a nurturing hand to guide her and then get the hell out of the way! God, I wish I'd had parents who recognized and supported me like that. But hey! Forward not back.

The bond was instant. I took that little peanut to every mommy and me under the sun. After dropping off Ax at school, Maddy and I would cut it up at Baby Zumba, create finger paint masterpieces at Lil' Picassos, and work off those baby rolls at Bouncing Babies. It was so fulfilling, the way she would gaze up at me while we churned our arms in tandem to "Wheels on the Bus." Our eyes would meet, and there's no better feeling in the world than connecting in such a pure way with your child. If you knew me before kids, you'd say I'd sooner stab myself repeatedly in both eyes than do that shit, but I'm telling you, love changes a person.

In my twenties, I put in sixty-plus hours a week selling ad space in Miami's hottest luxury magazine, *Magic City,* and I was damn good. I was out every night, hosting tables and popping bottles, entertaining every bigwig in town. How do you think I met my husband?

I had Ax at my peak, career-wise, and thought I could juggle it all. How naive, right? I must have aged ten years in twenty-four months while burning the candle at both ends. That kid didn't sleep! And my clients were so demanding, like a dozen more little babies to take care of. No one, not my baby or my clients, was ever fully satisfied with me. At the end, I might have looked like the crypt-keeper, but at least I *was* crushing it on commissions.

By the time Maddy came along, I'd learned my lesson. Ax was smiling wider for the nanny than for me, which kind of broke me inside, and I'd missed one milestone too many. That's when I decided to become a stay-at-home mom. At that point, no amount of money in the world could have kept me away from Maddy's intoxicating baby smell. Bottle that and you'd be an overnight billionaire! Eau de Madeline.

So we hit the baby class scene and I told myself, I'm going to be the best soccer mom, school volunteer, and playdate host this town has ever seen. If I could sell ads in a dying print medium to the biggest players in Miami, I can sure as hell bake some organic, gluten-free, sugar-free banana muffins for the pre-K bake sale. Sales is sales! I don't care if you're closing a million-dollar ad buy for twelve months of back covers, or up-charging for generic school supplies in the Sunset Academy school store, it's the same hustle.

I never thought I'd become quite this active on the fundraising side. But one day, Maddy came home from kindergarten and told me that, during recess, she and her friends were so bored that they decided to play catch with a napkin. Can you believe that's how underfunded the school was? That was the aha moment. I knew I had to do something bigger.

DARCY

O Captain, my Captain!" Jackson shouted down the stairs with out-stretched arms, wielding an invisible sword.

I'd like to say that my newly minted third-grader was a young prod-igy with an affinity for Walt Whitman, but in reality his mom just has a soft spot for *Dead Poets Society*.

It was the first day of school, which meant scrambled eggs, bacon, waffles, orange juice, and a late start to my workday. I cherish the first days. The truth is, most working moms do have to choose between a career and playing an active daily role in their children's lives. Sure, I'm always available for homework and bedtime at a minimum, with considerable sacrifice to my practice, but after that first-day drop-off, I'd be hard-pressed to tell you when it is "dress up like an animal day" or when the Student Artists' Craft Fair takes place.

I know that Jackson watches the long hours I put in, despite societal pressures to pack it up and "be a mom." Hopefully, the long-term result will be a respect for not only me but also for women in general. All the studies show that the children of working mothers are better adjusted and become higher achievers. And are less sexist in general. Yet the pang is still there, a deep gnawing worry that I'm not there enough or don't do enough.

So yes, I treasure the eggs and the bacon, and riding together to school on the first day, and even deign to smile and greet all the other parents who have so many opinions about what can make our school great. We have the highest teacher retention rate in the county, and our students are outperforming their peers at other schools at an impressive rate, but I suppose that's not good enough for some people.

Allow me to step off my soapbox. Jackson loves his school, and he loves his classmates. He is kind, empathetic, a good listener, and a hard worker. This year, he is hoping to try out for elementary school debate. It would be unusual for a third-grader to make the team, but he's going to try his best. Because that is who he is. Somehow, and I am acutely aware that I do not deserve this, I have been gifted the most wonderful boy in the whole world.

And to think, there was a time when I didn't think I'd even have kids. I was three years out of law school at the University of Miami, and on the fast track to partner at the largest firm in South Florida when I met, fell in love with, and married Elliot, a partner at the second-biggest firm. He and I were both working eighty-plus hours a week; the mere concept of work-life balance was a terrible joke. We decided that we were the type of couple that would utilize our vacation days to take lavish trips, a distinct counterpoint to our marathon workdays, rather than wipe bottoms and sing "Twinkle, Twinkle." Billable hours means putting in the work, so many hours, until your eyes start to bleed while reading contracts and your fingers spasm at the keyboard with every stroke. Ten years later, having each made partner and just an inch away from turning forty, I missed three whole periods before I even noticed something was amiss. Sure, my belt ring was barely hanging on to the last loop, but I assumed it was a combination of age and too many consecutive days of take-out pizza. It wasn't.

The news was shocking, but not apocalyptic. Elliot was the ever supportive "whatever you decide, we will make it work" husband. It was one of those now or never moments, and I did what had once been unthinkable and said "yes" to becoming a mom. Elliot and I left our respective firms and opened our family practice. At the risk of sounding cliché, it was the best decision I've ever made.

For most people, working with your spouse would put you on the fast track to divorce, but Elliot and I are partners in every sense of the word. Which doesn't mean he isn't the most annoyingly loud chewer in the world, and lord knows he can't do a load of laundry to save his life. But he's a brilliant lawyer, and there is no one I trust more in business and ethical matters. We try to tag team with Jackson as much as possible. Elliot throws cereal in a bowl while I get ready, and then I shuttle Jackson to school. We have an afternoon sitter on some days who can do pickup, and Elliot and I split the others. Dinner is usually some version of takeout, but sometimes I do manage to scrounge together the odd roasted chicken and salad. My husband tries to be fifty-fifty in every facet of our life, but parenthood often skews more toward me. I can't explain why; that's just how it is.

Sure, it's been a juggling act over the years. I've missed my share of client meetings and, gasp, PTA events to prioritize career-Darcy over mom-Darcy and vice versa. But I wouldn't have it any other way. There are multiple parts to me that create one whole, and some of these moms forget that the second they become parents. Which is just one of the reasons I find most of them insufferable. If you aren't in their playdate group, then your kids can't be friends. Who has the time and patience for all these playdates? And why do the dads get a free pass? I've not once seen a heterosexual father set up or attend a playdate. Have you? All Elliot needs to do is show up for a birthday party, and the moms will say, *You're so lucky to have such an involved husband. Dad of the year!*

At least now the kids are old enough for drop-offs, but back when they were tiny and all those bonds were formed, you had to literally sit there for hours and make conversation with adult strangers while your children were on the floor eating one another's boogers. I cannot and did not do it. Poor Jackson, his mama didn't have it in her. As a result, he hasn't been invited to every single party and I'm not in the "mommy inner circle," and that's fine with me. I find other ways and moments to mother.

I woke up that morning feeling grateful. For simple traditions that become meaningful with repetition and the passage of time. And for a darling boy who was all mine.

Interview Transcript with Patricia Walker

For profile in *Magic City* magazine, summer issue 2019
By Andres Castano
August 28, 2018, Session 2

PATRICIA: Please excuse my tardiness. I'm ready to begin whenever.

INTERVIEWER: It is no problem at all. If this isn't a good time, we can certainly reschedule. I know you are a very busy woman.

PATRICIA: Yes, I am. I am, but today! Today has just been extremely frustrating. You wouldn't believe what a morning I've had.

INTERVIEWER: I can only imagine. I know it was the first day of school, it must have been difficult getting everyone up and out the door on schedule.

PATRICIA: It's actually not, the nannies get the boys up and ready. We are a well-oiled machine. Very organized. It's other people who ruin it for us.

INTERVIEWER: Oh my. It sounds like a very frustrating morning, indeed! This is off the record, of course.

PATRICIA: Oh good. You wouldn't believe what happened.

INTERVIEWER: I'm very curious!

PATRICIA: In that case . . . [takes a sip of water] I send my boys to the public elementary school, Sunset Academy. Do you know how much it costs for a designated parking spot at Sunset Academy? Thirty thousand dollars, Andres. That is how much money the Walker Family Foundation donated to Sunset Academy, in return for a thank-you letter from the principal and a spot in front of the campus. So you can imagine my disappointment when, on the very first day of school, I found that spot *occupied*. My thirty-thousand-dollar spot!

Not only was that a huge slap in the face, but it also made us late for drop-off. My kindergartner and third-grader had to jump off at carline and walk themselves to their classrooms while I circled around to park across the street at the pharmacy. It threw off the entire first-day vibe. How is that fair? Explain that to my five- and eight-year-old, both of whom were in tears by the time I made it back to campus.

What do you think would happen to that place if Don and I stopped bankrolling every single tediously presented initiative that Sunset puts in front of us? Those crunchy recycling moms would sure miss my organic salad bar.

And yet someone still thought it was okay to park right in front of the school under a sign labeled "Walker." As if I don't even fucking matter.

INTERVIEWER: That takes some nerve! It was a completely tasteless thing for that person to do.

PATRICIA: Mm-hmm, I can't disagree, Andres. Unfortunately, not everyone is born with class.

CHARLOTTE

For heaven's sake, what kind of a nitwit parks in a marked space that doesn't belong to them?

After I hung up with Patricia, I raced back to Sunset and called Miami Beach Tow. By the time they arrived, the offender had already left the scene. Did you know that you still have to pay the tow guys just for coming out, even if the illegally parked vehicle isn't there anymore? It's like getting a UTI after a bad one-night stand.

By then, Patricia had gone nuclear, which honestly is just unbecoming on such a pretty girl. She was shaking and looked like an electrocuted giraffe, in her nude bodysuit and black miniskirt, crocodile Bottega pouch squeezed to death under one arm. She kept running her free hand through her hair and squealing, "My spot! Who would do this!" Like, come on, girlfriend, don't ruin a perfectly good blowout.

She was a mess, so of course I offered to pick up the tow tab. But not before I got slapped with plenty of "Charlotte, you need to find out who did this. Char, how do we make sure this will never happen again?" *Char, Char, Char!* So I told her we would send out a PTA email, which reaches every parent in the school, and let them know the rules and etiquette for drop-off and pickup. No honking, no stopping, no parking in Patricia and Don Walker's spot. Don't shit where you eat, people!

Officer Beatty showed me the security footage from the morning and, I'll be damned, the parking bandit was that grumpy too-good-for-us Darcy fucking Resnick. I'm telling you right now, I'll put my wedding ring on it, she did that shit on purpose. I mean, she reads fine print for a living, she can definitely understand the meaning of a giant block-lettered name in front of a parking spot.

This woman can't be bothered to send $10 in her kid's lunchbox for Ditch the Uniform Day, but she thinks it's her damned right to pull up on the most important day of the year and slide into the primo spot in front of school? If that doesn't reek of entitlement, then I don't know what does.

I can't say I'm surprised though. Back when Maddy and Jackson were in kinder, Darcy and I both signed up for classroom Halloween decorations. I asked for weeks what we should do as the theme, and she literally just kept saying, "Isn't Halloween the theme?" No, Halloween is a holiday. A theme is ghosts, spiders, pumpkins, spooky stories, monsters. Finally, I suggested we create a cutest-pumpkins-in-the-patch display, for which we could cut and fabricate twenty-two poster-board pumpkins, one for each child, and then do a little photo shoot to add their faces on each pumpkin and glue them to individual fence posts. Then we would scatter them into a little patch in the classroom and surround each sign with crafting moss, which we would also hang from the ceiling to extend the decor theme throughout the room. This bitch doesn't respond, and then shows up on October 31 with a bag full of decorations from the party store. Never mind that I'd spent the previous week cutting, gluing, photographing, and painting.

Darcy is a repeat "don't give a fuck" offender. Well, let's see her try to ignore this $200 tow bill.

From: Charlotte Giordani
August 28, 2018
To: All Sunset Academy
Subject: Parking Etiquette at Sunset Academy

Dear Parents and Guardians,

Welcome back to Sunset Academy! I am so excited to kick off the 2018 to 2019 school year with you and your children. It's going to be a great one.

Unfortunately, it has come to my attention that there was a parking incident at drop-off today that must be addressed. A parent, and I am sure it was done by mistake, parked in the dedicated WALKER space in front of campus. Because of this, the Walker family was forced to find alternative parking, which we all know is quite difficult.

Sunset Academy reserves parking spots for the school administration and staff, the PTA president, and one major gifts donor (in this case, the Walkers). Moving forward, if anyone illegally parks in any of these spots, we will be forced to tow the offender immediately.

Children may be dropped off in carline on the north side of campus or parents/guardians may park down the block on Sunset Avenue and walk their children to class. No exceptions.

Thank you for your time and attention to this matter, and Go Sunset Seagulls!

Warm regards,

Charlotte Giordani

PTA Vice President of Fundraising

PS. If any of you are interested in donation opportunities, please do not hesitate to reach out to me directly!

MELODY

The house was unpacked, my kid was in school, and I was alone. By. My. Self. For truly the first time in my life. Greg was working, and I wasn't. And I couldn't keep calling my one new friend to hang out, because she was a busy lawyer and working, too. Also, I didn't want to seem needy (even though I obviously was).

Despite that, Miami was growing on me. It still felt like a foreign country, but it was becoming one I was keen to explore. Greg's new hotel job was in Miami Beach, perhaps the most well-known city within Miami-Dade County. An international vacation paradise. Who wouldn't want to live here full-time?

The Beach comprised at least three distinct areas: South Beach, with its throngs of tourists, open-air shopping streets, and art deco buildings; Mid-Beach, with its more upscale hotels and tony residential streets, mixed with orthodox Jewish enclaves; and the Bal Harbour/Surfside area, with some of the nation's most luxurious shopping and hidden gated communities for the uber wealthy.

Greg's "office," the Palm Place Hotel, sat squarely within the Mid-Beach neighborhood, constructed behind one hundred feet of beach-front splendor. Miami Beach is a manmade island, bordered on one side by Biscayne Bay and on the other by the Atlantic Ocean. Our modest new home sat directly in the middle, between the bay and the beach, as most residences were. Sunset Academy was just five blocks away.

Before I could let the homesickness take over, I decided to explore my new surroundings, wondering if I could reinvigorate my former business from Wichita in our sunny new home. I had founded Melody Howard Consulting, my nonprofit management firm, eight years earlier, and it had become a huge part of my identity. They called me the Charity Doctor. We helped nonprofits with everything from financial reports to events to major gifts cultivation. "We'll keep the house in order so you can save the world," we told our clients. With Greg's promotion, I didn't *have* to work anymore, though we would certainly be more comfortable if I did. And, I loved my old job.

I had built MHC from scratch, starting with one client, my church's youth group, and a laptop set up in my apartment kitchen. By the time we moved to Miami, it had grown to two dozen clients and a six-person staff. We were passionate and we believed in the work, putting in extra hours because we truly wanted to make a difference. There's no way I could have managed all that from afar with the hands-on attention my clients deserved, much as it pained me to admit. So I had been forced to sell the business to my second-in-command, Lisa. Greg doesn't know this, but I still Skype with the office every day just to chat about the business.

Miami, on its face, was a philanthropic city. A basic Google search of "Miami" coupled with "charity" spawned a half dozen pages of unique results. There was everything from Samson Homeless Shelter to Miami Agency for the Advancement of Ceramic Arts (MACA). I visited all their websites, jotted notes in a Word document titled "Miami nonprofit prospects," copying names and contact information for management teams and each organization's board of directors.

Then I did an image search for the same query: "Miami," "charity." This is where things got interesting. My screen filled with glamorous event photos, women in gowns, men in expensive-looking black tie. I double-checked the search terms, making sure I hadn't stumbled upon images from some high-profile celebrity shindig. The search terms were correct and, when I remembered the bizarre

Back-to-School Night at Sunset Academy, it began to make sense. Minutes passed, maybe close to an hour, as I analyzed the pictures. For research, right?

The events seemed to fall into one of three categories: whimsical outdoor garden party, full production ballroom gala, and women wearing as little as possible without being pornographic. My personal favorite was the Fur-Ball, which benefited the Greater Miami Animal Rescue. Along with face-painted whiskers and fluffy paw gloves, many women donned furry catsuits, and at least a few of their male counterparts went shirtless, with bow ties and animal ears. This was not your grandmother's gala.

A good chunk of the images featured parents whom I had seen at Back-to-School Night. The Walkers, for example, seemed to support just about every charity in town, commendable really, and struck almost identical poses in each photo. Husband, gleaming, dapper, handsome, hand loosely touching wife's back. Wife, unsmiling, coquettish, one foot crossed over the other, hand on hip, creating a sideways V shape with her arm.

I was so curious about this glamorous couple. They did not fit the profile of *philanthropist* I was accustomed to in Wichita. Don and Patricia seemed . . . fancier? And also, more difficult to approach. Even in photos, they exuded a very *look but don't touch* vibe. At some point, I knew, it would make sense to get to know them better. They'd likely have more insight into local charities than I could garner with my Google searches, but they seemed hard to reach.

Charlotte was clearly close to them. She featured prominently in many of their Google images, and I had seen them mingling together at Back-to-School Night. And Charlotte *was* approachable. She came on strong but also had a warmth that I was finding myself drawn to.

Which is why, a couple days later, I was a little dismayed to hear that Darcy seemed to be on a crusade against Charlotte and her friends. Darcy and I met for coffee at Panther, a hip local café known for its laid-back warehouse feel and uber-caffeinated beverages. But the date ended up being more gossip session than casual catch-up.

In a corner table by one of the floor-to-ceiling windows, Darcy sat across from me and was practically vibrating. Whether from the cold brew or her rage, I couldn't tell.

"There are exactly two saved parking spots at school that are not for faculty and staff: the PTA president spot, and the highest-fucking-bidder spot." She shook both hands at me. "The rest of us wait for, I don't know, sometimes forty-five minutes to drop off or pick up. But then whoever happens to be the richest family at school can bypass the peasants in their golden chariot."

It did seem crazy to me, the whole concept of paying tens of thousands of dollars for a school parking spot. In Wichita, carline was an in-and-out type of deal, and if you wanted to park instead of waiting in the short line, you just parked. But that was another difference coming from a school of 275 to one with 1,000 students, I supposed.

Darcy explained her act of rebellion to me, which was funny in a movie scene kind of way, but a little cringeworthy as a real-life scenario. She had seen the open Walker family parking spot and took it on the first day. This caused the Walker mom to park blocks away and then her children were late for morning bell. That *was* pretty mean. Of course, the Walkers were expecting to have the spot ready, and they did pay for it. Regardless of whether you morally agree with the dedicated spot, it had already been decided.

So I didn't fully understand the fury on Darcy's end. She was the one who broke the rule, however distasteful the rule was. I agreed with her that the apparent elitism was problematic at best. But she was upset about how Charlotte reacted to the whole thing. I picked at my croissant and tried to keep an open mind. It wasn't like Charlotte had done anything wrong. If anything, she was on the receiving end of Patricia's wrath and had to make it right. Of course she was upset.

"Charlotte Giordani, she decides to make this a public stoning," Darcy said. (She loved to use Charlotte's full name.) "Sends an email to the school with a *blind item* about parking in reserved spaces. Of course, everyone had heard the damn story by then. Walkers, Giordanis, even damn Gabriela Machado couldn't let go of the *horror*.

Apparently, they are referring to me as the *PB: Parking Bandit*. Over a parking spot, Melody!"

If she seemed melodramatic, Darcy claimed, it was because she'd been the punching bag for these women one too many times. "I was idealistic about modern-day parenting once," she said, raising her coffee cup as though giving a toast. "I thought that we could teach our child about kindness, and morals, and that we were all born equal."

She said that the first incident happened when Jackson was in kindergarten. "Of course, I knew as a working parent that I wouldn't have enough time to be the most engaged mom in the class, but I was looking forward to having at least a presence, to learn all the children's names and perhaps read a story to them every now and then." Darcy sat back in her chair. "Enter Charlotte Giordani, the self-styled supermom and passionate school advocate. More like a card-carrying narcissist who cares naught but for herself. I should call her Charlatan Giordani."

Darcy was witty. I had to give her that. She went on. "In my naiveté, I dared to choose decorations on the sign-up sheet for the class Halloween party, thinking that I could buy some cute, ready-made party supplies and call it a day. Oh no. In the age of Pinterest, one must construct every piece of decor painstakingly by hand, with care to personalize wherever possible. Don't get me wrong, I admire those that have this talent, but I simply do not possess it."

This part actually made me feel bad for Darcy. Apparently, Charlotte was the other mom who had signed up for Halloween decorations, and I'm not surprised to hear that she was a perfectionist in that department. Even I would be intimidated! "I cannot pretend to have the time or ability to produce a theater-set-worthy re-creation of a harvest pumpkin patch, complete with homemade scarecrows," Darcy said.

Charlotte was not having it. In fact, she was so disappointed with Darcy's lackluster efforts that she banned Darcy from volunteering in the class for the remainder of the school year. Apparently, as room mom, it was within her power to do so. Ouch. "I'm sure that I could have petitioned to Jackson's very lovely kindergarten teacher, but honestly, the entire experience had been so mortifying and panic inducing, I didn't even bother," she said.

Darcy sat up straighter and looked dead into my eyes, as if giving me the most important warning of my life. "But the blackballing wasn't the worst part. When I came home from work on the day of the Halloween party, Jackson was slumped over his iPad with a look of complete dejection. I asked him over and over how the party was and kept being answered with a curt 'fine.' Finally, while we were reading *Don't Let the Pigeon Stay Up Late!* in bed, Jackson broke out in tears and revealed that Madeline Giordani, Charlotte's clone of a daughter, had told the entire class that 'Jackson has a dumb, ugly mommy.'"

I gasped, not wanting to imagine how I'd react if Lucy came home and told me about a similar experience. We are heroes in our children's eyes until someone tells them otherwise. And Madeline was Lucy's new friend. Did I have something to be worried about? But I shook it off. These were *kids* we were talking about. When my daughter was in kindergarten, she told me that I looked like a pretty little pig. They don't really know what they're saying at that age.

Darcy shrugged and eyed her coffee cup. "And now I'm the parking lot pariah."

I felt bad for her. Darcy was smart and witty and had welcomed me at first glance. But this pettiness didn't match her obvious intelligence. Why did this group get under her skin so much? She seemed better than that. It felt like we were always talking about them.

I tried to pivot.

"The real question is, Who *was* the masked parking bandit? Xoxo, Gossip Girl," I said.

Darcy finished the last sip of her cold brew and smiled. "I knew I liked you, Kansas."

Interview Transcript with Patricia Walker

For profile in *Magic City* magazine, summer issue 2019
By Andres Castano
October 1, 2018, Session 3

INTERVIEWER: It is so nice to see you today, Patricia. You are looking lovely, as always.

PATRICIA: Thank you, Andres. It is nice to be seen. How have you been?

INTERVIEWER: Very well, thank you. How about you? Did you ever find out the identity of that nefarious parking spot bandit?

PATRICIA: I did, and I'm still annoyed about the parking spot. It was that awful Darcy Resnick. She has so much nerve; it's unbelievable. She's a mom from school who flat-out despises Don and me.

INTERVIEWER: Such a shame. These things are almost always rooted in jealousy. Don't you think?

PATRICIA: You might be right. Charlotte, she's the PTA woman who does all the fundraisers, she called us after "ParkingGate" and was beside herself. She was on the phone with Don for half an hour apologizing. I almost felt bad for her. I mean, we support the school to benefit the kids, but of course I expect a certain level of respect for the many, many contributions we have made to Sunset Academy over the years. We even funded the new state-of-the-art performing arts center for Miami Beach Middle School, and our oldest won't be there for three more years. What has Darcy underwritten, a pencil sharpener for the classroom?

INTERVIEWER: Yikes. This Darcy seems like a piece of work. I'd think the school parents would be profoundly grateful for all your contributions.

PATRICIA: Exactly. You would think the other parents would appreciate everything we've done, but I guess that some people would rather starve than accept a free meal. Lucky for them, Don and I are committed to Maddox and Monrow experiencing the "real world" in public school to counteract all their privilege. It's character building. And the craziest thing is that we could send the boys *anywhere.* We could leave Miami-Dade public schools in a second for any of the tri-county's prestigious privates and take our generous support along with us. No offense, but that would literally affect every single student and family at Sunset Academy and even Miami Beach Middle.

INTERVIEWER: Do you think it's important to raise Maddox and Monrow as though all this privilege could disappear at any moment?

PATRICIA: . . .

INTERVIEWER: I'm sorry, I didn't mean . . .

PATRICIA: Why would it disappear? Am I on the record right now?

INTERVIEWER: Of course not, sorry. Would you like to get started?

PATRICIA: Yes, let's move on. There's so much I'd rather discuss than Darcy Resnick. I need to remain in a positive place as we put the finishing touches on Villa Rosé.

INTERVIEWER: Yes! Villa Rosé. *Magic City* is keen on getting an exclusive. Are there any details that you can share with me today?

PATRICIA: It would be my pleasure. Our new home has been my full-time job for the last five years, and I have managed every aspect of the project, from securing the half-acre waterfront lot to selecting the architect and interior designers, and finally overseeing the placement of every light fixture, power outlet, and baseboard. The result is Miami's first modern masterpiece that is appointed with all floor-to-ceiling rose-colored glass. It took some convincing to get Don on board (he can be such an old-fashioned man) but, in the end, he agreed that it was *the* quintessential Miami Beach color. And no one had been bold enough to do it before us. There's excitement in being the first.

We wanted the home to be a nod to the golden age of Miami Beach, with its pink art deco structures and gilded geometric patterns. But adding a modern sophistication. At great expense, we commissioned the best modern architect in Paris and had them cooperate with a local builder. Then we brought in a top-notch New York designer, the same one who did Gwyneth's apartment, to fill the spaces with all the warm touches of home, but with a distinct Walker flair, like our kidney-shaped blush velvet sofas, custom Rosa Portogallo stone dining table, artfully appointed seating areas, and Calacatta marble built-in bar. Currently, we are finalizing a well-thought-out collection with our art consultant. We worked to procure as many pieces as possible before the Art Basel craziness. All of those pseudo-collectors make such a rush on contemporary pieces, it artificially inflates the pricing for everyone. After the install of the new collection, the home will be photoshoot ready.

INTERVIEWER: Incredible. We will wait for your go-ahead, just give us a week or so of lead time so we can schedule the photographer. Do you have a date in mind?

PATRICIA: The home's official unveiling is in just two weeks, on October 12, so as you can see I have quite a lot on my plate. We are celebrating Villa Rosé with a weekend of back-to-back events, our opportunity to welcome Miami society into our new home. On Friday, we are hosting an exclusive dinner party for the Art Deco Preservation Society. It will be an intimate hundred-person black-tie event with a special musical performance and dancing under the stars—I wish I could divulge the singer, but we really must keep it a surprise for the guests. They've donated a thousand dollars a seat to be wowed. Then, on Saturday, we are opening our doors to the Sunset Academy PTA for their first general meeting of the year. Typically, the event is held at school, but really, who wants to spend their evening in a crowded auditorium that smells like unwashed gym shorts? Charlotte thought the Sunset Academy mission would feel more impactful if we wined and dined the parents a bit. For many of the parents, it will be a special opportunity to experience glamour they don't typically have access to, and I am happy to provide that.

DARCY

I'm sorry but who names a house? That grants you automatic inclusion in the douche and douchette society, in my book. Though it does make me smile that they named their fancy *villa* after a cheap wine that moms drink at playdates. Their next home should be called Franzia Estate.

Get a load of the invitation:

SUNSET PARENTS/GUARDIANS ARE CORDIALLY INVITED TO
KICK OFF THE SCHOOL YEAR WITH THE PTA AT THE
OFFICIAL UNVEILING OF VILLA ROSÉ

1800 Peacock Drive

Generously Hosted by Donald and Patricia Walker

Saturday, October 13 at 6 o'clock in the evening
Cocktail attire

Please RSVP by October 1 to Charlotte Giordani

I'd have rather administered myself an unmedicated colonoscopy, but I had already roped in poor Melody Howard, that nice, untarnished new mom from Kansas. It turns out, the newbie is something of a charity world maven. She left behind a successful consulting firm that focused exclusively on nonprofits to follow her husband's promotion and, lo and behold, it turns out she misses the challenge of restructuring and strategizing on behalf of struggling clients. Well, we have quite the struggling prospect for her! Struggling to find their moral compass in a storm of unethical initiatives, that is.

I have actually read the PTA bylaws, and the rules about preferential treatment for school-related services and conflicts of interest are both unequivocal. In other words, the Walker family's eponymous buildings at both Sunset Academy and Miami Beach Middle should not have been developed in a no-bid contract by a company in Walker Equities, LCC's portfolio. The Sunset Academy PTA might be Miami's most corrupt nonprofit.

I took Melody to the PTA-hosted "home unveiling" on October 13, where, in the garish pink glass house, Miami entitlement was on full display. Melody's husband was working late, and mine was stuck in a mediation, so I picked her up like the chivalrous date I am. Our hosts, Patricia and Don, were peacocking around their new home, martini glasses dangling precariously from extended fingertips, pointing out every handblown glass light fixture and custom throw pillow. Melody and I were greeted at the entrance with the soft sounds of a young violinist, perched between the grand foyer and the great room, and were offered the "signature cocktail" of the evening: a "sunset rosé" concocted with vodka, muddled strawberries, fresh basil, and a splash of rosé champagne. To be honest, it was delicious. "Lifestyles of the rich and famous, dahhhling," I drawled in response to Melody's bewildered expression.

"Is this a normal PTA meeting?" she whispered. No. Nothing about this should be considered normal.

As if on cue, Charlotte Giordani, the belle of the overblown public-school function, appeared at the top of the floating staircase, cradling a stack of papers and wearing a lacy fascinator, like it was the fucking Kentucky Derby. By her side was the elegant Gabriela Machado, lame duck PTA president. She had enjoyed a prosperous two-year tenure under the robust, if not completely immoral, Giordani fundraising boon and would soon be taking her talents, and only child, to Miami Beach Middle.

"Welcome, parents and faculty, to our first general PTA meeting of the year!" Gabriela said from the top step. Down below, the rest of us plebes were huddled together for a prime view of the spectacle. She continued with something to the effect of "We are so excited to kick off our most ambitious year yet, as we plan to increase after-school enrichment offerings, produce our first-ever school play, purchase two hundred new iPads for classroom use, and fully fund a new cutting-edge media lab and library. And what better way to launch a mile-stone school year than in the stunning new home of our most generous hosts, Don and Patricia Walker!"

Villa Rosé's king and queen held court midway up the staircase and nodded down to the assembled mass, arms around each other's waist.

The truth is, all these innovations and refurbishments would clearly be a benefit to Sunset Academy, but at what cost? What are we teaching our children when the wealthiest public school in the county is propped up with college-level technology and resources, while our inner-city counterparts can provide only a free lunch? One of my husband's pro bono clients this year was a tenth grader from Liberty High, a D-rated school in the very same district as Sunset, who was arrested for *borrowing* his classroom laptop to finish his homework. Why couldn't he just grab one from our prestigious elementary school, where dozens are still sealed in boxes in a storage closet, collecting dust?

Charlotte stepped into the spotlight. "And now, let us meet outside to continue the party with cocktails and canapés overlooking beautiful Biscayne Bay."

In the mixed bag of partygoers, there were PTA board members, school parents, and slightly embarrassed-looking Sunset Academy faculty and staff. Ms. Sanchez, Jackson's third-grade teacher, was smiling amiably next to the glossy grand piano, while shooting me a conspiratorial *what the fuck* glance. Meanwhile, Charlotte had slid her way next to Don Walker, expressing, no doubt, effusive gratitude for the evening's pomp and circumstance.

All thousand-ish Sunset Academy families had been invited to the soirée, and an astonishing close to six hundred people showed up. Definitely a PTA event record. I'd venture to say the typical meeting attracts a paltry ten to twenty, while parties can pull up to five hundred guests. I suppose this particular event was part meeting/part party, but I'll wager that it drew such an impressive crowd because people wanted to gawk at the shiny new mansion.

I explained the attendee breakdown to Melody. "About a third of these people actually care about the school and the PTA. Another third of them are here because they hate Charlotte and want to talk smack about her later. And the last third are here only for free food and booze."

"Which third do we fall into?" Melody asked. I hope rhetorically.

When we joined the others outside, the enveloping humidity marked the transition from blasting A/C to Miami night air. Autumn in Florida is really summer part two, sticky with a light breeze beginning to tease cooler days ahead. Melody and I joined the rest of the attendees spread out on the Walkers' massive waterfront lawn. With the glittering bay as a backdrop, a DJ crouched over an up-lit acrylic bar and played soft electronic beats.

"Well, hello there, how delightful that you came." A catlike Charlotte approached Melody, slinking in her skintight black midi dress. "And Darcy, how *interesting* to find you here. I didn't realize you had any interest in our PTA meetings. But this is a special one," she said through tight lips.

"Yes, I just love free drinks and finger foods. Can't resist them," I responded.

"Well, enjoy them, Darcy," she said, "especially after that sting of a tow bill from the first day of school. All such a strange misunderstanding. Live and learn, I always say."

She turned to Melody. "Now, I hear that you have quite the organizational background! We could use someone with your attitude and experience on the PTA." Then, as if having the greatest idea of all time, she clutched her chest and said, "Oh, you should take my spot as VP of fundraising next year! And we must get the girls together. Maddy goes on and on about adorable Lucy. And here"—she handed both of us a paper from her stack—"I'm running for PTA president next year. We will miss Gabriela, but someone has to try and step into her shoes!"

With that, she snap turned to solicit her next victim.

Charlotte's letter was typed on heavy stationery and emitted a subtle fragrance of lavender. Perfume?

FROM THE DESK OF CHARLOTTE GIORDANI

Dear Sunset Academy Parents and Guardians,
It is with great excitement that I announce my candidacy for Sunset Academy's 2019–2020 PTA president!

For three years, I have served our beautiful school as vice president of fundraising, lead room parent, event chair, cafeteria volunteer, and parent liaison. My efforts have resulted in the many renovations and upgrades that our children enjoy today. These include, but are not limited to: record-breaking fundraising, our beautifully upgraded basketball court, our new state-of-the-art STEM lab, the beloved organic salad bar I launched in the cafeteria, cutting-edge reading and math resources, and brand-new instruments for our children to enjoy during music class.

This is only scratching the surface of what I would be able to accomplish as your president!

I sincerely hope that you will endorse me for the role of PTA president, and vote "yes" for Charlotte Giordani. It would be an honor to lead Sunset Academy into the next decade!

Go Sunset Seagulls!
Yours Truly,
Charlotte Giordani

It was nauseating.

"Sounds like she's a shoo-in," Melody said.

The slow burn in the pit of my gut bubbled higher and higher, threatening volcanic eruption at any moment.

"You should run," I blurted. "You're looking for an entrance into the Miami philanthropic scene, and this is the perfect opportunity to prove yourself." I told her that Sunset Academy comprised many of the wealthiest families in the county. Collectively, they sat on the boards of every major charity in town and could recommend her to consult on their various causes. "Not only that," I said, "but Sunset *needs* you to run the PTA. Our financial statements are nonexistent, and we are alienating more than ninety percent of our families with elitist events and initiatives. I mean, just look around. Most of these people are horrified, as they should be. They don't want to be pressured into naming a building or spending five hundred dollars a seat for a cafeteria gala. You should hear them whisper about all the *innovative* initiatives that the Charlottes come up with. Even the ones that have the money find them ridiculous. And make no mistake, most of our student body families *do not* have the money.

"Also, the PTA's business practices are questionable at best. Trust me, there are so many of us ready to see Charlotte Giordani and her crew taken down. I've been having these conversations for years. There are the working moms who don't have time and the reasonable fed-up ones who don't have the experience. And now, here you are. We've been waiting so long for the right successor."

Exhale.

MELODY

The last thing I wanted was bad blood at a new school, in a new city, even if Darcy had made some compelling points.

The perfect opportunity to prove yourself in the Miami philanthropic scene. She was a good salesperson. It had been only a couple months, and not working was making me restless. I found myself baking obscene amounts of zucchini muffins and spent far too much time "exploring" local boutiques. Both things I didn't have much time for or interest in back in Wichita. I began to wonder: How much of my identity was tied to my former career?

I recalled my "Miami," "charity" Google search, the fancy clothing and diamonds the size of hard candy. I did want to start a new nonprofit consulting firm in town, and what Darcy said was true. I would need an introduction to the philanthropic community, and a cold call wouldn't cut it. Several of Miami's key charity-world players were Sunset Academy parents, so there was truth to what Darcy had said. Many of the same people who appeared on my Web browser in tuxedos and sequined gowns were at drop-off wearing fashionable work attire or workout gear. An active role at the school would be a smart way to meet them.

Still, running for PTA president seemed like a stretch. Charlotte was clearly the more likely candidate, and I did love the idea of serving as her VP of fundraising. I could establish myself in town, and also hope to make a positive impact at my daughter's school. But some of what Darcy had said lingered in my mind. I couldn't argue that something seemed *off* with the existing parental leadership at Sunset Academy. Lots of schools and even well-respected nonprofits can come across as insular, accessible only at the highest tier by those *in the know*. But this place seemed next level. There were special concessions for top donors and the PTA board, like unlimited access to teachers and administrators through their personal cell phones, and the children of this inner circle seemed to be placed in what were deemed the best classrooms and the most coveted after-school programs. And, of course, there was the pay-for-play parking spot.

Could I address these inconsistencies while also staying in the good graces of Sunset Academy's privileged class? Darcy claimed that there was a large contingency of parents who were eager for a regime change. Professionals with little time to involve themselves with school politics, and others that simply prefer to avoid conflict. Apparently, these parents whispered behind their paper water cups at school and side-messaged off the grade-level WhatsApp chats, but many were too nervous to speak out. I would be their mouthpiece. Darcy had made mental notes (and possibly even physical notes; this lady was committed) about *who* wanted change and *what* improvements they'd like to see.

It was also becoming clear that I'd have some trouble navigating relationships with both Darcy and Charlotte. I mean, Darcy *hated* that woman, though I couldn't fully understand why. On the one hand, Charlotte was very charismatic. But it was also true that she had a side that made me feel conflicted. So much of what came out of her mouth was offensive, like "Your daughter has the perfect body. Have you thought about putting her in modeling?" Which she said about my eight-year-old one morning at drop-off. I didn't know if I was more horrified or, I'm embarrassed to admit, flattered. Charlotte took up so much space, as though her energy created a force field around her, an impenetrable bubble. One couldn't help standing just beyond the glow, rapt at every word. Mesmerized, as by a cult leader. Honestly, I liked her. This strange creature. I was oddly drawn to her, like she was the bizarro Miami world version of me. In a weird way, I had been the Charlotte of my town, so part of me understood her. She was out there. But harmless, right? I really hoped neither woman would ask me to choose sides.

A couple weeks after the Villa Rosé event, Darcy invited Greg, Lucy, and me to a Halloween party with her and her family. Full disclosure: I *love* Halloween. Some of my fondest memories of growing up in Wichita are from racing down my neighborhood streets, unsupervised, trick-or-treating with a gaggle of friends. We'd all pull the pillowcases off our bedroom pillows and tear into our neighbors' stashes: orange plastic pumpkins on their doorsteps overstuffed with Skittles, M&M's, Snickers bars. We'd dress up in odd combinations of old playroom clothes, draw some whiskers on our cheeks or blood dripping down our lips, and voilà! Costume-ready.

I was excited to receive the call from Darcy, but also a little nervous. Everything in Miami seemed different from what I knew growing up. Even something as simple as picture day at school was bizarre to me. One mom had asked me, rather aggressively: *You're going to schedule a blowout for Lucy before school, right? Or at least the night before and have her sleep in a shower cap?* I wondered if Halloween would be sweet and whimsical or some kind of fancy juvenile masquerade ball.

"It's the best night of the year," Darcy had assured me. "You'll almost forget about all the terrible people who are there."

There was a neighborhood called Parkview, she told me, that went all out every Halloween. The houses went into fierce competition outdecorating one another and they all passed out top-quality candy. A sea of trick-or-treaters would flood the streets as far as the eye could see. The best part, according to Darcy, was that one of the third-grade families threw a raging preparty where all the parents got tipsy and all the kids got a preemptive sugar high before everyone dispersed to go house to house. Greg and I don't shy away from a good time, and Lucy was overjoyed to spend the holiday with her new friends, so we were in. Lucy wasted no time planning a coordinating costume with Maddy Giordani. *Zombie cheerleaders!* Her excitement was contagious, and I found myself counting down the days to the big event.

I found what I thought was a perfect zombie cheerleader costume at the big Halloween Depot off Lincoln Road, Miami Beach's sprawling outdoor mall. Lucy and I ambled the aisles together, trying on dead president and Pennywise masks for fun, until we spotted the perfect red-and-black dress, complete with splatters of fake blood. Size medium, 8–10 years old. We upgraded the look with a pair of black pom-poms and felt like we were all set.

Halloween arrived on a Thursday, and Lucy wore the costume to school. I was so excited for her to experience her first holiday in the new city, but she came home disappointed, telling me that all her other friends had worn a different costume than they had all discussed. Maddy was a unicorn instead of a zombie cheerleader; Lola was Wonder Woman instead of a ballerina. I worried that she'd been pranked, *Legally Blonde* style, and the thought almost sent me into a spiral. But no, she told me. As it turned out, everyone had been *saving* their real costume for the party. We just didn't get the memo.

That evening, I smeared some white makeup all over Lucy's face and drew stitches on her forehead with black eyeliner. Greg and I were dressed as the Big Bad Wolf and Little Red Riding Hood. Costumes also picked up from Halloween Depot. "Do you think this getup reads a little sexual?" Greg asked me while staring not so innocently at my red velvet skirt.

"Have you seen how these people dress when it's not Halloween?" I responded. "I think we'll be okay."

We pulled up to the party around four P.M., about an hour before trick-or-treating would be in full swing. The home was gorgeous. A sprawling modern house on a corner lot with a spacious, gated front yard. Waterfront, with a canal in the back. The third-grade parents who owned it, the Vogels, were in the exotic automobile business, and a trio of red Ferraris were parked on evenly spaced angles in the driveway. The hosts were, adorably, both dressed in race car driver jumpsuits. (Also Ferrari, definitely not from Halloween Depot.)

The party was over-the-top, which didn't surprise me too much after the Villa Rosé night. The decorations looked professional and were coordinated around a *Night of the Living Dead* theme. There was a DJ set up in front of the garage, playing a Kidz Bop mix at a volume that made conversation impossible. A buffet with rows of gleaming chafing dishes spanned one side of the driveway, containing hot dogs, burgers, and chicken fingers for the kids, and roasted brussels sprouts, grilled chicken, and steamed mahi-mahi for the adults.

Zombie-clad servers passed out nonalcoholic beverages from silver trays, and a bartender held court on the other side of the driveway, whipping up custom cocktails and pouring wine for the somewhere around two hundred costumed guests. Greg braved the lines for us and returned triumphant with the signature drink of the evening: the witches' brew, which was really just a pisco sour with dry ice smoking on top.

"I could get used to this," Greg said, as he cheersed my witches' brew.

"Me too," I admitted. "Miami has grown on me."

It was the truth. The scenery and weather couldn't be beat (back home we'd already be in long sleeves by now, but Halloween in Miami was a sweatfest if you were wearing anything but short skirts and tank tops), and we all seemed to be assimilating in different ways. Greg was loving the new job, and he often had a drink with his colleagues after work. It was comforting to see how fulfilled he seemed, how sure he was about following his career instincts. Lucy was practically a local with her new social circle and after-school activities. And I was feeling my way around the new people, too. Not to mention excited about opening a consulting firm in town. I really felt I could add value to the Miami nonprofit scene. I was good at that kind of work, and I wanted to find career fulfillment, too, like Greg had.

A few minutes after our arrival, Lucy squealed with delight and made a beeline to another zombie cheerleader, only this one had on what was clearly a much-higher-quality costume. Neatly pleated skirt, fitted top, hand-painted blood spatters. Must have been a custom-made Etsy purchase. My heart sank. Madeline Giordani was the American Girl doll to Lucy's Target knockoff. Even her hair and makeup looked to be professionally done. (It was, I found out later. Glamsquad.) But neither girl seemed to care, and as soon as they embraced, that was it. Lucy was gone for the night.

I couldn't help but feel self-conscious for my daughter. Or like I had failed her with my costume and home-styled face paint. But before I could sink any further into that doubt, a magnificent Cleopatra put her hands on my shoulders.

"Okay," she said. "Turn your face to the *side*."

I obliged, and the stunning Charlotte/Cleopatra pressed the side of her face gently onto mine. "Now, *that* is how you avoid an embarrassing lip kiss." She smiled, in her broad and inviting way, and I doubled over laughing.

"See! I just needed someone to teach me." I lifted my witches' brew.

"That's what I am here for, Melody." She remembered my name. "But oh my gosh, you must think I am the rudest person in the world." She patted me on the shoulder like an old friend.

"Why would I think that?" I asked.

Charlotte tilted her champagne glass toward my nose. "Because I keep telling you that I'm going to have you for a playdate and, you know, tell you all about Miami. And then nada. I swear, I'm not a flake! We are going to do this, Little Miss Riding Hood!"

I told her I was looking forward it, and I meant it. Charlotte was *really* starting to grow on me. I could picture us becoming good friends, sharing confidences over smoothies. Kind of an odd couple, but with more in common than we thought, maybe. She was feeling more and more familiar to me. The warm, easy conversation. She seemed like the type who would be up for fun, conspiratorial but always good-natured gossip.

Darcy found me a little while later. She and her husband were dressed as Lily and Herman Munster. It was an endearing throwback. Their son, Jackson, was some cute Pokémon character that I didn't recognize, and he was busying himself jousting with the other third-grade boys.

"Do you think the swords are Freudian?" Darcy asked, approaching me from the bar.

I shrugged and instead responded, "Love the costume! And thank you so much for telling me about this party. You weren't kidding when you said it was a good time!"

Darcy took a long look into the crowd. "Yeah, I do love this one. It sure brings everyone out. For better or for worse."

She nodded over to Charlotte/Cleopatra and a dashing Mark Antony. "We even have an appearance from the rare, endangered species known as Charlotte Giordani's husband, James. He is rarely seen in public, which is for protection, because he is married to an apex predator."

I chuckled and said, "Really, she doesn't seem all that bad." I hoped we could pivot quickly off the subject.

Darcy eyed me up and down. "Heaven help us. Kansas drank the Kool-Aid."

She pointed toward the buffet at a perfect ringer for Phyllis Nefler from *Troop Beverly Hills*. "Gabriela Machado is here? Her daughter is in fifth grade; this is a third-grade function," she said. And then, shaking her head, "I guess the PTA president is automatically invited to every party. Perk of the job! By the way, have you given any more thought to running?"

I didn't know how to tell Darcy that I wasn't going to run, that I didn't want to risk Charlotte hating me for some long-shot plan. "No. I don't think it's the right time. I am just getting to know everyone. I want to network, but I also don't want to step on anybody's toes."

"Well, it's a two-year commitment," Darcy said. "Lucy is already in fourth grade next year. If you don't do it now, you won't do it at all. But of course, no pressure."

It felt like pressure, and I wondered why she cared so much.

Darcy continued her explanation of the crowd. "There's my friend, the esteemed Judge Carol Lawson, and her husband, Samuel." She pointed her cocktail toward a beautiful couple dressed as the Tin Man and Glinda the Good Witch, the wife's gown tapered just enough to still look tasteful.

"And oh my god, there go the Walkers with their poor personal trainer slash indentured man servant." Darcy pulled my attention over to Don and Patricia Walker, who were with a young, handsome, and very fit young man. The three of them were all dressed like people out of an eighties workout video. Rainbow headbands and wristbands, toned bare midriffs. Olivia Newton-John's "Physical" played in my head.

"They brought their trainer to a kids' Halloween party?" I asked. I didn't love Darcy's snarky tone, but I joined in with her disbelief on this one.

"Oh, they bring him everywhere." Darcy took a sip of her drink. "It's weird. He's *part of the family*, you know. Rich people love to say that about the help. As if having them around isn't completely self-serving."

It was definitely odd. I mean, I could see them becoming close friends after spending so much time together. But why not meet up, I don't know, after a kids' party? The Walkers were kooky. But that was so often true of the very wealthy.

The day after Halloween, I received a text from Charlotte. She'd followed up, as promised, to invite me to a girls' lunch with her and Patricia Walker. To *get me up to speed* about things in town. It was a sweet gesture, and I was curious to get to know Patricia better, too. She was a pillar of Miami society, which was impressive, and I also looked forward to picking her brain about local philanthropies. It seemed like the perfect research opportunity for launching my new consulting firm.

I realized pretty quickly, however, that no such conversation would take place. I met the ladies at Opa, an upscale Greek restaurant a block over from the beach, and dressed way fancier than I ever would have back in Kansas for a weekday lunch: a belted T-shirt dress and new ankle booties. Charlotte was waiting for me at the table, stunning as usual in a neon pink cropped cashmere sweater and denim skirt. But as striking as she always looked, it was Patricia who just about took my breath away. Charlotte and I had started in on hummus, and the whole restaurant took notice when the third member of our party arrived. The society maven was decked out in a low-cut bodycon dress and wore five-inch crystal-studded pumps, which made her appear almost Amazonian.

"Hey, gorgeous!" Charlotte air-kissed her friend from the table. "Oh my god, is that the 19?"

"Hi, girls," Patricia said while seating herself. We hadn't at that point been formally introduced, but she air-kissed me just the same. "It is." She held up a quilted purse with a long two-toned chain. "Chanel is officially releasing it in a couple months, but my shopper got her hands on one from the runway."

"Amazing!" Charlotte looked genuinely impressed. "She is to die for." I think she was talking about the purse.

"I'll ask my girl if she can get her hands on another one," Patricia said. She took a celery stick and dabbed the end in a bit of hummus. "But you have to put me in touch with your flower guy."

This flower guy, Charlotte explained to me, put together the most beautiful arrangements and could have them delivered within the hour. Perfect for when you've forgotten a friend's birthday or there's a sudden tragic event. I nodded along, but inside I couldn't get over the fact that these women had a "flower guy" and a "Chanel girl." I tucked my own leather tote bag from Dillard's a little farther behind my chair.

We ordered our main courses, and the conversation moved to bullying, and I was hopeful that we had veered into something I could add to. It was a topic that concerned me, as the mother of a young girl, and I had read several articles on the subject. I was a little thrown, however, when Charlotte's take was something like, "The thing is, it is so important for girls to find their group. If they don't find it, there are all kinds of psychological problems." She explained that this is what *experts* said, and she had read it somewhere or other. "But when they do find their group," she continued, "they can never leave."

It was a dark take on girl dynamics.

Patricia agreed. "That's why it's so important to make friends with moms you trust. So you can control as much as possible in your kids' social environment." She ate a few bites of her steamed fish and declared herself *so full*. Then said, "Thank god I have boys. I don't envy the kind of drama you two will have to deal with."

"It's settled then," Charlotte said. "Maddy and Lucy will be best friends and we will never have to worry about bullying or mean girls or cutting or whatever else kids are doing these days!" She winked at me, actually winked. But what would have been a little weird and inappropriate if I tried to pull it off was oddly charming from her.

"Sounds like a plan," I said, and for some reason added, "You ladies are a scream."

Patricia and Charlotte exchanged a glance that made my heart momentarily race, until Charlotte cut the tension with, "I told you this Kansas girl was adorable."

"So cute," Patricia agreed, and I must have blushed, because all of a sudden my cheeks became very hot. From anyone else, it might have sounded condescending, but from these women it sounded like a real term of endearment. "We should introduce our husbands," she added, and my heart quickened. It seemed like it was coming so easily, getting to know this power couple. But my hopes were dashed as quickly as they rose.

"He's the best fund manager in town," Patricia continued. "He doesn't usually take in new investors, but I'm sure he'd make an exception for a friend."

I didn't know how to respond and took an extended sip of water to buy some time. There was no way that Greg's and my meager savings were big enough to invest with Donald Walker. "Oh, that sounds great," I finally answered. "He's a hotel manager, so . . ."

"No business at the table." Charlotte saved me. "Let's leave that to the finance bros, and we can stick to the actual important stuff. Like planning a boat day for Patricia's birthday."

I assumed she meant a day on a powerboat, maybe fishing or just enjoying the ocean, but thank god I didn't say that out loud.

"Well, our captain is usually off on Wednesdays, but I'm sure he can make an exception," Patricia said. She had a *captain*.

Charlotte spread her fingers into jazz hands. "Patricia's boat, *EBITDA* it's called. That's some financey name that all the husbands think is so clever. Anyway, she's gorgeous. Tri-decker, four bedrooms. And all the toys: Jet Skis, slides. Will be so fun for a day on the bay."

A yacht. This woman owned a yacht.

DARCY

The first time I met Donald and Patricia Walker was on Halloween night, three years ago. Jackson was in kindergarten (yes, this was the same fateful Halloween season that Charlotte and I became school mom enemies).

Trick-or-treating is still a thing in Miami Beach, yet another tradition that can make our world-class city sometimes still feel like a small town. And the absolute best neighborhood to solicit at strangers' doors is an affluent residential enclave in Mid-Beach called Parkview. It doesn't matter where in Miami Beach you live, everyone in the know will trek over to this particular area and park on someone's grass (hopefully a friend's) around four o'clock on Halloween to be in the prime trick-or-treating location. It's like the VIP vernissage of Art Basel, but for kids.

Every house for five glorious blocks outdoes the next with decor and candy. There's the haunted house with a tree full of Ring Pops, and the coffin that, once approached, has a grown man jump out holding full-size Hershey's bars. It's all a well-organized spectacle. Police block off the streets for pedestrian traffic only, and about two thousand costumed parents and children spend the evening miraculously not losing one another. For the most part, that is. It's a delight for the kid in all of us.

That year, Jackson was dressed up as Captain America. In the history of the world, there's never been anything cuter than my five-year-old in his blue-and-red spandex pants and puffy muscle shirt saying,

"Avengers: Assemble." He wielded his vibranium shield with such poise and authority, I swear he was a dead ringer for Captain Steve Rogers. Elliot and I played his backup S.H.I.E.L.D. agents, Coulson and Hill, but everyone thought we just came from the office wearing all black. A for effort?

By the end of the first block, Jackson's jack-o'-lantern treat bucket was halfway full of Twizzlers, Nerds, Snickers, and other classics, and he was vacillating between elation and a kind of spastic sugar overdose. Elliot and I had treated ourselves to a couple of vodka soda roadies and were feeling warm and lubricated.

We followed our Captain America from house to house, content as we passed werewolves, princesses, SpongeBobs, and vampires. The familiar call and response was sung at every doorstep: *Trick or treat! Here you go. Thank you!* The tradition, one of few things unchanged from the generation gap of parent to child, brought such contentment that I found myself zoomed into the present moment, living it without distraction. Or so I thought. I reached for Jackson's hand and gave a loving squeeze. But when Captain America turned around, it was not *our* Captain America.

My buzz evaporated. Elliot and I ditched impostor Jackson and raced back down Parkview Lane, shrieking our son's name. Six, seven, eight Captain Americas deflated us along the way. At that point, we lost all concept of time. Was it five minutes or fifty? Nothing made sense with the adrenaline pumping through our veins—not breathing, not screaming. But we were doing those nonetheless, automatically, our worst nightmare suddenly a reality.

Elliot and I had circled the entire block twice over when across the street we spotted our Captain America. About forty-two inches high, black Nikes below blue-and-red spandex. I bolted in his direction, lifted by elation and relief, and tugged hard on one puffy-sleeved arm to spin the boy around. Only, it wasn't Jackson. To our detriment, *The Avengers* had been released earlier in the year, and our costume choice had been far from unique.

In my heightened adrenaline state, I had accidentally torn the not-Jackson Captain America's sleeve at the shoulder, exposing a tuft of white polyester stuffing. The startled boy screamed for his mother, who then rushed to his side. A statuesque Catwoman, in head-to-toe latex, towered over my still-crouched body. "What the *hell* do you think you are doing?" she demanded.

Lacking any rational thought, I was stuck on an absurd query. *Why Catwoman? She's DC, and Captain America is Marvel. That doesn't make any sense as a family costume.*

"Get your hands off my son this instant!" Catwoman shouted.

I hadn't realized that I was still squeezing the terrified boy's arm. I released my grip. "I'm sorry!" I was sure this woman, another mother, would understand my terror. "My son is wearing the exact same costume. He's lost!"

"Well, it cannot be the *exact* same costume," the woman replied. "This is a limited edition, and it's customized with my son's name—Maddox—on the chest. And now it's ruined."

If it wouldn't have resulted in a lawsuit, I might have spat in her face. Jackson was still somewhere out there, alone.

"Darcy?" A she-devil joined the conversation. "What is going on here?"

"Well, this woman thought Maddox was her son, and she just ran over and grabbed him by the arm, and tore his sleeve!" Catwoman threw her hands in the air.

"Oh my god, Patricia, Maddox must be terrified." The she-devil was Charlotte. How appropriate.

"I need to find my son! My son is fucking lost!" I screamed.

She-devil Charlotte did not seem impressed. "Is this how you speak in front of the children?" she whispered.

She turned around to her trick-or-treating posse. "Listen up!" she instructed. "We have a lost boy, kindergartner, about Maddox's height, dressed as Captain America, answers to the name Jackson."

Grateful and mortified. Terrified and hopeful. I followed the she-devil like a whipped dog, as her minions spread out to cover more ground.

With her red lamé miniskirt, corset, and pitchfork, Charlotte looked more ready for the pole than a child's holiday, but the sun was starting to set, and she offered me the numbers I needed. She walked at breakneck speed, a necessary pace, and her little Madeline kept up with the same urgency. Five-year-old Madeline was the angel to her mother's devil. She wore what must have been a custom-made white-as-snow tutu, with a gorgeous sequined bodice and layer upon layer of ethereal tulle. But the costume's pièce de résistance was her delicate and stunning angel wings. They spanned twice the length of Madeline's tiny body and were adorned in pure white feathers. Following from behind, the small child did in fact appear to have descended from the heavens.

A Victoria's Secret Angel, I thought. She fucking made her kinder-gartner a Victoria's Secret Angel. At least there was no crystal bralette.

We were crossing Steinberg Park, at the entrance of the Parkview neighborhood, when I spotted him. *My* Captain America, red-faced, holding hands with a lanky Darth Vader. I blew past the devil and the angel and scooped up my precious boy, harnessing a strength that I didn't think possible. The force was so great, I almost tossed him into the sky, but instead managed to keep him in my arms, safe, together.

"Ace in the hole, Ax." Charlotte patted Vader on the shoulder. "You found our missing Avenger."

Axel Giordani, Charlotte's second favorite child, was from that day forward a hero in my eyes.

Wordless, Jackson and I trailed Charlotte and Madeline back to Park Lane, where her followers were informed that the mission had been successful, nothing to see here.

Batman marched toward me with conviction, to make sure that we were okay, I was sure. No. This, it turned out, was Catwoman's hus-band, Donald Walker.

"Hey, you! If you *ever* put your hands on my son again, you will be hearing from my lawyer. Do you understand!"

Behind him, Catwoman scowled.

She-devil took note. "Yes, well. I hope we have all learned some valuable lessons today," she said, leading Madeline and Vader back toward her friends. "Now, it's getting a little late. Who wants to go back to my house to sort some candy?" I hate to admit this, but I appreciated the redirect. Though I suspect she was just shielding her friends from further drama.

A chorus of "Meeeee!" rang out from her posse's children.

I hurried Jackson home, and never said thank you.

MELODY

A few days after our girls' lunch, Charlotte invited Lucy and me for an after-school playdate at her house. It was little things like that that made me feel like I was settling more and more into this new town. Charlotte was proving to be easy to talk to, and she was much more available than Darcy. We planned the playdate for Friday, because, she told me, her daughter didn't have piano or ballet, or tennis, or horseback riding, so it would be the perfect time to let the girls play while she educated me on everything about life at Sunset Academy and in Miami Beach.

The Giordani home was only six blocks from ours on Pine Tree, so Lucy and I walked the tree-lined street to their Mediterranean-style mansion. Our street comprised two giant one-way lanes that were sliced in the middle with a majestic line of Australian Pines (thus the name). The eighty-foot firs provided welcome shade from the Florida afternoon sun and added an almost remote residential feel to the otherwise bustling urban neighborhood.

The "dry" (or nonwaterfront) side of Pine Tree consists mostly of tight ten-thousand-square-foot lots with a myriad of mismatched homes. One-story ranches, Old Florida colonial style, historical art deco, the odd modern house. Humble but charming-looking residences with not-so-humble price tags. Real estate in Miami Beach comes at a premium, to put it mildly.

The other side of the street contains all the waterfront homes. There, price per square foot jumps exponentially, and the residents enjoy the beautiful intracoastal as their personal backyards. Lot sizes are sometimes double their stone's-throw "dry" neighbors, and the homes favor glass-and-concrete modern styles or are Scrooge McDuck–esque mansions.

Charlotte's house sat on a corner of the dry side and was classic Miami, with ivory stucco exterior, an orange terra-cotta roof, an impeccably manicured lawn, and hedges of lush fuchsia bougainvilleas.

As we approached the walkway to the home, the front door flew open and expelled a giddy and radiant Madeline. "Lucy!" she chirped, and took my daughter firmly by the hand to lead her inside and as far away from the mothers as possible. My heart swelled. It was such a simple gesture of acceptance and friendship for my Lucy, who was still the new girl in a very new environment.

Maybe, I thought, this crowd wasn't so intimidating after all. I had initially been feeling a little out of place and conspicuous among so much apparent wealth and glamour. It's not that Wichita didn't have well-heeled residents; they just *showed* it differently. They didn't wear it quite so . . . openly.

My host appeared in the doorway with a wide smile and open arms. Her thick brown hair tossed into a messy topknot, she wore a white bodysuit with high-cut denim cutoffs and no shoes. Even her casual look was polished, in a *celebrities, they're just like us* way.

"Pink water or bubbles?" Charlotte asked, as she led me to her neat-as-a-pin, all-white kitchen. I must have looked confused because she followed up with "Rosé wine or champagne, dear?"

"Oh, rosé sounds lovely," I answered.

Then she got down to business. This is the best pediatrician in town, tell him Charlotte sent you; you already know Publix for staple items, Whole Foods for produce, and Fresh Market for proteins. Here is a list of the best activities categorized by day of the week, time of day, and driving distance. What are Lucy's interests? Here is the best place for that, and then go here for dinner as a family, but then go here for dinner on a date night. Do you have a nanny? A good babysitter? You can always drop her here if you're in a pinch.

I tried to keep up, nodding along while sipping my rosé perhaps too eagerly. It was so much to take in! The crisp wine did its job to soothe my nerves as I peppered in "mm-hmm"s, and "oh, wow"s with each recommendation. It felt like I should have been taking notes.

After my crash course in Miami, according to Charlotte, the girls joined us for a cheese and charcuterie platter by the pool.

"Manchego, my favorite," Madeline said, while sliding a triangle of ivory cheese onto a water cracker.

"Me too!" Lucy said, mimicking her friend's movements.

I don't think you've ever eaten Manchego, I wanted to say. But they seemed so bubbly and happy together, I just smiled.

Their attention shifted to something in a second-floor bedroom window. Standing side by side, with long golden hair falling over tanned shoulders, crystal-blue eyes upturned at the same angle, the girls looked like twins. "Look at my weirdo brother." Madeline's delicate mouth twisted into a sneer. Behind the window, a curtain was parted to reveal a lanky adolescent boy with hollow eyes, a blank expression, and long, blue-streaked hair wrapped in a messy bun. I think all four of us shuddered when the curtains abruptly snapped closed.

"Oh, that's just my hormonal firstborn. Ignore him, he's harmless," Charlotte answered my daughter's concerned frown. Then she turned to me and said, "Boys! I should show you baby pictures of Axel. All towheaded curls and sailor suits. Now he's in a *phase,* I think. Never talks to me. Never brings friends over. Who knows if he even has friends at this point? He's not the social type. But if you want to learn how to build a whole world on *Minecraft,* well, he's your guy!" She raised her wineglass and rolled her eyes.

I felt for Charlotte in that moment. Every mother can sympathize with the pain of parenting an unhappy child. Maybe things weren't as perfect or easy for her as it seemed.

"My brother went through a tough time at that age," I told her. "I remember how hard it was for my parents. Always worrying about him, trying to help him. But he grew out of it, and I swear, he's the best guy now."

"That's sweet of you to say." Charlotte gave me a sad smile. "I have faith that he'll come around. I really do. But you're right. It is so hard as a parent." She sipped her rosé and looked back toward the window. "I hate to admit this, but sometimes when I'm watching Maddy at a tennis tournament or ballet recital and people ask me if she has brothers or sisters, I say no. I just don't want to get into the *Well, where is he? Does he play tennis, too?* How terrible is that?"

"Not terrible at all," I said. "It's nobody's business, anyway."

"Well, cheers to that!" Charlotte said, lifting her glass. "Moving on! Let's get some photos for my page! Melody, are you and Lucy following me at MomGoalsMiami yet? Girls, go pose on the pink flamingo floats and hold up your lemonade."

Lucy doesn't have any social media pages, I wanted to say, but thought it would sound silly. Of course she didn't.

The girls bounced into position, kneeling on their designated floats with lemonade in hand. Madeline angled one shoulder in front of the other, pursing her lips toward her mother's iPhone. Lucy followed suit, with surprising accuracy. They finished the impromptu photo shoot with a synchronized dive, holding hands and pouncing off the inflatables into the pool below. Lemonades tumbling in after them.

"Kids are basically born influencers these days," Charlotte said. And I have to admit, I couldn't tell if she was joking or not.

Later that night, I scrolled through Instagram and remembered to follow @MomGoalsMiami.

Wife, Mother, Philanthropist, Friend, Influencer, read her account description. I immediately recognized the page as the kind you love to hate, a guilty pleasure. Hundreds and hundreds of seemingly professional photos and videos followed Charlotte and Madeline on their daily adventures with tags like *Matching Monday* and *We live where you vacation!* It was completely addicting to scroll through, and apparently her 27.6 thousand followers agreed.

The most recent post was a *Vogue*-worthy photo of Lucy and Madeline cheersing atop their identical flamingo pool floats. The caption read *Flamingling on a Friday with our new Friends!*

I'm embarrassed to admit that I felt a rush of flattery at the inclusion. Charlotte was well respected in town and had a large following. And I understood why. She was magnetic, and even her shallowness was honest. She didn't seem like she was putting on an act. Unapologetically herself, which I've always respected. And she had been only kind to Lucy and me.

The Instagram post, though, made me feel conflicted. The parading of our daughters, the performative aspect of posting their photo. The little girl inside me, the one who still craves acceptance and popularity, was tickled to be included. But the moody teenager inside me was snarky and judgmental.

That night in bed, I took a screenshot of the MomGoalsMiami page and texted it to my girlfriend Gail in Kansas, saying, *OMG babe, check out this mom's page. She's either a complete sociopath or my new best friend. I can't tell! You should start @MomGoalsWichita as a competitor. #wefarmwhereyouvacation*

The guilt was instant. Charlotte had been so welcoming to me; it wasn't fair to take a dig at her.

Three bubbles popped up and disappeared. Then *Are you really that dumb?*

Charlotte. I fucking sent the text to Charlotte.

Oh my god, no. How do I recall a message? Shit, Charlotte clearly already saw it and responded. Deny, deny, deny. Lucy did it, it was her fault. Really? Blame it on my eight-year-old? Nice one, Mel. Honestly, we don't even like Miami that much, we can move back to Kansas.

Deep breath.

Two years ago, I helped a client back in Wichita with a social media training. It was for the YMCA, and they wanted to educate their entire staff on best practices, effective messaging, sensitivity issues, and, for embarrassing digital faux pas, crisis management. The specialist I brought in gave us a road map for turning potential disaster into redemption: admit the mistake, explain how your organization's staff and leadership are learning from the mistake, outline steps to ensure said mistake never again occurs, make reparations to those affected. Most reasonable people, the specialist said, would accept this response and move on with their lives.

This specialist had never met Charlotte Giordani, to whom these rules did not apply.

After the cold paralysis of panic began to subside, I unlocked my phone and started typing:

> Charlotte, I am so sorry. That was incredibly insensitive of me and is not an accurate representation of how I feel about you. I was attempting to be funny with an old friend, but I realize now that what I said was just offensive and not funny at all. You have been so kind and welcoming to me, and I truly hope that we can continue to develop our friendship for both our own and our daughters' sakes.

At that point, Greg had joined me in bed and, seeing that I was glued to the phone, slid on his sleep mask and gave me his back.

Five agonizing minutes passed before the response.

> It's 11pm. Are you drunk or something? I'm going to bed . . . You can continue to develop the imaginary friendships in your head, but please don't bother me with that shit. I've known you for five minutes. Thanks for showing your true colors so early! Saves me soooo much time. PS, your daughter is sweet. You can drop her off anytime.

I glanced over at Greg, hoping for a sympathetic ear, but found him gently snoring. By then I had passed the point of panic. The initial rush of adrenaline had come and gone, and now I was left with something worse . . . remorse. This was totally my fault. Charlotte had been nothing but nice to me. And I so quickly betrayed her, mocked her behind her back. Or, as it turned out, in front of her face.

This was a 911 emergency, so I kicked Greg repeatedly under the covers until he pulled off his sleep mask and said, "Sorry, was I snoring?"

"Yes, you were snoring, but also I just did something so stupid and I need help."

"Oh, Jesus," he responded, and sat up in bed, eyes half closed. "What'd you do?"

I explained the whole thing: the playdate, the Instagram post, and the dreaded text. I felt like I needed to make a pot of coffee so we could fully rehash the events and all possible outcomes, no matter how unlikely.

Greg didn't seem to share my sense of urgency.

"I've told you that social media is toxic," he said. "Nothing good comes from it. Also, a phone call is always better than text. No paper trail."

I've told you. Just what every wife wants to hear.

"This is serious, Greg," I said, desperate. "I think I just committed Miami social suicide."

"Like an honor suicide or . . . ?" He tried to joke.

"Can you not?" Where were your girlfriends when you needed them? It was too late to call in reinforcements, and I was not getting any comfort from my soulmate.

Greg gave me a *when am I allowed to go back to sleep* look, and said, "I'm sure this will blow over." He leaned forward and kissed my cheek. "It will look different in the light of day."

CHARLOTTE

When I was a little girl, all wide eyed with auburn curls and chubby cheeks, my mom said I was a living Little Debbie. So she did what any housewife in Weston, Florida, would do and put me in pageants. I'm talking *Toddlers & Tiaras:* flippers, $500 custom tutu dresses, drag queen makeup, enough hairspray to single-handedly burn that hole into the ozone that people kept talking about in the nineties. That was me. My talent was singing "On the Good Ship Lollipop" in a sailor dress. It killed, every time.

Photos lined my childhood staircase. Me, looking like a four-year-old Madonna in the "Like a Virgin" video: giant hair, mini tiara, lace bridal tutu, white Chiclet flipper that had been slid over my teeny gap-toothed toddler teeth. Another one of me dressed like a peacock, giving an early version of duck face. A half dozen of me wearing 1st Place sashes.

I was a natural to the stage and I say that without arrogance. It's just a fact. The pre-stage jitters would melt away when the emcee called my name and I'd tap, tap, tap onstage and, according to my mom, illuminate the room.

By kindergarten, I already had a dozen trophies that were twice my height, and ribbons hanging from my walls as far as the eye could see. The kids called me Miss Goody Two-Shoes and stuck their tongues out at me when I'd come back to school triumphant after every pageant.

God, those little brats made me cry! But my mom would say, *You know they're just jealous. They wish they had what you have.*

And she was right. After pageants, it was catalog modeling, cheerleading, class president, sorority president. The haters kept hating, and I kept on living my damn life. I learned a long time ago not to feel sorry for my success. No one handed me a trophy that read "Congrats on being you!" I worked for every medal, honor, accolade.

I guess you can say that I've always been in the spotlight. All eyes on me. In the pageant days, it was my competitors' jealous mothers and creepy old men in the audience. You should have seen those Lester the Molester smiles, eyes blinking mechanically like the shutters of old-fashioned cameras, taking mental pictures of my barely formed self. These days, it's snarling school moms, threatened by my clout. Which is grosser? I couldn't tell you.

Most people don't realize that Miami is actually a small town. A population of around two and a half million, but Miami *society* is a close-knit circle. Think one to two degrees of Kevin Bacon max. If you're in, you're in, but if you're out, goodbye! This is not a place where you want to burn bridges.

You know what I think? If you've got something to say, show me you can do it better. I'm curious to see how Miss Melody will fare on her own, since she *clearly* thinks she's too good for me. Is she serious? This is a hard town to break into, and I was trying to do this woman a *favor*. She strutted in from butt fuck, not knowing one thing about Miami, but she sure brought along her condescending opinions and her snide comments. Well, she can scurry down to the back of the line where she belongs.

MELODY

When Charlotte Giordani began icing me like Elsa on coronation day, it stung. I spent weeks trying to warm her up at drop-off, my most apologetic smiles waiting for her by the classroom door, only to be met with her cold blue gaze piercing through me. I sent a bouquet of flowers with a heartfelt note and left a batch of my homemade banana muffins on her doorstep. Silence.

By then, I had magnified the impact of my mistake into countless different catastrophic scenarios: *Charlotte told Madeline to stop playing with Lucy. Lucy is now a pariah. Lucy is going to become a victim of bullying. Lucy is soon to be a disenfranchised teen with no friends and suicidal thoughts. Charlotte took a screenshot of my screenshot and blasted it out to the entire school. All the parents, teachers, and students know about my shame, and they all judge me and whisper about me at all times day and night.*

More than that even, I was sad at how dramatically I had ruined any chance of being friends with Charlotte. We had hit it off, even though I thought we'd be an odd couple at first. But that lasted all of about five minutes before I acted out like a bratty teenager. What the heck was I thinking when I sent that text? I couldn't blame her for turning cold on me. I came across like a mean girl, which is so not me. And I really felt guilty for hurting her with my callous words. If Charlotte was a little intimidating when I was first meeting her (and was in her good graces), this woman was downright terrifying when I was on her *out* list.

The text fallout haunted me every time I stepped on campus. I started wearing my biggest sunglasses and baseball caps, and hung my head down low during drop-off, like a celebrity at the mall trying to blend in, but really just making herself all the more conspicuous. Battling heart palpitations, I braced myself for any dreaded run-in with Charlotte. Eventually, I started dropping Lucy off at carline in lieu of walking her to class.

Usually, these things are always bigger in our heads than in reality, right? Not true when you're talking about Charlotte Giordani.

Thanksgiving was fast approaching, and Sunset Academy sent out an invitation for parents to "Gobble till you wobble!" with their kids on the Monday before the holiday. The flyer was adorned with autumnal leaves of cayenne red, burnt orange, and mustard yellow, which was a little funny because those leaves wouldn't naturally be found among Miami's tropical foliage. "Come one, come all," it announced, "to the annual Sunset Academy Friendsgiving, as we share in the spirit of gratitude with our little pilgrims and loving families." On the bottom it read, "Hosted by the PTA, with generous support from the Walker Family Foundation." If I were consulting for the PTA, I'd warn them that they had a donor concentration problem with the Walkers.

My stomach lurched at the thought of showing my unwelcome face at a school-wide function. I imagined myself onstage, while Charlotte Giordani pulled back a rope and dumped a gallon of pig's blood on my head, the entire campus pointing and laughing.

But I was not Carrie, and this event wasn't about me—it was about Lucy. My only child, my greatest gift. Back in Wichita, I'd volunteered for every school activity. I'd put together three hundred treat bags for Wichita Elementary School's Halloween Festival, I'd served chicken nuggets and mashed potatoes (it's almost universal that little kids hate roasted turkey) for the annual Giving Thanks for Our Friends lunch, and I was always, without fail, the room parent in Lucy's class. Being involved gave me a window into her little world and let my sweet girl know that Mommy was always within reach.

So I pushed my fear aside, for the moment, and drafted an email to Lucy's teacher, Ms. Sanchez:

> Dear Ms. Sanchez,
> Thank you again for the wonderful instruction and classroom environment you have provided for Lucy this year! She is thriving academically and socially, and we are grateful that her transition to a new school has been so smooth.
> Lucy and I are looking forward to the upcoming Friendsgiving event. It seems like a sweet way to meet other families and celebrate the holiday!
> I know these things can be incredibly labor intensive to produce and would love to volunteer to help in any way.
> Kind regards,
> Melody Howard (Lucy's mom)

A couple days passed, which seemed normal, of course, as public school teachers have so much on their plates. Then came the response:

> Dear Melody,
> Thank you for the kind email. Lucy is a bright girl, and I really enjoy having her in class.
> Friendsgiving is a PTA event, so I forwarded them your generous offer. Apparently, they are overcommitted on volunteers and are unable to take on any additional helpers.
> I hope to see you at the event, and perhaps we can discuss other opportunities for you to become involved at Sunset Academy.
> Regards,
> Ida Sanchez

Snubbed.

My cursor hovered over the reply button as I weighed my response.

So the PTA was pulling a *you can't sit with us*. I'd ticked off the alpha mom, and now my child had to suffer the consequences. It was cruel and unusual.

> Dear Ms. Sanchez,
> Thank you so much for your response, and for looking into the volunteer opportunity for me. How wonderful that there are so many involved parents at Sunset Academy willing to lend a hand! I'm sure there will be another opportunity.
> See you at Friendsgiving!
> Warm regards,
> Melody

I rage typed the tepid response and plotted my next move. No Miami bitch would stand between my child and me. Not when I had been the most active mom at Wichita Elementary. Not when I could run circles around these ladies in hands-on parenting. When you mess with family, you better stand back and be ready for what's coming. Game on, Charlotte.

DARCY

Friendsgiving! It's a delightful politically incorrect way to celebrate cultural appropriation and colonization all at the same time. What is this, the nineties? Aren't we supposed to be woke now?

Wading through the sea of "pilgrims and Indians" (hundreds of black construction paper top hats with white square buckles and brown felt headbands with assorted feathers glue-gunned to the side), I found my way to the apple cider table. Charlotte Giordani stood at its helm, wearing a skintight brown leather dress, fringe hanging from the waist, her head adorned with a chieftain's feather headdress. "How!" she said, with one palm facing forward, elbow bent at a right angle, as she passed each paper cup of cider with her opposite hand. How is this woman not her own feature story about American ignorance?

Sunset Academy has a painfully outdated sensitivity issue, I'm sorry to say. I honestly have no idea how some of these event themes get the green light. Last year, for example, the school decided to celebrate Black History Month with a Dress Like an African Day. I shit you not. Forget that we were supposed to be celebrating Black contributions in the United States. Oh, and it gets worse. One little girl, a first grader, showed up to Dress Like an African Day in a leopard costume. She dressed like an animal to represent the most culturally diverse continent on the planet. Let's just say a concerned group of parents complained and we petitioned to cancel that particular dress-up day.

And don't get me started on the Hispanic Heritage Appreciation parade. We are trying to unravel these things one at a time.

I decided I wasn't thirsty, and then sidestepped the cornucopia to make a beeline for the pumpkin pie. Kitsch and generational offenses of the spectacle aside, I've always loved a good pumpkin pie. Give me a thick muddy orange slice with a generous swirl of canned whipped cream, and I could forgive many things. Or at least forget for the moment.

Jackson had scurried away to pin the tail on the turkey and my husband had pulled a hall pass to watch Monday Night Football, leaving me to contemplate cultural stereotypes and the miseducation of today's youth in the solace of my festive dessert.

Then, a tap on my shoulder. Blond and wholesome Melody Howard. "Hey," she opened, with almost a look of regret. After the small talk and the typical *how are you's*, she said, "Do you really think people would vote for me for PTA president?" I feared I had lost her to the dark side when she started ditching playdates with Jackson in favor of Charlotte's Madeline. But there she was, tail between her legs. I didn't fault her for chasing the shiny ball, but ventured to guess that, by then, it had smacked her in the face.

"I'm confused," I said. "I thought you were going to be Romy to Charlotte's Michele and serve as her fundraising lackey?"

I felt bad after saying it. Melody looked so meek and bruised. Then she said, "Let's just say that's not going to happen, and I think you're right. The PTA needs a complete overhaul with new leadership. Not more of the same."

You're right. Possibly the sweetest two words in the English language.

"Nice to see that you've come around. I promise I had faith in you all along." I meant it to sound playful, but it probably came out with a little edge.

"Ha ha, I appreciate that." Melody fiddled with her hair. "I've been meaning to ask you for coffee to discuss but I know how little free time you have."

"I'm pretty sure you could get the votes," I replied, answering her original question. "But if you need further validation, talk to her." I nodded over to Judge Lawson, who was deep in conversation with Principal Garcia. "Her Honor is quietly seeking a new regime to take down the old guard and, with her demanding career, doesn't have the time to overhaul things herself. No offense to you and your stay-at-home cohorts, of course."

Judge Lawson, the elegant jurist who happened to be a mother of four, marathon runner, and community leader, was my favorite fellow Sunset Academy mom, and not just because she was the first one to invite me to a weekend playdate (aka one my child and I could actually attend). She played her cards close to her chest but was deft in getting things done. A well-placed word here, a suggestion there. Lawson never publicly lost her cool but was assassin-like in exacting justice. And she was very mistrustful of Sunset Academy's largest benefactor.

Lawson joined us and chimed right in. "Melody, I'm interested in what you have to offer. We need to make some real changes around here. This school is a banana republic, and Charlotte Giordani and the Walkers are its abhorrent dictators."

"I always told you they were terrible." At this point I was just shamelessly gloating. Lawson had been listening to my rants for years with little more than a nod and mm-hmm, but recently she'd finally admitted that something needed to change.

Her Honor explained that she'd been keeping an eye on some PTA characters from a distance and had grave concerns about their efficacy.

She told us, "You know how the Neiman Marcus Christmas tree in Bal Harbour has all those beautifully wrapped presents underneath? And every child passes them on the escalators and squeals with excitement, hoping that one is somehow for them? Well, one day my Elizabeth dropped my hand on the way to the cosmetic counter and snatched one of those gleaming presents for herself. She was probably five years old at the time. She tore off the bow and ripped into the pretty paper before I could reach her, and do you know what she found? An empty box. You can imagine her disappointment, the betrayal. Melody, the PTA is that brightly wrapped box."

JUDGE CAROL LAWSON

Friendsgiving, cringeworthy as it was, was not the right venue for me to have the audience I desired with Principal Garcia. The entire school (staff, students, and parents) had congregated in yet another bedazzled spectacle of PTA malfeasance. While sipping spiced apple cider, Garcia and I discussed experimental education strategies in Europe and how they might be implemented at Sunset. Mundane at best. What I wanted to do was deliver a warning, of sorts, that a ruse was in play with Sunset Academy's parent leadership. But I was bound by confidentiality, so instead I told her that perhaps they could test certain methods in the accelerated classes and gauge their merit for wider integration. It was like knowing that a train would explode on its way to MiamiCentral station and telling the conductor, "Maybe you should serve sparkling wine in the café car, in addition to red and white." I don't mean to be evasive, but I could be disciplined for sharing what I know.

How opportune, though, that on the very same day, I met a possible solution to the school's troubles. Melody Howard, as fresh as they come in Miami with her khaki slacks and minimal makeup, had an interesting pedigree as someone to take over the PTA. She was experienced in every aspect of nonprofit management, was probably not a sociopath, and I liked her. She had ideas, like "full transparency for finances, creating an ethical code of conduct." These things matter.

Our children deserve to be educated in such an environment. I told Melody that I would consider being her ally in what would likely be a contentious race. Lord knows she'll need all the help she can get. The PTA queens will not accept any new challenger without a tussle.

Does Melody Howard have what it takes to be PTA president? Certainly, we could do no worse than the current administration. I've known that those people were morally bankrupt for years.

When my third born, Elizabeth, finished pre-K, I found a group of fellow incoming Sunset Academy kinder parents on a Facebook group: *Miami Moms on the Go!* I was still at the law firm in those days—this was about four years ago—and I was nervous about little Elizabeth starting elementary school without having friends in her grade. So I took a day off to join a group of mothers for a playdate. It was an informal "getting to know you" get-together of Sunset kinder parents, none of whom I'd previously met, and hosted by a woman named Rebecca Turnberry, the PTA's vice president of membership.

We all met, round-faced five-year-olds in tow, at Rebecca's home and sipped prosecco while exchanging pleasantries. *We did Montessori for two years, now we are making the big transition to traditional education.* That sort of thing.

The home was one of those Tuscan villa–inspired things that Miami loved to build in the nineties. Grandiose archways and tiled terraces with lush foliage, but more than a little out of place in South Florida if you stop to consider it. The other moms (I hate to be gendered, but no dads were there) seemed to mostly know one another but were polite enough to me, a new face for them. *Your job sounds so demanding! And a mother of four, how do you do it?*

We sat in lounge furniture around the infinity pool while the children entertained themselves in a giant sandbox on the grass. Elizabeth mixed in with ease, shoveling little plastic castles with damp white sand and flipping her molded masterpieces over in a neat line.

There were about a dozen of us: Rebecca Turnberry, the host; two yoga teacher moms; three real estate agent moms; four stay-at-home moms; one Patricia Walker, however you'd like to define her; and my-self. Things started out innocently enough with the poolside prosecco and kids in the sandbox. I don't raise an eyebrow at the occasional day drink or indulging from time to time in front of the children. But then I started noticing a kind of . . . look. Like the kind you give your hus-band when you need to have a private talk away from the kids.

Then a few moms decided they had to use the restroom. At the same time. Rebecca, Patricia, and one of the yoga teachers. They came back jubilant. The music grew louder. More prosecco was poured. Then five moms declared that they were in need of a little washroom relief. Rebecca, Patricia, the yoga teacher, one real estate agent, and one stay-at-home mom.

Our host reemerged as my new best friend. *Oh my gosh, Carol, I'd die for your tan. You never have to spray, do you? Jealous! You have such beautiful skin.*

It wasn't until the third bathroom break that I snatched Elizabeth up from the backyard playhouse and made curt goodbyes. What they were doing was illegal, immoral, and dangerous. And they didn't offer me any, because? I was in the legal field? I look like a Goody Two-Shoes? At least they spared me the awkwardness of having to speak my mind against it.

I didn't call the police, and I didn't report it to DCF, and I don't know if that was the right call or not. God knows, I wouldn't be able to forgive myself if one of those children accidentally got their hands on that stuff. But I definitely would never again expose my child to a cocaine playdate.

A few weeks later, school started and Rebecca reached out to me about joining the PTA, also suggesting that I join their board given my *impressive résumé*. I sent my $10 membership fee and never spoke to her again.

Sometimes I wonder if this is an *only in Florida* thing or if the rest of the country deals with the same level of sleaze. The state that houses us is a running joke of national embarrassments. How many salacious news stories begin with the sensational Florida Man? "Florida man uses alligator in armed robbery attempt." "Florida man saved the bodies of his entire family in deep freezer for twenty years." We keep the country entertained with our ongoing misdeeds. Although "Florida women accidentally invite future judge to cocaine playdate" is a decidedly more *only in Miami* story.

MELODY

We discussed school politics over three slices of pumpkin pie, like vigilantes staging a coup. Darcy and Judge Lawson pitched me on the prudent opportunity to *make a name* for myself before relaunching my nonprofit consulting firm, while assuring me that not only did I have a chance of being elected PTA president but also that a long list of parents, faculty, and staff would rejoice in my returning Sunset Academy to its former ethical standards.

"It sounds like we need a code of conduct," I told them. "If these board members are writing rules to benefit only themselves and their biggest donors, that will be the best way to curtail the favoritism."

"Amen to that, sister," Darcy replied, toasting with a whipped-cream-dotted fork. "I know we are talking about school conduct, but would it kill us to serve a little wine at these things?"

"It seems I forgot my Corkcicle," Judge Lawson said. "But, Melody, tell me more about your ideas. Darcy, me, and a silent majority of concerned parents who are unimpressed by fancy party invitations or Birkins or overvalued real estate want what is best for the school, for our children. And I believe that might be you."

Their playful banter put me at ease for what felt like the first time in weeks. I had found actual friends at Friendsgiving, or something close to it. Fledgling bonds. It felt like enough. A little safety to feel at home in this environment, and confidence to take on the woman in town who most intimidated me.

I had little to lose. Charlotte Giordani had already turned her loyal PTA posse against me, as evidenced by the shunning I was experiencing at school. It was like being in a cliché high school movie where the new girl, once tentatively accepted by the "it" crowd, was now the object of attack for the mean girls.

After being denied as a volunteer, exhibit B came the morning after Friendsgiving, when I dared to walk Lucy into class for the first time in weeks. In the courtyard, a six-foot folding table had been dressed up with burlap linen and various sizes of orange and white pumpkins. An easel was propped next to it with a sign beckoning, "It's the season of giving! Open your hearts to the less fortunate by donating a Thanksgiving meal to families at the Samson Homeless Shelter." Two PTA moms that I didn't recognize stood behind the table and collected money from the huddle of families that had gathered to contribute. They both had that *just stepped out of the salon* look, at 8:30 A.M. no less, and I wondered to myself: How does one manage perfect beach waves, family breakfast, and dressing children all before the morning bell?

I approached the table to wait for my turn. Minutes passed. True, there was no rhyme or reason to the line (or lack thereof I should say). The table attendants seemed to point at random to select who was able to donate next. But one by one, all the parents who had assembled before me and then all who came after me were called on to make their donations. At some point, Lucy broke off without saying goodbye and walked herself to class. Finally, several minutes after the morning bell had rung, all the other parents had dispersed and I was the last person standing at the donation table. I considered leaving, taking my contribution and stomping off like a chastened toddler. But I had to confirm my suspicion that the snub was personal. I stared motionless at the PTA moms, and they stared back at me.

I broke the silence. "I'd like to donate to help the families at Samson Homeless Shelter receive meals on Thanksgiving." The words sounded robotic beneath my frustration.

The one holding the credit card swiper responded through

unmoving lips. "It's twenty dollars to sponsor one family of four. How much would you like to give?"

"I'd like to donate one hundred," I said, reaching into my purse. Shit. I hadn't brought it. "I'm so sorry, I seem to have left my wallet at home. Can I just give you my credit card number?"

"You should just do it online," the other woman answered. "It's a fraud risk to input that information manually, and we really need to protect the charity from things like that."

I nodded and smiled through clenched teeth. "Is there a website then?"

The second woman pointed to the sign. On the bottom, the charity's website was listed. Her partner hadn't bothered to look up from her phone, which now contained something so fascinating that it required her full attention.

"Have a wonderful Thanksgiving," I said, and with a huge knot in my stomach, speed-walked to my car.

Fighting back tears, I called Greg. He answered on the first ring even though he was at work, immediately asking, "Hey babe, everything okay?"

He knew that I'd been on edge at morning drop-offs since the text incident, so when I explained the public shunning I'd received that morning, he was sympathetic. "Mel, that is kinda mean. I'm sorry." Maybe I was being dramatic, but these women had pushed me to the edge.

The tears flowed unabashedly after that. "I'd never treat anyone like that," I said through labored breaths. It was pathetic, and, in that moment, I realized that I needed to be stronger than some helpless baby chick. This never would have happened back home in Wichita.

I was persona non grata, that much was clear. But it wasn't spite that made me move forward with the PTA presidential race. It was a combination of genuine desire to make an impact and professional strategy, blended with not giving a fuck what anyone else thought. Charlotte and her friends had gifted me that freedom. From that moment on, I was in it to win it.

JUDGE CAROL LAWSON

You know how people get all worked up about landfills going in their backyards? I'd argue that it's preferable to the stink of a pink glass house across the street.

I've lived on Peacock Island for twelve years. We moved into the gated Miami Beach enclave when my oldest, Alexander, was only two years old, back when the current hot spot was still affordable for two young lawyers. And we made this peaceful community our home. Samuel and I brought three more children into the world while living in this neighborhood, pink or blue balloons floating from our mailbox with every arrival. It was while living on Peacock that I was elected to the bench at Miami-Dade civil court, district 5. Here, where my mother came to live with us after my father passed one year ago.

Like other gated communities in Miami Beach, Peacock Island comprises public land that is legally accessible to anyone who wishes to enter. The gate and security guards are merely a deterrent, a ruse meant to intimidate would-be burglars and riffraff. If security could truly keep out the bad actors, they'd have to go after some of the residents, too. But I digress.

My parents emigrated from Kingston, Jamaica, to Queens, New York, in 1975, two years before I was born. They remained there until my father took his last breath, having fought a fierce and futile battle for thirty-six months with pancreatic cancer. When he died, my mother was left with a hole bigger than all five boroughs could fill. A few months later, Samuel and I begged her to come and live with the kids and us, and she agreed.

Over the past year, my seventy-year-old mother has, with painstaking effort, worked to write her next chapter, refusing to resign herself to the labels *widow* or even *grandma*. She joined a book club in Coral Gables, meeting women of various ages and backgrounds to discuss modern American literature. She took up yoga for the first time and can balance a headstand against the wall for fifteen breaths. And finally, my brave and audacious mother decided to learn how to drive an automobile.

There was never a need in Kingston or Queens for my mom to own a car, but when she moved to Miami, spread out and unwalkable as most of the city is, she decided that it might be nice to go for her own groceries every now and then. Maybe, on occasion, she could help pick up the grandkids from school, or even drive herself south to the Gables for her book club meetings.

Mom did her own research and found a nice Jamaican driving instructor to practice with her in the neighborhood, where the one-way streets are wide and traffic is sparse. She studied for her driving exam and carried herself with pride when she came home one morning with a freshly minted learning permit. Driving lessons began in earnest the second week of November.

Two months earlier, our newest neighbors had moved into their ostentatious pink glass house, the one that took two years of incessant noisy construction to build. I recognized the owners as parents from Sunset Academy, where my two youngest are in school. Cold and soulless neighbors for a cold and soulless house.

On the fourth day of lessons, a Thursday, Mom was practicing parallel parking—an essential driving skill if you live in Miami. Behind the wheel of the instructor's car, an older model Toyota that was identifiable by a JB'S DRIVING SCHOOL sign affixed to the roof, she circled the park at the center of Peacock several times, practicing cutting the wheel and backing into a parked position a few times with every lap.

After successfully learning the skill, JB dropped Mother back off at my house.

Later that evening, I was walking my dog when Don Walker ran across the street to approach me. "Carol!" he said, as though we were best friends. Mind you, I'd gone out of my way to avoid him ever since I'd realized that his wife was the cocaine-playdate type.

I nodded and said hello, hoping it would end there. But he went on to praise me for the "very smart decision" to buy my "nanny" driving lessons. "So much easier than having to hire two people," he said.

"Wanda has been driving for years." I smiled. "It is a huge help. And now that my *mother* is learning, I may need to apply to the city for a larger driveway."

Don shuffled awkwardly. "I'm sorry, right. Your mother. That really is great." He looked across the street as if analyzing my driveway was suddenly very interesting to him. "But those city permits are notoriously slow." He pointed to his new construction embarrassment. "We added some little extras at the end, off the books. Would have taken years longer to get approval."

"I'm a judge," I reminded him.

"Right," he said, looking at his feet. Then he laughed. "That was a joke! Little legal humor. Anyway, enjoy your evening."

As if not pulling a permit was the worst of his problems.

CHARLOTTE

Three years. I've spent three years putting in a full-time job's worth of unpaid work in service to Sunset Academy. This is a public school. There is no admin staff helping to execute my fundraisers and initiatives. There's just me. At two A.M. on weeknights, you can find me reconciling school rosters with micro donations the kids have raised. We have a thousand students, mind you. Or you can find me writing sponsorship proposals, sending invoices, tracking invoices, and writing detailed runs of show for special events. So yes, it is extremely upsetting when Sally New Girl waltzes in and thinks she can do it better.

Growing up, I worked my hardest to be the best damned me I could be. I put that pressure cooker lid on so damned tight that in my senior year of high school it nearly exploded. Sure, I was homecoming queen and head cheerleader, with a 3.7 GPA. But nothing was enough. Why not a 4.0 GPA? Why not a better SAT score? Why is my boyfriend, Tucker, still going behind my back with that hooker Heather? This is hard for me to admit but, little by little, I inflicted that pain back on myself to try to release it. It started when Mr. Fisher, my AP Psychology teacher, accused me of cheating on my term paper. *Plagiarism*, he said. Which was ridiculous, because I properly cited all of my sources. Isn't that the point of using sources? To borrow someone's research to prove your point? He threatened to fail me on the paper, which accounted for a third of my semester grade. It would have tanked my entire GPA! Three and a half years of near perfect grades, and this prick wanted to humble me with my first C.

I lobbied the principal, the school counselors. I asked to do extra credit, even anther god-awful term paper. But this man wouldn't budge. So I found a new outlet that stayed with me through my college years. There was a specific spot, on the top of my left thigh, where I would pierce myself every night. Like trying to let the air out of an overfilled balloon by pricking it with a little needle. One drop of blood, no more, using a rusty old box cutter. Lord knows how I didn't get tetanus.

Sometimes, I wonder if my son, Ax, has a little bit of that tendency in him. Like, maybe he's actually wound very tight but can't cut himself to bleed just a little bit, so his whole life is a rebellion against the pressure.

Anyway, no need to Baker Act me, I'm not reaching for the X-ACTO this time. The great thing about being an adult is that you have wine for these sorts of things. But my god, my blood is boiling.

I'm not saying that it's war. I'm not a sociopath. Besides, Maddy and Lucy have become such good friends, and we all know that hurting the kids is a line that we just don't cross. Also, Lucy is an absolute doll, one that Melody probably doesn't deserve. It's not Lucy's fault that her mother is a cringey loser.

I told Madeline, "Lucy's mommy and I don't talk much anymore, but I don't want that to affect your friendship." And poor thing. She wrinkled her little nose and asked, "Is Lucy's mom not a nice person?"

You have to be so careful what you say to these little sponges. "I'm sure she's lovely. She's just not my cup of tea," I said. "But Lucy is an absolute doll, just like you." Maddy looked satisfied at that and just nodded. "Yes, Lucy is one of my best friends. I feel bad that her mom is that way." And I swear, I had never said anything in front of her. Kids are very intuitive. They pick up on these things.

DARCY

Do I sense a crack in the shellacked armor? Charlotte has been acting almost unhinged since Melody threw her name into the PTA race.

At carline yesterday, she was pacing back and forth among the cars—a big no-no by the way, no one is allowed outside of their vehicles at drop-off and pickup, for both safety and efficiency purposes. But the rules don't apply to Charlotte apparently—anyway, she was squeezing her athleisure that's never been sweated in self from car to car while shoving VOTE FOR ME! collateral through all the windows. Every two or three cars, she stopped and widened her pageant grin with an "Oh, so good to see you! Cute top, by the way. Where'd you get it? We must get the kids together!"

Imagine the scene: every afternoon at three P.M., all one thousand Sunset Academy students are being dismissed, causing almost as many cars to wrap around the entire campus and wait for their offspring to be flung into their back seats. And here is Charlotte Giordani, holding up traffic to promote her PTA election. Then 3:10 hits (by the way I can't believe it wasn't me who started it) and some brave soul dug into their horn and didn't let go for a solid three seconds. The act started a chain reaction, and the carline erupted into a chorus of horns, long and short, rhythmic and staccato.

I wish I had brought my popcorn.

Charlotte's eyes were as big as soup spoons, stretching the limits of her Botoxed forehead. "Just a second! Just a second!" She waved her hands toward the line of cars.

Then, chest heaving, she went back to passing out flyers.

Beep, beep, beep, beep! Beep!

By then, her hands were shaking as she passed the papers through the windows. Fran, our school crossing guard, had jogged across the street to Charlotte and held her Stop sign up to shield their heads, creating a modicum of privacy while she whispered into her ear. Finally, Charlotte stepped back onto the sidewalk, glanced up and down the line a couple of times, and shuffled away toward the parking lot.

I hate to admit that I relished watching Charlotte squirm; it sounds so juvenile. But I do think that she needs to be taken down because she is a corrupt presence at the school. And also . . . I can't stand that woman.

MELODY

Do you want to know what Miami looks like during the holiday season? It's similar to *Home Alone 2*: packed beaches, 80 degrees and sunny, twinkling lights strung up on palm trees. It feels like some make-believe holiday, a Christmas in July, acting out cherished holiday traditions for show. Not that I'm complaining about the weather.

On the last day of school before holiday break, Sunset Academy put together a lovely winter show, where all the children were invited to showcase their special talents. The auditorium had been transformed into a veritable winter wonderland. Ubiquitous fluffy homemade snowflakes hung suspended from the ceiling. Just seeing it made me wrap my sweater tighter around my body with a phantom chill. Onstage, ornate hand painted sets created a scene of snow-covered cottages, a candy shop with icicles dangling from its windows, and a cuddling family of furry polar bears. It was magnificent. The level of detail was exceptional and gave off the effect of a professional theater production. The entire set was, of course, orchestrated under the watchful eye and direction of Charlotte Giordani.

You had to hand it to her, she could plan events with the best of them. To be honest, it was a little crazy that she didn't use her talents professionally. At my old firm, I definitely would have hired her for my client events. The familiar doubt, the insidious fear of failure, came back. Could I really do any better? I certainly had the requisite experience to be PTA president: excellent managerial and back-office skills, marketing acumen. But people seemed to adore and respect Charlotte, who had also been a mainstay at the school and in the community for many years. So many people seemed to love her.

Lucy and her constant companion, Madeline Giordani, daughter of my now mortal enemy, decided to present a spirited rendition of Ariana Grande's "Santa Tell Me." With their blond hair pulled back into migraine-inducingly tight ponytails, oversize red-and-green-striped hoodies, and tiny black biker shorts, the girls looked like a cross between backup dancers from the "Simply Irresistible" music video and extras from the *Elf* movie. But cute. They were adorable and they did a great job.

After the show, with Charlotte glaring from the opposite end of the auditorium, Maddy approached us to give Lucy one last hug goodbye. Their friendship only grew as my tenuous relationship with Charlotte disintegrated, and somehow the girls seemed uninterested in their mothers' awkward détente (at least Lucy never mentioned anything about it in my presence).

"I'll miss you, bestie!" Maddy said to Lucy. "We'll be in Aspen until the third, but I'll FaceTime your iPad every day. I hope you get a phone for Christmas."

Fat chance, kiddo.

While Greg and I, the ever-dutiful chauffeurs, waited for Lucy to say "See you next year!" to all of her school friends, Darcy greeted me with a tight hug.

"Hey, Mel. Lucy did great," she said, turning her head to make sure no one was listening. "By the way, I've been campaigning for you since you don't seem to want to do it yourself."

"Ha! Thanks, friend," I responded. "Though I'm not sure how far I want to take this thing. Can we at least table it until after the holidays?"

Darcy scratched her nose. "You can and should do whatever you want. But you are going to disappoint a lot of Sunset parents if you step away."

I wasn't sure that I believed her. But on our way to the parking lot, a well-dressed mom with three candy-cane-clad children pulled me aside.

"I hear you're running for PTA president against Charlotte Giordani," she said. "Hallelujah! The woman is a sociopath. Did you know she has an older child, a son, that she might as well hide in the basement? The poor kid, she pays zero attention to him while showering all her love and affection on Madeline. Supermom? Ha! Isn't that rich. Someone should send social services to her house to check on that boy."

It was mean-spirited and ugly, but also . . . comforting? I knew I shouldn't have indulged in such gossip, but in truth it was nice to hear validation of Charlotte's ugly side. It's an awful feeling when you think that everyone around you should be horrified by a car crash, but most people simply move around it and get on with their day.

I tried to answer graciously. "Thank you so much for your support," I said. "I can't speak for my opponent, but I plan on bringing my extensive professional experience in nonprofits to the table. I think there's work to be done here." Better to keep personal business out of it, I thought.

The woman, it turned out, was not alone in her distaste. Over the next week, I was stopped at the grocery store, flagged down at the park, even interrupted mid-jog. I had often wondered, when Darcy called Miami Beach a small town, if she had ever visited such a place. Ever heard of Goddard, Kansas? I wanted to ask. But I was starting to see her point. Everyone was up in everyone's business here. If you weren't a tourist, you were probably part of a tight group of residents. If you were a parent, the circle was even smaller.

The busybodies made bold accusations.

~You're Melody Howard, right? I've heard so much about you. Welcome to Sunset Academy! We've been waiting for someone like you. This school is going down the tubes. It's basically modern-day segregation.

Wealthy families with their kids in gifted, poor folks stuck in the so-called regular classes. Did you know that Charlotte's daughter isn't actually in gifted? My friend is the therapist who gave Madeline the test and—this is obviously completely confidential—but she did not test into gifted at all in kindergarten. We could all see on the grade-level group chat that Maddy was assigned to a regular class, and then guess what? The first day of school arrives and Maddy had magically been moved into a gifted class.

~Melody! Darcy told me the good news. You're going to be an excellent president. You know all this PTA fundraising crap is a total illusion, right? Follow the money. What percent of what Charlotte has raised comes from the Walkers? And why do you think they are giving so generously? Well, Patricia likes to look rich, and Don, on the other hand, likes to play hide the pickle with Charlotte. Between you and me, of course. It's a house of cards. And pretty soon it's going to come crashing down. This is Miami, after all!

Character assassinations mostly. Vile and vicious accusations even. But Charlotte, and also the Walkers, for that matter, no longer seemed untouchable.

It gave me the spark I needed. I spent the following two weeks of winter break setting up playdates with other Sunset families. While Lucy played and expanded her social network, I networked my experience and ideas to new groups of parents.

"You're really taking this seriously," Greg said to me one evening, as I cleared up art supplies from another playdate. And then, irritatingly, "Are you all of a sudden super passionate about Sunset, or . . ."

"Or what?" I asked, sounding sharper than I wanted. I felt like Greg had been oddly judgy lately. Accusing me of *changing*. I mean, how else are you supposed to adapt to a new place? A place that *he* made us move to, no less.

"It's just that you always said being PTA president was for masochists, and that this school is kind of bizarre and out there." He gave me a weak smile. "I just hope it's not a single-white-female thing because of your fight with Charlotte."

I managed, with great effort, to keep my voice even. "Umm, no, Greg, I'm not a psycho. This is a *strategic* move to meet important philanthropic people in town so they can recommend hiring me as a consultant to their boards." I threw him a warning glare.

"Got it," he said, and grabbed the palettes from my hands to toss in the sink. I made a mental note to try not to discuss the PTA race with him again.

CHARLOTTE

It's the most wonderful time of the year! I mean, what a crock. I haven't had a second to myself since early October. Someone should really tell kids to soak up all that Christmas magic while they're young, because guess what? Santa Claus is real. Santa Claus is the grown-up version of you! Making a list, checking it twice, and shopping, decorating, wrapping, and creating holiday magic on repeat until you literally fall into bed every night for three months next to an already snoring husband. Good teamwork, babe.

The shopping starts in October, the holiday cheer starts in November, and the anxious diarrhea starts in December. It's a hoot! This year alone, I had two hundred people on my shopping list. Two fucking hundred family members, donors I need to impress, kids who are friends with my kids (or kid—luckily in this case Ax isn't creating much of a demand), teachers, coaches, oh and my girlfriends, of course. And if you've ever received a gift from me, you know that it's going front and center under your tree. That's what takes up most of my time, rustic artisan wrapping paper adorned with perfectly tied ribbons and a single golden jingle bell.

My mother was a wrapper, though not a fancy one. And growing up I coveted presents in gift bags. The glittery colors, the ethereal tissue paper, they seemed so luxurious. Of course, that was because I almost never had them. It had to be my own birthday and maybe some lovely friend would bring me a gift in a sturdy, elegant bag. It would hold the promise of something beautiful and special. But as an adult I know better. Gift bags are the easy way out, the lazy person's packaging! Run to Target, grab a shiny bag, throw in a piece of tissue, and *boom*, you're done. Taking the time to wrap a gift with care shows respect and patience. The precise cuts, the meticulous folds, the rush of pleasure when you've placed the last delicate strip of tape and created a taut little masterpiece. It's both my calling card and the thing that keeps me up until two A.M. (or until the wine bottle is empty, whichever comes first).

But it's not just the gifts! Every year we seem to add another event or two to our "traditions," which have exploded into dozens of burdens that absolutely cannot be missed under the threat that Christmas would be ruined. We have the kickoff, Mickey's Very Merry Christmas Party at Disney World on the weekend between Thanksgiving and Art Basel, followed by gingerbread house making, Santa at the Bal Harbour Shops, The Polar Express train ride, cinnamon buns and strawberry milkshakes at Knaus Berry Farm in Homestead, Santa's parade on Lincoln Road, Christmas caroling in the neighborhood, the Sunset Academy Winter Show, and the ballet's *Nutcracker* brunch. Just to name a few.

The Giordani Christmas Eve Eve Bash, on December 23, has become Miami famous. You'd die at how many randoms are sucking up to me between Halloween and Christmas for an invitation. It's laughable but flattering. It started seven years ago, when Maddy was barely a toddler and Axel, an adorable six-year-old, still believed in magic. I hired a top-notch Santa to bring gifts and read *The Night Before Christmas* to a select group of friends. There were champagne toasts and small-batch cheeses, and we all sang carols in front of my tree. It was warm, magical, and everything Christmas is supposed to be. The next year, I added a table of caviar and charcuterie, and the kids decorated homemade cutout cookies after Santa's visit. The year after that, we did the same but added a hot chocolate station and gingerbread houses.

The fourth year, I couldn't help myself, so I really kicked it up a notch, and here is where we went from magical to over the top. I'll put it this way, celebrating the holiday season while sweating in cutoffs and tank tops is kind of a buzzkill. So I had the bright idea to have the backyard covered in real snow, sixteen tons to be exact, and let the kids have a good old-fashioned snowball fight. James thinks the whole thing is a bit too much but lets it slide because he knows it brings me joy. "Just don't show me the bill!" he says. Well, you would have thought I invented dry shampoo, because the sucking up from people trying to get their kids invited to my "White Christmas in Miami" is next level.

I try to be inclusive—I mean, the money has already been spent—but you can't make everyone happy. This year, there are sixty-five guests confirmed, and that's about my limit before the snow turns into a muddy, slushy mess and kids are spilling out of my gate and onto the street. On top of that, I am getting the house staged and entertaining these people less than twelve hours before James, the kids, and I need to be on a plane to Colorado!

By the time we board the Christmas Eve flight for Aspen, I look more like Jack Skellington than a cheery elf, but it's all worth it. Watching Madeline glow from the inside out like a winter angel fills me in a way that is even more magical than having lived my own childhood Christmases. The payoff makes me forget, year after year, how much I sometimes loathe the setup. Even Ax gets into the spirit when he thinks no one is looking. You know, I actually heard him singing "When Christmas Comes to Town" in the shower after The Polar Express this year? I should have recorded it as proof that my sweet son is still inside that angsty teenage body, but I was too frozen to reach for my phone. It was a moment.

So the holidays and I have a love-hate relationship. This year will be the fourth annual Giordani family Aspen Christmas, which is definitely my favorite tradition. By the time we push back from Miami International Airport, my hard work is done. Presents have been shipped, the holiday house has been rented and is ready, reservations have been made. From there on out it's s'mores, snuggles, and skiing. The group gets bigger every year. This year they might as well call the Little Nell, our favorite hotel for après ski, Little Miami Beach.

Pretty much all of my Sunset crew is going, which is great for the kids, and also fun for me. And James gets off on talking finance with Don Walker for a week straight (even though my husband is so condescending about the Walkers' success) so he's happy, too. Sounds like a tedious way to spend a ski trip to me, but boys will be boys.

We'll all meet after breakfast and ski school drop-off at the base of Aspen Mountain, then the girls will go off and cruise blues with Patricia's instructor, and the guys will compare penis size on black runs all day. Maybe they'll meet us for lunch or maybe they'll slam protein bars and ski through. Either way, we will all hook up again for après along with basically half of Miami.

Honestly, Miamians, for all our bragging about stunning tropical winters, crave a white Christmas. Not everyone can afford it, but we all want it.

DARCY

The best thing about winter break is that half of Miami leaves for a ski holiday, the proverbial "other half," to be specific, and we working folk are left with a little at-home holiday of our own. Why anyone would want to *leave* the Sunshine State in December is beyond me, but that's on them.

Also, how exactly do so many people have the types of jobs that allow them to take off for an entire two weeks, like the schoolchildren? Sometimes it seems like no one actually works in Miami. Group text chats and local cafés are lit up all day. There are no lulls in traffic anymore, more like all-day rush hour. Doesn't anyone need to be in an office?

Anyway, along with the humidity, a lot of dead weight slowly starts to drift away from the Magic City in December, and I breathe a little bit easier. The air takes on an electric kind of energy, beginning with the cultural boon of Miami Art Week in early December. As exhausting as Art Basel can be, the omnipresent cultural production that week is amazing. Sure, there's the douchebaggery of the party set. The *let's put together my wildest outfit and try to get into Soho House* crowd, as though the whole thing is a giant costume party. But the access to such creativity—the outdoor performances, the live graffiti paintings in Wynwood—fills my soul. And then, a few weeks later, with the blessed exodus of Charlotte and Co. during the holidays, my freedom is complete.

You know that song from *Pinocchio* about how he used to be burdened down with strings, but now is free? That was me from December 21 to January 7 this year. My law practice was slow, with most of my clients celebrating one thing or another, which gave me time to reorganize my comically chaotic desk, update my spreadsheets, and clear out my inbox for the new year. It also afforded me some extra time with Elliot and Jackson, evening card games and slow walks around our local museums.

My guy and I even snuck in a few date nights, which we always forget to do. It's hard when you work all day together. You just kind of think, What else do we have to talk about? But date nights always remind me why I fell in love with Elliot in the first place. We are different people when we aren't being parents or colleagues, people who laugh at the same inappropriate jokes and are still very much in love.

There was social time, too, and I took one of those two-hour wine lunches that just aren't happening the rest of the go-go-go year. The girls and I, call us the Aspen outcasts, met for a leisurely afternoon bite at the Palm Place Hotel, where Melody's husband is the general manager. They have this beautiful art deco revival courtyard among lush potted greenery and rich velvet lounge seating. Very cozy. Melody, Carol (Judge Lawson, if we are being formal), and I exchanged the kind of idle gossip that makes one feel simultaneously guilty for being petty and comforted to be in the presence of good friends.

We looked like some kind of early-middle-aged Spice Girls situation. Carol was classy in a white button-down tucked into perfectly hemmed skinny jeans. Melody had ditched her Midwestern sensible for something closer to Miami sexy, wearing a silky black crop top over high-waisted cream pants. Close, I thought, but not quite nailing it. Unfortunately, Miami fashion is contagious, so I wasn't too surprised by the effort. I was comfortable in my oversize T-shirt dress. Who wants to be worried that their imperfect posture is creating some kind of belly roll when they sit down? Certainly not me.

We started harmlessly enough, with the casual *How have the holidays treated you?* and *What are the kids up to over break?* But with two bottles of prosecco down and main courses yet to be served, our lips and inhibitions loosened.

I threw the first stone. "Carol! How are your lovely new neighbors, the Walkers? Has Patricia borrowed a cup of sugar yet?"

Carol sucked her teeth. "Don't even go there. I'm drinking right now to forget that I have to look at their ridiculous pink house every time I pull into my driveway."

We all laughed.

Carol lit up. "What about you, Melody? How are you holding up after taking on the Queen Bee?"

Melody covered her mouth, but the belly laugh betrayed her. "That woman gives me the chills! But I guess I'm not the only one, so at least I have strength in numbers."

"That's right!" I held up my wineglass. "We are behind you all the way to the White House. Ahem, the schoolhouse!"

"You ladies are the best," Melody said, blushing. Or was she flushed from the wine? "But it's not only this table. Apparently, there are a lot of parents at Sunset who really don't like Charlotte and her cast of cartoon villains." She took another sip.

"Oh, you can't just drop that morsel on us, Melody." Carol sat back in her chair. "Come man, talk di tings dem."

Melody laughed again, but then tensed. "Oh, I shouldn't."

"Don't be shy," Carol said. "Those ladies are ridiculous. Charlotte once told me that I was *so brave* for wearing flats to a charity luncheon. It had nothing to do with bravery, just sore feet."

"Oh, I can definitely see that," Melody said.

I was forceful, not to mention sauced. "Oh, come on, Mel! What are you hearing? Don't leave us hanging now. Besides, you are in the company of friends. Nothing leaves this table."

"Okay," Melody said. "But please don't repeat this to anyone." We all crossed our hearts. "People have been approaching me with some, let's say, unflattering stories about Charlotte. Honestly, it's mostly personal gripes that shouldn't be repeated. The point is, Charlotte definitely isn't as put together as she'd like us to think. And she probably shouldn't be leading Sunset Academy in any capacity if she's as amoral as people say."

"For example, Ms. Howard?" I teased.

"Am I on the witness stand?" Melody laughed. "Okay, again, this doesn't leave the table. But people have told me . . . and who knows what the truth is . . . but people are saying that Madeline isn't actually gifted, and that Charlotte paid to get her into the program."

"Charlotte and eighty percent of the other parents with children in gifted," I responded. "Next!"

"Really? Ha, okay," Melody continued. "Well, she has another child. A teenage son. And he basically gets ignored even though he clearly has some needs that aren't being met. I saw him with my own eyes. I guess he doesn't fit the Giordani profile enough for Charlotte."

"Poor Ax," Carol said. "I remember when he was in fifth. Even then, Charlotte didn't dote on him like she does Maddy. It's like she worships that girl. Ax was always the shy type. But sweet."

"It is sad," Melody added. "And then the bombshell." Melody squeezed her eyes shut and opened them, glassy and suddenly afraid. "Sorry, I can't!"

You can imagine the commotion at the table. It was just getting spicy, and we were ready for what sounded like a stunning reveal. We goaded her.

"Okay." Melody seemed to concede, and took a long drink of water. "I don't think you gals understand just how bad it is at the Giordani home."

"I can imagine." I inhaled a breadstick, trying to sober myself up. "What, does Charlotte keep Ax locked up in a closet or something?"

Melody shook her head. "No, nothing like that, but . . ." She suddenly averted her gaze, wildly searching her half-empty salad plate. "But she does pretend that he doesn't exist. I mean, she confided in me that she sometimes pretends Maddy is an only child." Her hands flew to her face. "Oh my god, please don't repeat that."

"Of course not," Carol said. "But Lord knows that is so sad."

"Tragic really." I felt genuine disgust. "That poor kid deserves so much better." We were all silent for a moment, and it occurred to me that as awful as this revelation was, it could hardly be called a *bombshell*. "So . . ." I broke the silence. "That's the big reveal?"

Carol seemed to pick up on it, too. "Yeah, hon. That's terrible, but why do I sense you've got more to say?"

But Melody had become so awkward, it was painful for even my inebriated self to watch. "There are some lines that you just don't cross. Sorry, ladies," Melody said.

"Okay, okay, yentas. Let's save it for another day. I need to get the check before someone starts dancing on the table."

A few groans later, the three of us were safely in Ubers, headed back to our respective homes, hoping to sneak in some late afternoon naps.

Here is the thing about telling people not to repeat something. It doesn't work. Even with the best intentions, the secret you told is repeated over and over again. Your original confidant tells a spouse, who tells a best friend, who tells a hairdresser. Everyone chooses someone whom they think won't repeat the gossip. But invariably the secret is retold and warped a dozen times over until it reemerges, ugly and scandalous. The lesson? If you don't want something repeated, don't say it out loud.

GABRIELA

January 5, 2019
From: Gabriela Machado
To: Sunset Academy Parents
Subject: Sunset Academy PTA Elections: Code of Conduct

Dear Parents,

I hope this email finds you well after the relaxing winter break.

As many of you know, Sunset Academy will be electing a new PTA president this year. It has been an honor to serve your children over the past two years. I am sincerely going to miss each and every one of you.

We currently have two parents who have been nominated to replace me next year.

It has come to the board's attention that one of these candidates has been making slanderous claims about her opponent's child(ren). This is completely shocking and inappropriate.

Please allow this email to serve as a notice to anyone who takes it upon him- or herself to attack a candidate's personal life or family while commenting on this race. We would never allow our children to behave in this way. We are better than this and will immediately dismiss any candidate who shows characteristics unbecoming of the Sunset Academy PTA.

Thank you for your time and attention to this matter. May the best candidate win, and Go Sunset Seagulls!

Regards,

Gabriela Machado

PTA President

CHARLOTTE

There is a line. There is a clear fucking line that literally everyone knows not to cross, and that is the children. My Madeline—straight-A, two-reading-levels-ahead, teacher's-pet Madeline—belongs in the gifted program as much as anyone else at Sunset. Maybe even more so. I'd put her GPA against Lucy Howard's any day, if someone is really in the mood to compare. How *dare* Melody spread vicious rumors that my daughter isn't actually gifted? Does putting down an eight-year-old make her feel better about her own pathetic life? That's just sad, and honestly reeks of jealousy.

But putting Axel in the middle of this? That's a low fucking blow. God bless the parents of easy children. They have no idea how lucky they are! Do I approve of everything that my teenage son does? No, not even close. But to insinuate that I don't love him as much as Madeline is absolutely disgusting. I loved him first, and he made me a mom, which is my favorite thing to be. Sure, you can look at his artificially colored hair and grungy jeans and see that he isn't cut from the same cloth as my Maddy, but that's Melody's judgment, not mine! What will she do if Lucy goes through a *phase* and cuts off her pretty blond hair and, I don't know, gets a nose ring? What, she's going to disown her? Honestly, I feel bad for her daughter right now. If she doesn't continue to live up to Melody Howard's high expectations, well, she's going to be in trouble.

And anyway, do you think Ax even wants me hanging around his school 24/7, decorating doors and planning dances? Hell no! That would literally be a cruel and unusual punishment to him.

This was some grade A bullshit. I mean, how badly does this lady need to win a damn PTA race? Don't worry, I'm not going to stoop to Moronic Melody's level and hurt her child in some way, which I could so easily do. I mean, one word from my Maddy, and Lucy would be on the permanent loser list. No, I would never do that, because I'm a good person.

Maddy asked me what was wrong the other night. She is so in tune with my emotions. I wasn't my typical sunny self and was trying to get lost in the meditation of chopping garlic for my famous tomato sauce. It was spaghetti night: good old gluten for the husband and kids, spaghetti squash for me. (Gotta be ready for Miami gala season; god, I miss carbs.)

"Mom," she said. "Is everything okay? You've been giving the cutting board dirty looks."

There is a delicate balance in these situations because you want to have a loving and open relationship with your child, but you also have to maintain some boundaries.

"Oh, sweetie," I told her. "I'm not mad at the cutting board, but I am dealing with some frustrating adult things at the moment. You don't need to worry a hair on your head about it, though."

Maddy didn't miss a beat. "Is it something with Lucy's mom?" she asked, killing me softly with her baby blues.

"What makes you think that?" I asked.

"Well," she said, "Lucy told me that she overheard her mom on the phone, and she was complaining about you. She called you a tyrant."

"Oh did she?" I said. My garlic at this point had been chopped finer than Morton's kosher salt. Whatever Melody had said in front of her daughter is exactly the kind of parenting that breeds shitty children. I decided to make it a teachable moment.

"Maddy, my love." I put down my knife and looked her in the eye.

"When someone has something nasty to say about you, it's like they're holding up a mirror to themselves. So if Lucy's mom is saying something ugly about me, maybe it's a reflection of what she sees in herself."

Maddy seemed to really consider this. "So, Lucy's mom is the one that is actually a tyrant?"

I grabbed my knife and started on the plum tomatoes. "Maybe."

Interview Transcript with Patricia Walker

For profile in *Magic City* magazine, summer issue 2019
By Andres Castano
January 18, 2019, Session 4

INTERVIEWER: Hello, Patricia. Happy New Year! Can we still say that?

PATRICIA: Hi, Andres. We can still say it, until February first, I believe.

INTERVIEWER: Good to know. How did the holidays treat you?

PATRICIA: Very well, thank you. We spent the majority of it in our Aspen home; we will be back and forth for the rest of ski season, and then will spend the entire summer there.

INTERVIEWER: How lovely. It must be nice to have the mountain house as a counterpoint to the bayside home in Miami.

PATRICIA: Yes, it is. Villa Rosé is our family estate in our favorite city, but the Aspen house keeps us connected to nature. Balance is so important in life. You have to make a commitment to it, or your emotions will get the best of you.

INTERVIEWER: That is so true. Of course, we are now entering the fast-paced Miami philanthropic season. You are the undisputed queen of galas and luncheons. How do you find balance between all these fundraising events and time for yourself?

PATRICIA: Well, I meditate every morning, that is my nonnegotiable. But you're right, from now until April I'll be sitting for hair and makeup several times a week to get ready for all the events we support. It can be exhausting at times, but it's all for such good causes. So I cannot complain.

INTERVIEWER: Great causes and you look great doing it! You bring such style and flair to the Miami social scene. Have you always had such a keen sense of fashion?

PATRICIA: Well, I have always had an eye. I didn't always have the means for high fashion, but I understood how to put a look together. Everyone has the ability to look their best. You have to make the most with what you've been given.

INTERVIEWER: And you do it magnificently. If I may say, the Valentino gown and tiara you wore to the Diamond Ball . . . that look could have been at the Oscars.

PATRICIA: You are so kind, Andres. I've learned over the years that it's not what you wear, it's *how* you wear it. One must dress authentically, or even a Chanel will come off like a Zara. It doesn't have to be haute couture, of course, but so many women get it wrong.

Let's keep this story between us, but we used to have this friend, Sabrina Quarles, bit of a tragic case. She was a regular on the scene with us: charity luncheons, fashion shows, private shopping events, store openings. Always wore a current season designer outfit and a different *it* bag. She had the Valentino cape dress before I did even, the newest Dolce prints.

She was, without fail, dressed to the nines, and she did not miss an event. In Miami we like to say, *She'd go to the opening of an envelope.* But I could tell something was *off.*

Well, one day I go over for a playdate (this was a couple years back). We were outside saying a long goodbye, I'm ready to leave, and you wouldn't believe it. The UPS driver comes up and delivers a giant box from Rent the Runway. I felt awful. Sabrina was more or less hyperventilating while trying to explain. Listen, I don't think there is anything *wrong* with renting, but don't pretend to be something you're not. That isn't fashion. Then it comes out that her finance husband was just a run-of-the-mill banker and, this is what sank her, *all* those looks and bags were borrowed or rented. Not one piece owned by her.

I think Sabrina has her kids at Miami Shores now, but honestly I couldn't tell you. No one has seen her since the whole scandal came to light. How could anyone trust her after that?

INTERVIEWER: Such a shame that she wasn't comfortable enough in her skin to just live within her means. I'm curious. You've mentioned that you grew up in different circumstances than you are now afforded. Can you give our readers a glimpse into your childhood?

PATRICIA: Oh, it's a not good story, Andres. I don't really want to focus on that.

MELODY

I'm still kicking myself. I woke up the day after my boozy girls' lunch with Darcy and Carol to that awful taste of regret and sour wine, not to mention a 4.5 magnitude headache.

According to Greg, I had stumbled home around four P.M. in a morning-after-worthy level of dishevelment. After declaring myself "ready to party," I did a little jig on the coffee table—thank god he didn't film me—shimmied to our bedroom, and slept for fourteen hours with all my clothes on.

I'm not sure if the headache or the heart palpitations woke me up first but, when I opened my eyes, it seemed there was a 95 percent chance I should go to the hospital. Two Tylenol and a glass of water had been placed on my nightstand, along with a note that read, "Thanks for the show yesterday. Thought you might need these." If ever I made a wise decision, it was in choosing a husband.

It turns out that I wasn't dying, though death would have been almost preferable to morning-after panic. *Did I say something bad? What the hell was I talking about?* I had a vague memory that it was probably shit talk. Something I try to avoid, but damn, this move to Miami had put me through an *American Ninja Warrior*–level obstacle course. It felt like I kept falling into that cold pool underneath the monkey bars, when all I wanted was to press that red buzzer at the end!

I sent a group text to Carol and Darcy:

Hey ladies! You sure know how to show a gal a good time! So much
fun yesterday . . . question . . . was I a little . . . loose-lipped? I feel
terrible. :(

Carol responded first. *Oh honey, I think we all feel terrible. But no,
you were fine. It was fun!*

Darcy followed suit. *Oh please, you haven't been corrupted . . . yet! We
are certainly working on it though.:)*

Good enough. My panic abated, I almost forgot that I might have
said something offensive. Days went by, and then the infamous PTA
email, Gabriela's *not so subtle* item.

My life in Miami has been the Gravitron. The ride that spins
around and around, and you have to lean back and hold completely
still, because if you lean forward, you will instantly spew a mixture of
funnel cake and giant fountain soda onto the other miserable spinning
riders. You could honestly say that my short tenure in Miami has been
a carnival roller-coaster ride. It's not quite off the rails, but I definitely
need to puke.

There's a self-help quote that I've stumbled on a couple of times
that says something to the effect of "it's bigger in your head than it is
in reality." Isn't that charming? I wonder if whoever wrote that pearl of
wisdom has ever been publicly shamed in front of his or her daughter's
entire school email list.

The more pressing question, however, was who the eff talked?
What happened to my *safe space*? Now, I know I shouldn't have been
so loose-lipped at the holiday lunch with Darcy and Carol. Thank god
I didn't slip with that *other* rumor. But really? My first two friends in
Miami, my ardent supporters? On top of being hated by the catty overgrown women children on the Sunset PTA, I had to question which of
my only two allies took an ice pick to my spine?

They both called me after Gabriela's panic-inducing email went
out. It went like this:

10:10 A.M.: Gabriela puts me on blast in front of all the parents in school. Sure, she didn't name me, but it was pretty damn obvious who she was talking about.

10:15 A.M.: *OMG* text from Darcy.

10:16 A.M.: Phone rings. "You have *got* to be kidding me," Carol said.

"Hold on a sec," I said, not concealing my annoyance. "Darcy is buzzing me on the other line."

"Patch her in," Carol responded.

All three of us got on one line. "Mel, I'm so sorry this happened. These women! I don't know what to say," Darcy said.

I had to tighten my grip so my sweaty hand wouldn't slip off the phone.

"Me too," Carol added. "You don't deserve this. I just can't imagine how—"

I didn't have the patience for their hedging. "Did you girls tell anyone what I said? I didn't mention those things to anyone else," I butted in, my voice a little too high.

"Ah, I don't think so, not really?" answered Darcy. I noted a slight hesitation. Confession will set you free, I thought. "I definitely mentioned it to Elliot," she continued. "I can't imagine that it spread through him. Um, I was talking about it when I was drunk in the Uber? On the phone with . . . I can't even remember. Oh god, Mel, I am so sorry!"

"Oh ladies, come on now. Let's not beat ourselves up," Carol chimed in. "The villains in this story are clearly Gabriela and Charlotte. Were we having a little fun at Charlotte's expense? Yes! Are we allowed to gripe and vent about a couple of serial offenders? Yes! The word should not have gotten out, but what those sociopaths did in response is just *wow*."

It was true, but the fact remained that someone had betrayed me.

"So . . ." Darcy responded. "Carol, you didn't tell anyone?"

The judge let out a heavy sigh. "Shoot. I may have, not in a malicious way, of course. I'm sorry, Melody, really. This is unfair to you."

I couldn't disagree on that point. It seemed like there was no one I could trust in this cursed town. But I was the one who had made the bad decision to gossip in the first place. How could I fault anyone harder than I would myself? I wanted to ask Carol who she'd told, but was afraid of sounding like a bruised teenager. And what difference would it even make, anyway? The damage had been done.

"Melody, what can we do to make this up to you?" Darcy asked.

I thought about it a minute. Secret keepers they may not be, but Darcy and Carol were good people. Also, I didn't have a ton of options at that moment and certainly couldn't afford to lose any friends. But even if I were the most popular woman in town, I would have forgiven the offense. I had to be the bigger person.

"Well, nothing really," I said. "But maybe don't get me in trouble like that ever again, please. The last thing I need right now is another embarrassment."

"Cross my heart, Mel," Darcy responded, sounding uncharacteristically somber.

"Loose lips sink ships," I teased. And we all laughed.

Greg didn't see the humor in it, though. Not at all. I told him the story that evening while Lucy swam in the pool.

"What, are you auditioning for the *Real Housewives of Miami Beach*? Your tagline is *I'm Midwestern nice: I'll bake you an apple pie while I stab you in the back.*"

"There's no backstabbing on my part," I told him. I love that man to death, but guys like him can be so damn holier than thou when it comes to social dynamics. They just don't open the door for emotional responses like we do when they're grunting and talking about football. I'd rather have real connections and conversations, even if that means experiencing lows with the highs. "Listen, I know I shouldn't have been talking trash, but what does Charlotte expect after all the psychological warfare?"

"Babe," Greg said, super annoyingly. "If you know you shouldn't do it, aren't you answering your own question? And these new friends of yours. They ratted you out? I actually feel bad for you about the quality of people you've been meeting lately."

"Wow," I said, grabbing a towel to coax Lucy out of the pool. "Condescending is not a good look on you." I mean, really? The only *friends* he'd made in Miami were colleagues. Does that even count? Sometimes, it feels like our social lives are 100 percent my responsibility. And he was implying that I was doing a poor job?

Greg put his hands on his hips and started backing away. "I'm just saying." He was wrapping up the conversation while we still had a modicum of privacy. "I'm worried about what this town and these people are doing to you."

Forget that he was the one who made us move to Miami. Forget that I had been thriving professionally and socially back in Kansas. This was my fault? That didn't seem fair. Had there been missteps? Of course, and I hated that. But I wouldn't have even been in this position if it hadn't been for *him*.

DARCY

Melody said it herself. Loose lips sink ships. It was so simple. I had everything we needed to sink Charlotte's empire and had just been too timid to use it.

Charlotte, Gabriela, and all their cronies were guilty, no question about it, of malfeasance: the illegal parking spot, the no-bid construction contracts, the complete lack of financial statements, the misuse of grant money. At a minimum, these offenses would open the door for an IRS audit. At a maximum, perhaps worse. It was so easy to prove. But where to start?

If I led with the parking spot, it would look like I was getting revenge for the Walker incident on the first day of school. Too petty. On the other hand, I wasn't sure how much support I could garner on the no-bid controversy for the Walker Auditorium at Miami Beach Middle. The namesakes did pay for the damn thing, which didn't make it right, but in the hearts and minds of the masses . . . They might let it slide.

Financial statements. Literal snooze. So proving that Charlotte and Co. misused restricted grant money was my best shot to get Melody elected. The Walkers aren't the only wealthy family at Sunset Academy. They act like they are, but it's far from true. Sunset Academy is located in one of the wealthiest zip codes in the state, so you can imagine the kind of money that's funneled into the PTA coffers from all the family foundations.

One of those foundations is the Palacio Family Endowment, whose scion, Manuel Palacio, happened to be my law partner before I went into practice with my husband. Manuel, or Manny to his friends, is the grandson of José Palacio, the storied Cuban immigrant who built Florida's largest sugar conglomerate on the heels of escaping communism. He was living proof of the American dream.

Faced with the enormity of his wealth and an inoperable cancer, a septuagenarian José created the Palacio Family Endowment with three goals: to leave a lasting impact on the Miami community that gave him so much opportunity, to avoid bestowing the kind of wealth that makes one lazy to his children and grandchildren, and to shield some of his fortune from federal taxes, because—as most Cuban immigrants from that era would agree—fuck communism. (His theoretical words, not mine.)

One of the caveats of these large endowments is that the executors must spend the money, a certain amount every year, on 501(c)(3) nonprofits in order to maintain their tax-free status. And my friend and former colleague, Manny Palacio, happens to be one of the twelve board members in charge of spending that fortune. Wielding such power to fund nonprofits has made Manny somewhat of an unwilling celebrity. Never has there been a person who cares less for being in the public eye, for being wined and dined, or being celebrated in magazines. Quite the opposite, Manny prefers to write checks quietly and pray that no one asks him to walk a charity's fashion show runway as their honoree of choice.

That is why, when his children (Carolina, aged ten, and Simon, aged six) enrolled in Sunset Academy, Manny was happy to support his local public school with generous annual grants. I don't know the exact amounts, but let's just say that "Palacio" could be on the marquis for all the buildings. Here's the kicker, while Manny doesn't want or need anyone to know how much and to whom he is donating, he does like to specify *how* those donations should be used. These are known as restricted grants, and legally, that means that organizations must spend those funds toward their intended purposes.

Last school year, when Charlotte Giordani ascended to her vice president of fundraising throne, she created a "safety and wellness" fund to upgrade Sunset's archaic security system. "Anything for the safety and welfare of our most prized possessions!" she would crow to anyone within earshot.

A few months ago, Manny had confided in me, over a catch-up lunch of stone crabs and key lime pie, that he had made a five-figure contribution to the security and wellness fund and had yet to see any evidence of the promised upgrades. "Are you surprised," I pressed, "that a self-absorbed debutante might be peddling false promises while she establishes herself as the most important person at school?"

"Aggressive!" Manny had laughed, and then mused that he didn't care to discuss or pursue the matter any further.

Well, since I have now established myself as one who can easily betray confidences, why not go all out? Tell the truth, betray a friend, but isn't it for the greater good?

Sure, Manny would be disappointed with my lack of discretion. But he would understand! We must hold people accountable for their actions! Especially when it comes to nonprofits! Even more so as it pertains to our children!

I've already disappointed a new friend, one who had no reason in the world to doubt me. Why not add a respected former colleague to the list?

All I need to do is send one email, from the comfort of my desk, sitting behind my laptop screen. Invisible. Except for the tiny name in the "from" section to one thousand inboxes. Or maybe two thousand. There are one thousand students at Sunset Academy, so let's call that two thousand email addresses, assuming that most children have two engaged guardians. Though I hate assumptions. Between one thousand and two thousand inboxes that belong to people who see me at drop-off, pickup, and special events. They will associate me with the whistleblowing email and associate my son with the mother who sent the email that was trying to bring down an established PTA dynasty. And I'll have to see their potentially judgmental faces for only two and a half more years before Jackson goes off to middle school somewhere. And then, maybe I'll see 20 percent of their faces, depending on who matriculated to that new school from the pool of current third-, fourth-, and fifth-graders. Simple.

Fuck. I really need to grow a pair.

MELODY

Show your face, they said. It will be good for the campaign, they said.

The Be a Kid Again Gala was in February, the height of Miami magnificence as I've come to learn. This is the time when residents have almost forgotten what 100 percent humidity feels like, and tourists from across the globe pour in like my mother and her friends to a Black Friday sale. The fashion is what I can only describe as *regional* this time of year, with women donning ankle boots, cutoff shorts, and tight sweaters as if to say *We know it's cold everywhere else, but we are still going to show some skin.* To my Midwestern blood, even a sweater was too heavy for the afternoon sun.

Darcy and Carol encouraged me to attend. If I were to become president of the Sunset Academy PTA, surely I must be seen at the largest school fundraiser of the year. The theme was the Pax Romana. I imagined myself as a leather-clad gladiator, entering the Colosseum in chains to face a trident-wielding Charlotte, riding around the rink on the back of an enormous lion. Gabriela and Patricia would watch us from the podium, cheering on their champion with a warlike bloodlust. The angry mob would pelt me with rotten fruits as I ducked and slid to avoid the pierce of Charlotte's weapon. Greg, crying from the rows of plebeians, would cast a single rose into the arena, to carry with me into death.

Or maybe everything would be fine. I told myself it was going to be just fine.

The invitation came in the mail (how very in keeping with the *ancient* theme) on ecru card stock, wrapped in a gold leaf liner. In beautiful calligraphy (another unnecessary expense) it read:

FRIENDS, ROMANS, COUNTRYMEN, LEND ME YOUR EARS!

*You have officially been summoned to Carpe Diem
at the 3rd annual Be a Kid Again Gala*

February 8, 2019, at the Sunset Academy Cafeteria

6 P.M. in the evening until . . .

Ancient Roman attire strongly encouraged

As Darcy noted in her distinct way, "It's a toga party."

My contempt for the theme evaporated when Greg, a dashing Bacchus, emerged from our bathroom wearing only a linen tunic, a crown of plastic grapes, and leather sandals. The temperate winter had inspired him to maintain a rigorous running routine, and to imagine my husband as a Roman god wasn't much of a stretch. "Grapes," he said. "I should be holding a pod of grapes."

"A bunch," I corrected. "And maybe we could skip the gala and you can feed me grapes in the bath, instead. Lucy is sleeping out tonight."

"As tempting as that sounds, Goddess Diana"—Greg plucked an arrow from the quiver on my back and tickled it underneath my robe—"we paid five hundred freaking dollars apiece for these party tickets, and I plan on eating and drinking my money's worth." The price tag was ridiculous, something we never would have paid in Wichita for a school event.

I grabbed my bag and headed to the door.

"That new?" Greg asked, pointing to my boho chic evening bag.

"Yes." I did a little turn. "It's Chloé. I know it's a splurge, but it's been so long since I treated myself. And I've been going through such a tough time. I thought it might cheer me up to get something nice."

Greg opened the car door for me. "Did you give the purse a name? What kind of a splurge are we talking here?"

"No, the brand is Chloé," I said, and thought about lying about the second question. Greg definitely wouldn't understand. The most expensive thing he wore was a pair of $100 Nike Air Force 1s. I rounded down a little. "It was, umm, fifteen hundred."

I closed the car door quickly, forcing him to process that bombshell as he walked around the other side of the car to let himself in. "Are you serious right now?" He buckled his seat belt with such force that I thought he'd snap the clasp. "Mel, what is going on with you? Are we not sending Lucy to college anymore? Since when do we spend like that?"

"Come on, Greg." I tried to lighten the mood. "Lucy is obviously going to get a scholarship. And what's wrong with enjoying your success a little bit? We live well below our means."

He started the engine but kept his eyes on mine. "Yeah. I'd like to keep it that way. I thought we both did. Babe, I'm not one of these finance guys. You know that. Who are you trying to impress?"

I bit my lip hard, struggling not to say something I'd regret later. "Can we table this for now?"

He sighed his agreement. "It is a very nice bag. You wear it well." We continued on to the gala in silence.

When we arrived, we were greeted with two giant stucco columns draped with green fabric leaves framing the cafeteria's entrance. In front of each column, lithe young women in togas swayed rhythmically while pretending to strum white and gold lyres. Additional muses greeted us with trays of champagne at the check-in table.

"Don't mind if I do," Greg said, as he plucked two glasses from the first tray.

I must have rolled my eyes, because he responded with "I'm Bacchus."

"Yes, I know. Meanwhile, I'm trying to avoid becoming the hunter turned prey," I answered. Our argument had briefly distracted me from the fact that I was about to step into enemy territory. Greg softened.

"Mel, come on. You're way too smart to let these desperate housewives get under your skin. This is classic schoolyard intimidation. You have two choices. Either let it go or find the biggest one and punch her in the nose."

"Great advice."

He was right about one thing, at least. Alcohol. Alcohol was clearly the answer. I helped myself to two glasses of champagne from the next tray and double-fisted my way into the event.

If transforming an eighty-year-old public elementary school's stale cafeteria into a luxurious, $500-per-ticket affair sounds like a Herculean task, well, there's a reason for that. Inside, the cafeteria lunch line, which would usually contain a dozen or so vats of mac 'n' cheese, sloppy joes, and vegetables boiled beyond recognition, had been repurposed as a Roman banquet buffet, housing polished nickel chafing dishes of lemon poached salmon, cheesy gratin potatoes, herb roasted chicken, and steamed asparagus. Trays of charcuterie preceded the assortment, and a carving table with brisket and rack of lamb was stationed at the end.

Rows of round tables covered with gold satin linens and white floral centerpieces stood atop the weathered cherry-red linoleum flooring, an effect similar to placing perfumed candles in a prison toilet. A dance floor had been stanchioned off on the west side of the cafeteria, with a caffeinated twenty-something DJ at its center blaring Top 40 hits from his laptop computer.

"Is it me, or is this more Fall of the Empire than Pax Romana?" Darcy, as Justitia for the evening, found us in line at the bar.

"I was expecting a little more polish, but at least the booze is flowing," I admitted.

"Yes, in the same room where our children sometimes hide during code red drills," Darcy added. "It appears our generous underwriters have grown tired of throwing their checkbook around like dollar bills in a gentlemen's club. Well, what we lack tonight in finery is made up for with hedonism, gluttony, and completely insane leadership."

"So the theme is a success!" I toasted to no one.

After I took a few spins on the dance floor, a nearby Isis gave me a curious look. "Carol!" I shouted to her over a Maroon 5 chart topper, "Do you need a drink?"

She sidled next to me. "Honey, you're drunk."

I extended my thumb and pointer finger in front of my face. "Just, like, this much."

"Well, keep it together, yeah? Because after tonight you might be well positioned to help take over this kingdom. All you have to do is smile and not black out."

"I have no idea what you're talking about but consider it done." I tried to nod convincingly.

"Okay good. Now let's dance like it's our last night in Pompeii."

The dance floor was sticky, probably with the remains of a thousand dripping juice boxes, but none of the assembled gods and goddesses seemed to mind. Through the din, I spied Charlotte Giordani and Don Walker, as Venus and Julius Caesar, respectively, conversing with their heads tilted toward each other. Don was gesturing wildly and then Charlotte threw her head back in laughter. I haven't spent that much time with him, but I never got the sense that he's that funny. Then Don leaned in closer and placed a hand on the small of her back, glanced around them (to see if anyone was watching?), and started whispering in her ear. If any man who wasn't my husband pulled that move with me, he'd have a glass of champagne in his face. But Charlotte just smiled and sort of cuddled into him.

They really are an item! I gasped at the realization. These people, it seemed, had no limit to their moral failings.

Charlotte was draped in a short gold tunic, belted tight at the waist, and wore a crown of fresh white roses woven with green myrtle leaves. From deep within my ribs, I suppressed a spark of longing for our brief friendship. But that harvest had long spoiled.

Maybe it was some newfangled self-confidence or maybe it was the champagne, but I found myself walking toward the golden goddess. I fantasized along the way about removing a single arrow from my quiver, nocking my bow, and striking directly into the Venus's heart. Ribbons of fresh blood would unfurl onto her golden toga, and her eyes would widen with the sudden recognition that she had been defeated by her mortal enemy. And then I'd go to jail.

"Congratulations," I said over a dance remix of a Whitney Houston song. "It's a beautiful event. I know how much work goes into these things."

Charlotte stared back at me, unblinking. "Oh, cut the crap, Kansas. This thing is a bust. I was working with a fraction of my gala budget from last year. I'm not a magician! I'd like to see you try to do better." She started to turn away, no doubt looking for someone, anyone, else to talk to.

"No, I mean it." I tried to double down on the lie. "The food is phenomenal and this DJ is really getting everyone going."

"Well, that's true," Charlotte conceded. "You have to put money where people will remember it." She set her empty cocktail glass down on a passing server's tray. "Listen, if you want to talk about what happened with Maddy and Lucy, it's fine. I'm sorry it even happened. Our grievances aside, I really like your daughter. She's a good kid."

I had no idea what she was referring to, but a block of ice formed in my stomach. "What are you talking about?"

Charlotte squinted. "You don't know? Well, last Monday Lucy came to our house after school."

To this I nodded. Of course I know where my child is after school, and at all times, for that matter.

"And when they changed into dry clothes after the pool, Maddy found one of her favorite charm bracelets in Lucy's backpack." She widened her eyes at me, looking both obnoxiously beautiful and obnoxiously smug.

I couldn't be hearing this correctly. "Okay wait, wait, wait, wait.

You're not insinuating that . . ." I felt a splash of champagne on my arm and made a mental note to steady my hands.

"Yes, Melody, your daughter stole something from my daughter's bedroom. The only reason I didn't pick up the phone and call you is because you're a complete asshole. I told Lucy to go home and tell you what she did, which she clearly did not."

I know I had been drinking, but honestly I think I would have reacted the same way stone-cold sober. The party around me disappeared, and a heat took over my body. Charlotte was accusing my daughter of stealing from her daughter. And then implying that my relationship with Lucy wasn't strong enough for her to admit it to me?

"You are out of your fucking mind! You really are!" I shouted. All eyes diverted to me. Greg reached for my elbow, which I promptly jabbed back in his direction. "My daughter doesn't need anything from you or your spoiled-brat daughter. How dare you accuse her of this!" It felt like she was going out of her way to make me look bad. And using my kid as a tool.

Charlotte's chest was heaving as she made a loud exhale from her nose, like an angry dragon. "Yes, Melody, your daughter did try to steal from my child, and she admitted as much to me through hysterical tears! Maddy said she never wanted to see her again, but I stepped in and said that we all just need to cool off for a while. We all make mistakes. She's a sweet kid, Melody, thank the lord she doesn't take after you!" A crowd had formed around us.

"Take after me? And what kind of influence are you, Charlotte? Dressing your prepubescent child in crop tops and miniskirts and giving her a phone while you're off gallivanting around town fucking your friend Patricia's husband under everyone's nose!"

And that, ladies and gentlemen, was my final act of the evening. I swear, it just slipped out in a moment of temporary insanity.

The oxygen left the room. I found Carol in the crowd that was still watching us, and she offered me the kindness of a sympathetic frown. Greg felt a mile away behind my back. *I went for the big one*, I wanted to tell him. *I punched her right in the nose.*

Patricia, her face an icy mask, appeared next to Don and, with a whisper in his ear, the Walkers left the building. I cringed, imagining their car ride conversation.

"I think that's enough for tonight." Darcy gently took my shoulders and guided me out through the entrance.

I can't remember the look on Charlotte's face when I accused her. As soon as the words left my lips, my world turned dark and foggy, and it didn't settle until I was home and shivering under a cold shower. Then, the clarity. Not only had I publicly shamed someone, I had possibly ruined that person's life, potentially ripped a family apart, because that someone had said something I didn't like about my daughter. Something that might have been true. Something that, in fact, turned out to be true. That person, Charlotte, who I had so vilified, had even defended my child while explaining the offense, and I spouted such hatred back in her face that I could no longer claim to be a decent human being at all. I wasn't even sure if my accusation was true.

Greg didn't mention my outburst at all, and the silence spoke volumes. I think that part hurt the most. We had been bickering so much lately, but I really needed him in that moment. Yes, I was making mistakes. But how could you blame me after being thrown into this pressure cooker of a new environment? I was still the same Mel.

CHARLOTTE

Do you ever feel like you've stumbled into a pool of quicksand, and you're just standing there, slowly sinking deeper and deeper, watching the world around you continue on? Like the people on the *Titanic* who didn't make it into a dinghy, watching, sinking, while their friends drifted closer and closer to safety. Death would be a mercy if only you could just get on with it!

I'm not suicidal; it's a metaphor.

If you've ever chaired a gala, especially a top-to-bottom one for a public school with no admin staff, you'd know what a soul-crushing, life-force-depleting drain the whole affair is. The hundreds of cold calls asking for sponsorship dollars or in-kind donations. *Would you like a kidney or my firstborn for those discounted flower arrangements?* Then there's the incessant glad-handing to sell tickets to people who should be supporting the damn thing anyway. This is benefiting *your* kids, people! This isn't paying for my summer in the Maldives! But no, I have to call every parent in the school and put on my most endearing voice. *Oh Carol, haven't seen you in so long! How are the kids? Congrats on that job you're doing. Are you planning on joining us for Be a Kid Again?*

When I finally remove my lips from all the Sunset butts, it's time to compare catering and production quotes. *Shrimp cocktail or arugula and strawberry salad? Ivory satin linen or sequins overlay?* And after that misery, I'm hijacked by the *why is everyone late/deliveries wrong/AV doesn't work/decor missing* of setup logistics!

So maybe I was distracted those last couple of weeks leading up to Be a Kid Again. Can you blame me? I'm trying to run a nonprofit. That means no profit. Just my blood, sweat, and tears for the welfare of others.

The gala was on Saturday and I received the phone call on Friday— the type of call that every mother dreads. We glance at our phones an average of three times per minute, every single weekday, for as long as our children are in school to see if said call is coming. Compare the number of daily phone pickups for a mother and a childless woman. I'll buy you a bottle of rosé if that mother didn't pick hers up at least twice as often!

Mrs. Giordani, there's been an incident with Axel at school. We are going to need you to come in immediately.

No, we can't discuss this over the phone. Principal Nelson will explain when you get here.

Mrs. Giordani, you're not helping the situation right now.

This kid. As if my third-degree vagina tear to bring him into this world wasn't pain enough, my firstborn child and only son told a history teacher that her class was "medieval torture" and, when sent to the office, left a very questionable journal on his desk. *A manifesto.* That's what the principal called it. Page after page of detailed ramblings from a troubled boy who is expressing his pain. Yes, the images were graphic, cemeteries and crucifixion self-portraits and the like. But things haven't been easy for Ax, my boy is *different*. He always preferred LEGOs to playdates, is more the solitary type. Hell, I don't always understand it, but haven't we all gone through some dark days? I did! I didn't write poetry about how much I hate my entire existence, but I might have had the thoughts. I just didn't write them down. And Ax has always been more *creative* than I ever was.

The pictures he drew, I pointed out, were quite well done. They showed an impressive technique and skill. He was obviously expressing himself. That's what artists do! I had not, until that moment, considered him an artist, but the images were almost breathtaking in a way.

The precise pencil strokes, wispy and delicate, though they were portraying startling images. Skulls sketched to almost look unassuming, feminine even. Bleeding crosses, with Gothic-looking gargoyles peering from behind them. It reminded me of the old buildings in Prague. Romance from another time. But the school was calling them *incendiary*.

I'm not saying they weren't shocking. The images and poems were definitely provocative, like great art can so often be. I'm just saying that they didn't present a threat. A grievance, maybe, a lack of acceptance, but not a threat. It actually seemed to me like a healthy expression of Axel's pain. I'm telling you, these public servants don't know how to think outside the box because they just kept repeating "very serious" and "red flag" whenever they could squeeze them in. Honestly, this is their fault. The establishment has let my son down, failed to recognize his potential.

Okay. Ax needs therapy, but I am also prepared to foster his inarguable creative talents. It is completely my fault for missing it in the past, and I can own that. As fury inducing as it is to be on the opposite end of someone attacking your child, I also saw the opportunity. So I guess you could say I was grateful in a way.

But first, those cunts decided to make an example of my boy. Suspension, to start. Axel was to be sent home for two weeks, during which time he was expected to begin regular therapy sessions. A psychological evaluation would be required for him to return to Miami Beach Middle. Those snotty condescending fucks. And that wasn't all! The police had already been notified, and I was forced to consent to a full search of our home.

The afternoon of our *intervention*, the officers arrived in their tactical gear—talk about dramatic—and pushed their way into Ax's room like he was some kind of murder suspect. They flipped over his dresser drawers, flinging boxer shorts and T-shirts all over the floor. They confiscated his laptop, threw his mattress upside down. And then they had the nerve to leave it that way. They were looking for weapons, for Christ's sake!

They didn't find any. And they didn't find any *manifestos* either. Really, all this was for some left-of-center drawings and depressive rantings. Haven't these administrators ever met a thirteen-year-old? It was ludicrous. Offensive, even. To make an example of my boy because he wasn't some YouTuber making unboxing videos like the other mainstreamers. I love unboxing videos, so I'm not knocking it. Just saying, my boy isn't that type.

And maybe he feels left out because of that. He has always kept to himself, as I said. Never was interested in the spotlight. When he was little, my MomGoalsMiami Insta featured him and me on the daily. It was how I first cultivated my following! Mommy and me on a boat, matching captain's hats. *Ahoy! From Ax and Char! #comesailaway.* But as he grew, he started refusing. Full-blown tantrums when I asked him to pose for the camera, give me a peace sign, a side profile. Admittedly, it drove me nuts that he fought me on it. *What's the big deal, it's one picture!* No ma'am. Wasn't happening. Maddy, on the other hand, could teach *me* a thing or two about influencing. Girl's just got it.

First, it was the pictures, then he rebelled at literally any clothing I tried to put on his body. No more little man button-ups or suspenders. Nope. Sweatpants on Easter. I hired an occupational therapist to try to work out his *sensory issues*, but it was worthless. Eventually I just gave up.

Time marched on, and he retreated more and more. I would try to set up playdates for Ax, almost desperately. I'd pick up moms at Pilates, school events, wherever, trying to drum up some friends. And every single time I planned one, my boy would sit in the corner and ask when we could leave. I honestly do not understand that impulse. Who doesn't want friends? James kept telling me, *It's a phase. Let it pass.* As if he was ever home enough to see his son for more than five minutes at a time. Well, there Ax was, suspended from school, labeled some kind of weirdo by people whose humanity I'm really concerned about.

I called James, who was on a business trip to New York, and he was incensed by what the school had done. "This is small-minded thinking," he said. Which was spot-on. "When I get back, I'm going to reach out to the school board directly." James and Ax don't have a ton in common, but he loves his son and believes fully in his essential goodness.

Meanwhile, I was one day away from welcoming more than half of the Sunset Academy parents to our biggest fundraiser of the year. One I had to pull off, mind you, without the ace-in-the-hole underwriting that the Walker Family Foundation has so graciously provided in the past. That bombshell exploded square in my lap while we were celebrating Christmas dinner with the Walkers in Aspen. It turns out they needed to *tighten up* their contributions for some Goliath planned gift to who knows what. Probably some uber anticipated new museum that they wanted to throw their name on. James gave me that judgy look of his when they said it and it took every ounce of my restraint not to pounce on him.

Well, that left me with an Applebee's budget when these parents had grown accustomed to a Nobu experience. Sure, I sold a good amount of sponsorships: there was Vogel, the luxury car dealership, and Bank of Florida, and all the liquor was donated (great exposure for the brands). But do you have any idea how expensive it is to completely transform a public school cafeteria? The draping alone would have been upward of $30,000, which I couldn't afford with what I was lucky to scrape together.

So there I was, juggling calls from vendors, dealing with last-minute plus-ones, and personally stuffing all the gift bags, and suddenly I needed to carve out a Hallmark moment with my teenage son, who had just been suspended from school and nearly arrested for making an alleged disturbance. Gimme a break!

I said something to the effect of "Listen, honey. You and I both know that this school reaction is bullshit. But really, what the hell were you thinking?"

And do you know what Ax did? He went to his room and slammed the door in my face. Moody or not, what happened to a little respect for the person who brought you into this world? I was trying to be on his side!

I also wanted to cry—like really ugly cry—punch some pillows, bury my head in the mattress to scream. But as adults we are rarely afforded that time, right? So I had to plug along.

That night though, I couldn't sleep. I always get a little jittery before a big event, but this was different. The pillows wouldn't lie right under my head and every time I closed my eyes, I saw Ax's drawings coming to life and becoming more sinister. Cartoon machetes hacking into my bedroom door, skeletons coming to life and chasing me down the hallway. Blood raining from the ceiling. Grotesque and evil versions of what he had actually doodled, but terrifyingly real in my sleepless nightmare. I couldn't imagine that my son would ever make the jump from off-color artwork to actual physical violence, but my heart was racing. It was like a friend telling you that they saw your husband sneaking into a hotel with his sexy secretary. Even if it's not true, the shadow of doubt is always there.

At three A.M., I called James and told him, "You need to come home! Things are not okay here, and I can't do this on my own!" Well, I told it to his voice mail. To which he responded the next morning with a text saying, *I'll be home in three days. Can you hold it down until then?*

Dark circles aside, I shook it off the next morning. The light of day made the whole idea seem absurd, and I just had so much to do! After a nine-hour day of setup, I opened the doors to the Be a Kid Again Gala, and welcomed the Sunset Academy parents to an event I'd rather not have my name associated with. The Pax Romana was more like a Little Caesars pizzeria, and I had to plaster on my pageant smile and act like it was a hit.

All I kept thinking was *never again*. There was no way I could let another marquis event fall from grace without the proper funding. So I found Don Walker and made sure he felt the love and appreciation that I do genuinely feel for his support.

Don is that type, you know. Powerful man, self-made, and he likes special attention. He feeds off an appreciation for his wealth and masculinity. This is my sweet spot. When I worked at the magazine, I killed with the entrepreneurial types. Males, mostly. Guys like Don can't resist an attractive woman stroking his ego. We've always played this game. The benevolent king and the enamored subject.

We found ourselves in these comfortable roles as I tried to ignore the living embarrassment around us—Roman nobility eating dinner off plastic plates among other indignities—when Melody, who possesses a preternatural penchant for kicking someone when they're down, decided to accuse me of adultery in front of a rapt cohort of Sunset Academy parents.

Fucking your friend's husband under everyone's nose.

If this was her campaign strategy, it was a good one. Now half the school thinks I'm the cuckolding type; it's quite the reputation killer. I might have accepted it—with rage, but accepted nonetheless—if there was any truth to the claim. Picture this: Don Walker, holding on to his high school athletic achievements like a seagull desperately clutching a wriggling fish in its beak, taking me into his arms and whispering, "Let me tell you about the time I drove the ball for forty yards to score a touchdown junior year." Then I'd get soaking wet and moan, "Oh Donny! I want you to touchdown between my legs!" No thanks.

But now that it's been said out loud, most people will just believe it because why on earth would anyone publicly declare something so salacious if it was, in fact, false? And then Don and Patricia fled the situation like a couple of escaped convicts, which made us look even more guilty! Typical, a man and a woman are accused, but only the woman needs to stay and explain herself. Let the mob sew the scarlet letter *A* to my chest!

Isn't it rich that *I* was the one being accused? When half of the other parents at the gala are so clearly bonking each other? I mean Gabriela, and I do love her, is having the worst-kept secret affair with

Kevin Duffy, our school board representative. You don't hear anyone shouting that in a public forum!

Of course, at the gala my husband is notably absent, as usual. Adding fuel to the fire. *Char, would you rather I show my face at your little parties or provide the lifestyle you've been privileged to live? Can't have it both ways.* I'm so sick of the same stupid excuse! No, James, you can't possibly have a business trip every single time I have something important to host. You can plan ahead and find a way to be there.

But what would Melody Howard know about the intricacies of my marriage? Or anything else about me, for that matter. Seriously, what kind of a person just unleashes an accusation like that? With no regard for marriage, children, nothing.

That whole thing about Midwesterners being nice? Total crock. Melody Howard is more Wicked Witch of the West than an innocent Dorothy. Did I drop a house on her sister or something?

So then I was dealing with a public shaming on top of a troublesome teen and thought I was just going to burst at the seams. Thank god for my angel baby, Maddy. At least that one wasn't adding to my gray hairs. The morning after the gala, I couldn't even get out of bed. Just lay there, staring at the ceiling, thinking about how the housekeeper really needed to dust the A/C vents. And you know what Madeline did? She ordered Uber Eats and brought me a croissant and coffee in bed. Then I just felt like, well, maybe everything will end up okay.

MELODY

I needed to surgically remove the foot that's been stuck in my mouth since I moved to Miami. I had been making so many mistakes, really stupid ones. And it felt out of character. I'd spent my adult life trying to be diplomatic. A good friend. A good wife and mother. I thought I'd left behind my days of rash emotional behavior with my homecoming queen sash.

The worst thing I ever did growing up was betray my friend Katherine Zilber while we were in high school. Kat and I had been close since elementary and, by the time we were fourteen, our friendship was almost an assumption. It required zero effort.

She and I weren't best friends exactly, but we were part of a group that was as solid as can be. There were no real issues among us, just a natural bond. Until freshman year, that is, when the hormones hijacked my brain and good judgment got buried down deep. This was before Greg and I were a thing, but let's just say I noticed him pretty quickly. While most of the boys our age were still pimply, gawky, and scrawny, Greg was an absolute stud. Already pushing six feet, he played varsity lacrosse and was toned and tan. He looked like a man.

Well, Kat noticed him, too. And with her genetically blessed teenage chest, Greg noticed her back. The two of them started dating. You know, high school stuff: movies, the odd kegger. It was all I could think about; the whole situation devastated me. I couldn't process the emotions. The friend I'd loved from childhood, and this paralyzing crush. I wanted to accept it, but I fantasized all day about them breaking up. I knew it was wrong, but the emotions were so strong!

I never thought I'd act on those feelings, though. That's why I even surprised myself when I took the opportunity to destroy Kat and Greg. We were at a house party on Sullivan Street. Matt Jenkins was hosting because his parents were out of town. It was straight out of that movie *Can't Hardly Wait:* Puff Daddy and Biggie blaring from the speakers, baby tees and wrapped miniskirts, dark lipstick and brightly colored Jell-O shots. Kat was grinding on Greg in the living room, and I remember gripping my red Solo cup so tight that I crushed it and spilled its vodka and Gatorade contents all over the Jenkins's Oriental rug.

Finally, Kat went to the bathroom, leaving Greg unattended, and I zoomed in like a Green Beret assassin. I slid my hips next to his to the beat of "Big Poppa," and together we threw our hands in the air like we just didn't care. I figured we had about sixty more seconds before Kat would be back and find me going hard for her boyfriend, so I wasted no time and went straight for Greg's lips. It was a bold move, and so unlike me, but my sweet guy took the bait and there we were, hard-core making out in the Jenkins's living room, while my friend/his girlfriend stood not ten feet away in disbelief.

Kat didn't talk to me for two years, and I definitely didn't blame her. I hated myself for how it all went down, but eventually everyone just realized that Greg and I were the real deal and just kind of accepted it. Even Kat. We never meant to hurt anyone. Greg said he secretly had always had a thing for me but didn't think I felt the same. I told myself that, while it was terrible, this was *my* guy, and we were supposed to end up together one way or another. So it wasn't actually so bad when you think about it.

But that was the worst thing I had ever done to someone else . . . until the Be a Kid Again Gala, that is. Publicly accusing Charlotte Giordani of adultery was a new low. And this time I wasn't sure if I'd ever forgive myself.

"What the hell were you thinking?" Greg asked me the next morning. This conversation was becoming all too frequent. We were still lying in bed, and I couldn't even make eye contact with him for fear of exploding into tears.

"I wasn't thinking at all," I admitted. "I was just so mad that Charlotte would accuse Lucy of stealing from her daughter. Like she was trying to embarrass me or something."

Greg rolled over and put a hand in my hair. "Why would something Lucy did be embarrassing for you? You are two different people."

"Like she was using Lucy to make me look bad, like a bad mom, or saying I'm not raising her well. Or her daughter is better behaved." I sounded ridiculous, I knew. My eyes were getting wetter by the second.

"Maybe Lucy did steal, in which case, don't you think we need to address this with our daughter?" Greg wiped my tears with his thumb, and I grabbed his hand and pressed it hard onto my face.

I'd been acting like a hormonal teenager. It was embarrassing. And Greg was right, of course. The stealing accusation needed to be addressed.

Lucy got dropped off after her sleepover with another girl from class, and I approached with caution. "Hey, honey, do you have a minute?" I asked as she slid off her overnight bag. "Maddy's mom mentioned something to me yesterday and I just wanted to discuss it."

It didn't seem plausible that my rule-following daughter could be capable of something as base as stealing, and I felt guilty even asking her about it. But as soon as the words came out of my mouth, Lucy tensed. She paused while kicking off her shoes and, without looking at me, said, "Sure. What do you want to talk about?"

My hands went cold. The truth was plain on her face before I even had to draw out her confession. It didn't take much for her to fold. Tears spilled, and I might have felt sympathy if I wasn't so enraged.

"What on earth were you thinking, Lucy Ann?" I shouted. Greg smirked at my outburst, and I realized that I had mirrored his words from earlier that morning.

Lucy gasped for breath between sobs. "I'm so so sorry, Mom. I just . . ."

"This is not how we raised you!" I felt out of control and willed myself to calm down, but the words kept flying out. "Stealing? That is so beneath you. Why would you do that?"

"I just love her so much. I just wanted to take something home to remind me of her." She took a tissue from Greg and blew forcefully into it.

I took a beat and closed my eyes. Fuck. Why did we have to act so crazy around girls we admire? "Oh, sweetie." I began to soften. "I know you look up to Maddy. But you had to have known that stealing from your friend was just going to harm your relationship."

Greg gave me the side-eye. "Yes," he agreed. "Hurting people you care about, that you want to be your friend, that doesn't go well."

I cringed. I had been behaving worse than an eight-year-old.

"I, I know," Lucy said. "I just want to be okay with her again. I'm so so sorry. I just want to be friends again."

"I understand," I said, and walked over to the foyer to wrap her in my arms. And I meant what I said. I could definitely understand how she felt.

As terrible as it felt to be on Charlotte's bad side, seeing Lucy in a similar predicament hurt more. I felt responsible for her bad decision, as though watching my questionable actions over the past months had transferred to Lucy by osmosis. We grounded her, of course. Isolated her to her room for a week with no iPad. But I did sympathize.

That next week at school, I almost wished I had given my daughter a phone so I could check in. I imagined the worst: Lucy being pelted with sandwiches in the cafeteria, having a DORK sign taped to her back while she wasn't paying attention. But everything seemed fine. Lucy said that she'd apologized to Maddy, and Maddy had accepted. And that was the end of it. Could it be that easy? It certainly wasn't with Madeline's mother. I didn't trust it.

Then the weekend arrived, with Lucy officially off grounding and the entire third grade invited to my friend Carol's house for her daughter's ninth birthday. I mean really, another grade-wide event? It was a little bewildering that these people who cannot stand one another insist on celebrating every holiday and milestone together.

The party was extravagant, which no longer merited even a mention between Greg and me. Though I did worry about how we would keep up with a grade-wide soiree for Lucy (should we ever attempt to have one). The theme was *Girls Rule* (of course Carol's daughter would have a socially conscious birthday party). The grand affair was catered with a full bar, and it was clear that a professional production company had handled the decor. I was a little surprised to see Carol so fancy because, I mean, while she has class written all over her, this seemed more like a Walker/Giordani type event. But hey, Samuel did well as a partner/litigator at a huge firm and it was their daughter's birthday!

Lucy had dressed like a mini Amelia Earhart, with a faux leather jacket, matching helmet and goggles, and a pink headband (everyone had to wear something pink). We hadn't been there for more than five minutes when a bouncing Maddy was in front of us saying, "Love the aviator look, Luce!" The two girls embraced and didn't hesitate to leave us behind for the rest of the afternoon.

"Was Maddy dressed like . . . Ariana Grande? Again?" Greg wrinkled his eyebrows.

"Gotta say, she can pull it off," I answered. "And Ariana is an empowered woman. I think. She's got like . . . seven rings for all her friends."

I wasn't making any sense. It was a relief that Lucy and Maddy were okay, but it didn't leave Charlotte and me in a better place. And she was bound to be close by. I was a bundle of nerves.

Darcy found me by the chocolate fountain.

"Who can we take down today?" She patted me on the back. "Should we announce that the Bakers have been cheating on their taxes? The Vogels upgraded their driveway without a permit?"

The joke eased a bit of my tension. "I'll be happy to fly under the radar today, if that's at all possible," I told her.

"Well, you're in luck today, Kansas." Darcy cheered my plastic champagne glass. "Charlotte isn't here. Issues with her son, Ax. Poor misunderstood Ax." Darcy looked genuinely concerned when she mentioned Charlotte's son. "Maddy was dropped off with the nanny today."

I had gotten off easy. A Sunset Academy event with no awkward run-ins? That was a first for me. I was free to enjoy the party with minimal anxiety.

Yes, I know that a child's nine-year-old birthday party doesn't sound like a rocking good time, but as I've mentioned, parties in Miami are anything but mundane. Carol had hired a well-known DJ, and after a couple of drinks the dance floor had been taken over by the parents. These adults could *dance*, too. No awkward Elaine moves or white-boy shuffles to be found.

Gabriela Machado was holding court in front of the DJ booth (her daughter was a fifth-grader but apparently the PTA president receives an invitation to every Sunset Academy event, official or unofficial) and she was giving Shakira-esque hip roll lessons to some of the girls. I didn't dare try and keep up; my Midwest skills were definitely not comparable.

Carol and her husband, Samuel, worked the backyard like a bride and groom at their wedding, making sure to greet each guest at least once. "Amazing party, Carol," I told her. "I love that your daughter chose such a mature theme!"

"Thanks, hon." Carol kissed me on the cheek. "My socially conscious nine-year-old! What can I say?"

Greg and Samuel stepped aside to discuss the Miami Heat's playoff chances, and Carol leaned in close to my ear.

"Don't be alarmed, but the Walkers just showed up. I'm actually surprised—they never go to the kids' parties. It's usually the nanny brigade."

I shivered. This I had not anticipated. It was rumored that the Walkers would never grace a children's party with their presence.

Though in this case they lived just down the street, so there was the convenience factor. And now the anxiety was back. The golden couple sauntered into the party, arm in arm, with the air of a royal family. Patricia was striking in a white eyelet sundress, and Don looked like he'd just stepped off a boat, wearing loafers, red chinos, and a linen button-down. This was the first time I'd seen them since accusing Donald of having an affair with Charlotte.

"I think I'm going to throw up," I whispered to Carol.

Carol rolled her eyes. "Don't even worry one bit." She patted my arm. "There is nothing to be afraid of with these two. Don may or may not be adulterous. But either way, I don't trust them."

JUDGE CAROL LAWSON

The rule for hosting children's birthday parties is this: you either invite fewer than ten kids or you invite everyone. By everyone, I mean the whole class, siblings, the entire grade, any child that has ever been on a team with your kid, and your hairdresser's cousin's twins.

Fear not, though, because this social edict has an expiration date. Middle schoolers are way too cool to be seen with who they consider tier two and tier three classmates. So the party budget has time to replenish from around when your child turns ten years old and their sweet sixteen (unless your family celebrates quinces, which ours does not).

Elizabeth, my third child and bona fide social butterfly—we call her Madam President because she was born to shake hands and kiss babies—turned nine in March, and we had long ago resigned ourselves to commemorating the occasion with the most lavish, cringeworthy waste of money possible.

At a certain point in every new Miamian's indoctrination, the city invades you like a virus. It sneaks in through your nostrils and begins to spread and multiply. At first, it's the liberal use of the word "literally." Next, you find yourself getting blowouts on your lunch break, and before you know it, you're driving a splashy luxury car that costs significantly more than you should be comfortable spending. Once you've succumbed to the extravagant child's birthday party, the transformation is complete.

You can try to fight it. You can endlessly criticize and deride it, like I so often do. But if you are honest with yourself, part of you probably *enjoys* the Sodom and Gomorrah aspects of Magic City culture. A guilty pleasure to be sure, but a pleasure nonetheless. And isn't it just so damned *easy* when it seems like everyone else is doing it? I can hear a stern, cancer-free version of my departed father's voice in my head. *If everyone went and jumped off a bridge, would you do it, too?* I don't know, Dad, it depends on if there's a Chanel waiting at the riverbank below?

Elizabeth chose the theme—*Girls Rule!* Her idea was to throw a coed bash that celebrated strong women and their allies. All of the vendors were required to be women-owned businesses, and the invitation featured a montage of her heroes: Marie Curie, Harriet Tubman, Ruth Bader Ginsburg, Nanny Granny, Malala. Girls and boys alike were encouraged to come dressed in at least one article of clothing in a pink hue, an easy enough feat for Miami-bred kids. In Miami Beach, even the sidewalks are painted a deep salmon. The maintenance is a disaster, but the color is almost synonymous with the town, so the upkeep persists.

My daughter explained her choice thusly: "I want to reclaim pink, which has been attributed to girls and women as a symbol of subservience and weakness, and turn it into a symbol of our power." It turns out the girl does listen to her old mother. You go, Elizabeth.

The party was on a Sunday. One hundred children were invited, parental drop-off optional (but strongly desired if anyone cared to ask) and one hundred children attended. Our backyard swelled with sweaty bodies. On top of the pool (which we had covered with custom-fitted wood panels), the dance floor vibrated with twerking nine-year-old girls, the boys not yet interested. Is the booty shaking they do an expression of their feminine power? In my day it would have landed me extra hours in church, dusting the hymnals, but they do know how to move. I let it slide, for the moment, and watched the girls have their fun.

Elizabeth was beaming in a hot pink T-shirt dress, layered with a white lacy RBG collar. Her curly hair was pulled into a stylish topknot, and, for good measure, a pair of pink lens-less glasses rested on her face. She was a modern, multiracial, Supreme Court badass.

The other third-grade girls surrounded her on the dance floor, where they took turns jumping into the middle of the circle to show off their solo skills. There were cartwheels, lots of flossing, a couple of hilarious sprinklers, and even a show-stopping backflip. Already one glass of rosé in, I was tempted to push my way in and teach these youngins a thing or two.

Next to the dessert table, which overflowed with tiers of doughnuts, cupcakes, and an assortment of pink candies in apothecary glass jars, the boys entertained themselves by taking pictures with their faces inside the cardboard cutout holes of feminist heroes. Dorothy Pitman Hughes and Gloria Steinem would cringe to see Maddox and Monrow Walker's smug faces on top of their bodies but there they were.

I had invited those very fine people from across the street, the Walkers, in their pink glass castle, because I had invited all of the third-graders who had ever been in a class with Elizabeth. Also, I was curious to see if they'd show up.

Sure enough, Don and Patricia deigned to bring their boys into my backyard soirée, sans nanny, which to my knowledge they had never done at a child's birthday party. Ever since the *incident* at the Be a Kid Again Gala (when a lubricated Melody accused, quite publicly, Charlotte Giordani of having an affair with Don), the Walkers had been increasingly conspicuous in showing up to events together, hand in hand.

Their united front did little to dispel the rumor, which was hardly a scandal to begin with, whether or not it was true. The general indifference to the whole affair mimicked every other salacious piece of news that happens in Miami: five minutes of curiosity, then everyone moves on to the next piece of dirt. In Coral Gables, such a huge number of people are having affairs and even swapping partners, they don't even waste group chat messages on adultery anymore. We are slightly more chaste on the Beach, but still.

Don and Patricia found me by the food stations and made sure to marvel at and praise the *fabulouuuuuus* party. "And what an inspiring theme, your daughter is going to blaze quite a path. I can already see it," Patricia said.

"A pleasure to have you," I told them.

"We should really get the kids together sometime," Don said. "One of the reasons we moved to this neighborhood was the community feel, where kids can run around from house to house. Like I did, back in the day."

Were we living in the same place? People barely waved from their mailboxes on Peacock Island.

"Well, that would be just lovely. Thank you, Don," I said, knowing I'd never let any of my children step foot onto their property. "Now please, help yourself to a drink and something to eat."

I didn't point to Patricia's nose and ask if she'd already helped herself to a powdered doughnut. I was determined to *go high* with the Walkers.

Don sauntered over to the food table. "Thank you, Carol. Everything looks delicious. What are these . . . empanadas?"

"Those are Jamaican patties. Mother made them from scratch."

Don took one theatrical bite. "Delicious!"

I thought about their pink glass kingdom across the street. Tinting their lives in rose for the world to see. A meticulously curated fishbowl. A perfumed lie.

CHARLOTTE

Oh my god.

Does anybody in this town have a fucking moral compass anymore? Doesn't anybody think about repercussions? You know what they say: Florida is a *sunny place for shady people*. It should be on our damned license plates. Oranges, sunshine, white trash meth addicts in the northern part, sleazy businessmen in the south.

It was Monday after drop-off, and my phone had been lighting up like a Disney fireworks show. No exaggeration, in the car ride from Sunset Academy to Beach Pilates, I missed eighty texts and five calls.

Police cars surrounding Villa Rosé! Do you know what happened?

Have you talked to Patricia? I heard someone tried to rob their house this morning!

Miami is constantly playing a giant game of telephone.

I never made it inside Pilates. How could I? I was worried sick. These were my good friends, and my most generous patrons! Not to mention, my fictional lover and his poor suffering wife.

So I started dialing Patricia on repeat. When she didn't answer, I tried Don. Nothing. Now I'm thinking the worst. Maybe it was an armed robbery and they're in the hospital, or holy hell maybe a body bag. And what about the boys? Now, that's a thought of sheer fucking terror. What kind of sick person would hurt such a beautiful family and precious children? I was on the verge of tears, agonized with worry.

I called the police station. Nada. Called Mount Sinai hospital. No one named Walker admitted. Clearly, something was very, very wrong.

Eventually, I gave up on standing there in front of Beach Pilates making frantic phone calls, looking like some psycho housewife who just found a highly suspicious GPS ping on her husband's LoJack.

I drove to Villa Rosé, braced for chalk lines, bloodstains, crying neighbors shaking while explaining to detectives for the hundredth time every single detail they witnessed. What I found instead was a peaceful Peacock Island, silent except for the occasional whirring of a landscaper's lawn mower.

I parked in front of the Walkers' gate and peered inside, easy enough to do with the floor-to-ceiling windows. All I saw was a pair of men in windbreakers, walking down the stairs, each carrying a large bankers box, their normal complexions turned peach behind the rose-colored glass. FBI agents, not Miami Beach PD.

No fucking way. I must be the biggest idiot in the southeast United States. Don's words echoed in my ears, his canned answer every time I politely asked about his business. *Oh Charlotte, it's complicated and boring. You don't want to sit through a long drawn-out explanation. This is MBA-level stuff.*

More like BS level.

Patricia called me back a couple of hours later, sounding like she'd just gotten off a three-day bender with Charlie Sheen, circa 2011. *Robbed*, she said. Some thugs with guns, thank god no one is hurt.

Suck my dick, Patricia. You won't fool me twice.

Of course, I told her I was so sorry and please call me and blah, blah, blah. We are here for you and the boys, send them over, the whole thing. I mean, did she really think we wouldn't figure it out? She was holding on like a frog to a windshield speeding down I-95. It was sad in a way, but my fury wasn't allowing me to pity her just yet.

Show's over, lady! Let it go! The curtain is down, the audience is gone, and you're all alone.

Later, at Maddy's tennis lesson, it was all the talk. Of course it was! The other moms and I huddled under the shelter and took turns guessing at what white-collar crime Don must have committed. Was Patricia in on it? How much did she know? I mean, she had to know. How dumb can you be?

Then, as the girls were gathering their bags and heading back to meet us, it happened. Like dominoes falling, all the moms, and the few tennis dads, were glued to their phones. Breaking News: Prominent Miami Philanthropist and Money Manager Arrested for Fraud.

Below the headline, Don's and Patricia's arrogant fucking smiles smacked me like a cat-o'-nine-tails. It was a photo that had circulated among all the Miami social pages back in December, from the Three Wishes Ball. The Walkers were "honorary chairs" for the night, which means they did zero work but cut a check for a butt load of money.

Patricia looked like she had just come off a thirty-year juice cleanse, with her hollow cheeks and her shoulder blades cutting a sharp angle out of her Versace couture gown. That dress was perfection though, a flowing crimson skirt with a gold bodice and intricate hand-sewn details throughout. Her hair was pulled back into a messy updo, and long beams of a sunburst headpiece created a halo around her bun.

Donald had one hand placed noncommittally behind Patricia's back as if to say *inquiries accepted*. He was dashing in a made-to-measure Tom Ford tuxedo (he'd spent twenty minutes that night talking to me about the damned thing), a burgundy velvet handkerchief peeking from his jacket pocket.

I felt sick.

All eyes were on me at the tennis shelter now. Maddy was hugging herself and giving me her best *read my mind right now* look. After a moment, she said, "Mom, everyone is staring at you."

What, am I the Walkers' keeper? It's not like I was sitting at their dining room table, scheming how to steal money from investors to then fund my Sunset Academy capital projects. I was a victim, too! I was taken, just like whoever Don allegedly defrauded to enrich himself and build a *making up for what is probably a tiny penis* landmark architectural home.

Ginny Squire, the mom of Maddy's tennis partner, stepped closer to me and whispered, "Charlotte, did you know?"

It's a good thing I'm not a physically violent person.

"Are you fucking insane, Ginny? Do I seem like the kind of person who just traipses around with criminals for fun? I spend all my free time planning events for charities and then just fund them with stolen money?" She looked at me like I'd punched her grandma, but honestly, who cares.

By then the salt was so thick on the back of my tongue, I thought I might puke. I tried to take a deep breath, but the air caught in my throat. There was no stopping the waterworks. The ugly cry came like a waterfall, and I mean snotty, gasping, dripping ugly crying. The other tennis moms exchanged looks, like *well, doesn't that explain everything*. Whether the alleged affair (thanks, Melody), or me supposedly knowing something. I can only imagine the ridiculous assumptions they must have been making.

Maddy. Poor Maddy was red-faced and looked hell-bent on fighting back her own tears. So I grabbed her by the hand and got the hell out of there. I didn't click on the rest of the article until after she went to bed that night.

March 11, 2019

Donald Walker, of Walker Equities LLC, was arrested Monday on charges that he defrauded investors to the tune of $700 million, federal agents say.

The prominent businessman and his wife, Patricia Walker, are mainstays of the Miami social scene, often photographed at glamorous charity events and known to donate large sums of money for naming rights at various buildings around town.

A criminal complaint against Walker alleges that he and his firm stole investor money to fund his lavish lifestyle and, when clients started asking questions, used new investor money to repay those looking for an "out."

Patricia Walker has not been arrested, and sources are not aware if she had any involvement in the alleged scheme.

This is a developing story.

Thank god I never fucked him. Despite what everybody thinks.

MELODY

Well, I hope you feel less bad now," Darcy said.

I didn't. I took zero pleasure in watching the fall of Donald and Patricia Walker. Their alleged crimes, no matter how terrible, did not absolve me of my violence against the accused. If anything, it amplified my guilt toward Charlotte.

When you lie down with dogs . . . That's what Greg said. He thought that Charlotte's proximity to the Walkers implied some complicity, or at least similarly amoral decision making. But my mind kept replaying the kindnesses. The first day of school welcome. The invitation for a playdate. The warm reception. The way she treats my Lucy.

I claimed for myself a moral authority, branded myself the beacon of ethics and good behavior. I had the audacity to believe myself better because, what, I have a more demure social media account?

It was easy to judge Charlotte, fun even. But now that her closest allies had been taken down in spectacular fashion—a public shaming worthy of *Game of Thrones*—it felt like I'd been picking on David instead of Goliath. The mouse instead of the lion. The sheep instead of the . . . you get the point.

The balance of power abruptly shifted, but I took no pleasure in it. Quite the opposite, actually. Every sinew of my being was compelled to somehow *make things right* with Charlotte. Lucy and Maddy were back on, after my daughter's embarrassing klepto moment and subsequent grounding, and the two were in a steady weekend sleepover rotation between the Giordani and Howard households. Awkward curbside handoffs had become commonplace, typically with the husbands handling the child swaps.

The week the Walker story broke was mayhem. Sunset Academy buzzed with gossip and accusations; every conversation at drop-off seemed to be centered on the scandal. Walking Lucy to class, my ears piqued with fragments of "I *told* my husband that something wasn't right there," and "Those poor boys. A father in prison?" Seemingly dozens of families from school had been invested. According to Darcy, it was the latest in a *Miami is always trying to be New York* saga. In Don Walker, they'd landed their very own mini Bernie Madoff. I'd never been so grateful for not being rich enough to be part of something. People were also speculating on how strange it was that the Giordanis, as close as they were with the Walkers, weren't invested. Did Charlotte know something? It did seem a little suspect.

I first heard what happened on a Monday evening. The Breaking News story spread like mono at a seven minutes in heaven party. Darcy and I had taken the kids to look at graffiti murals in the artsy Wynwood neighborhood, followed by pizza at Wynwood Walls.

After taking photos in front of an expansive Shepard Fairey piece, an impressive collage that included images of the Dalai Lama, lotus flowers, Martin Luther King Jr., and Andy Warhol, we tucked our foursome into a cozy booth. Darcy gasped and let out a startled "Oh shit!" She found my gaze, widening her eyes in a *we are going to need to speak in private* gesture, while Jackson and Maddy giggled over their menus.

"I don't know why you guys get so weird with your crazy mom fights." Jackson rolled his eyes. "We always figure out what's going on."

"Agreed," Lucy chimed in. "It's like, embarrassing. You have more problems with people than we do."

From the mouths of babes.

"Well, sweet children," Darcy said, "not that this is any of your business, but this has nothing to do with moms fighting. And I'll have you know, I only fight on the side of righteousness."

Double eye rolls from our progeny.

While the news would inevitably reach our children the next day at school, Darcy opted to text me the link to the *Miami Times* article.

There, in Helvetica Bold, was the takedown of Sunset Academy's most prolific donors, a public stoning in the form of breaking news, where words like "alleged" become lost amid "fraud" and "stole."

I was surprised at my rush of sympathy for the dethroned couple. Their children, who were innocents, would forever be wounded by scandal. I imagined their boys in college meeting new friends from different cities, perhaps a girlfriend or boyfriend. Naturally, the new acquaintances and/or lovers would sooner or later type the Walker boys' first and last names into whatever space-aged search engine was in vogue at the time and—surprise! The parents turn out to be white-collar criminals, or least the father, but everyone will assume that the mother was either in on it, or very stupid. So really, either way the boys will be branded with the stench of failed aspiration, greed, and, ultimately, failure. Maddox and Monrow Walker certainly did not deserve that future.

But I couldn't help feeling sad for Donald and Patricia Walker, too. For all their pretense, pomp, and condescension, something within me didn't want to resign them to frauds. There was something deeply disturbing about the realization, a level of emptiness and despair to their characters that was almost too much to think about. I wondered if I, too, would resort to extreme artifice if my insides were too painful to view as is, if my authentic self was so disfigured and grotesque that living a lie was preferable.

Darcy was impudent. *This is so typical Miami, it's almost cliché. They didn't even have the decency to be original,* she typed to me from across the table.

Allegedly, I wrote back.

"You older folks." Jackson crossed his arms. "Always staring at your phones."

That boy had inherited some lovable snark from his mom. He was right, too. All the Sunset PTA mom drama had distracted me from being present with Lucy, my husband, and especially myself. I had made zero progress in building my consulting business in Miami, because I had made zero effort. I'd placed all my eggs in the PTA election basket, what a farce, which was feeling more like a popularity contest than a decision between two qualified candidates. Suddenly, with scandal whispering closer and closer to my opponent, I was looking like the prettiest girl in school. And it felt dirty.

I resolved to speak with Charlotte, in person, to look at her face and have an actual conversation while sober. I took Lucy to her sleepover at the Giordani house that Friday, ignoring my daughter's panicked expression when I parked the car and walked her up to the front door. The manicured lawn and lush pink bougainvilleas belied a sense of mundane suburban safety as I pressed my finger into Charlotte's doorbell. I counted my heartbeats until the door opened, enveloping me in a wash of crisp air-conditioning and an underlying scent of English rose.

Charlotte stood in the doorway with a halo of light behind her, an expression of neither surprise nor disappointment on her face. She pursed her lips, then looked down at Lucy and transformed into her bright stage-Charlotte self. "Hi, sweetie! Come on in, Maddy is upstairs laying out all her Rainbow Looms so you can make some bracelets."

"Hi, Charlotte." The sound that came out of my mouth was ridiculous, high-pitched and dripping with neediness.

"Hi, Melody," she responded, half closing the door.

I put my hand out to catch the door before it closed. "Wait, I'm sorry. Can we talk for a second?"

I don't know what I expected. She could have either slammed the front door shut on my hand, breaking several fingers, or invited me inside for a glass of wine and some charcuterie. Both options seemed entirely plausible.

Instead, she stepped outside and folded her arms. "Well, this should be good." She half smiled.

"Listen, first of all, I owe you an apology. More than one probably. But I really, really can't tell you how sorry I am about my outburst at the gala. It was wrong and it wasn't me at all."

"Go on," she said.

"I also wanted to tell you I'm sorry about what is happening with the Walkers. I'm sure it's affecting you. I know how close you've been." My own words made me cringe, wondering if I sounded completely disingenuous or just condescending.

"I didn't know anything, if that's what you're implying." Charlotte stood up taller, surveying my face with her piercing eyes. Talking to very attractive people has always made me nervous. As if the gorgeous are somehow superior in every way, not just physically, and my words must sound like jumbled rambling to their special ears. Standing in front of me, even in her homey tie-dyed sweatsuit and messy topknot, Charlotte was beautiful, in that effortless kind of way.

"No, I know that. I'm saying this as a friend." I immediately winced. Charlotte cackled. "I realize how that must sound."

"Well, thanks for your sympathy, Mel. The last month has been a hoot, let me tell you! If you're looking to step away from this guilt-free, well then, you're in luck. You're fine, I'm fine, everything is fine. I don't give two shits about you and our little rivalry. I have bigger fish to fry. Is that all?"

"It is," I replied, deflated. "Just know that, as ridiculous as this sounds, I am here for you. If you ever need. And I really am sorry."

"Noted," Charlotte said, and turned around to let herself back inside. "I'll text you after the girls have breakfast tomorrow so you can pick up Lucy."

And then she was gone.

I'm not sure how long I stood there on the Giordani doorstep, ten seconds, one minute, five minutes. Part of me was wishing she would come back outside to give me a big sitcom hug and invite me in. Pathetic. It was embarrassing to admit that I still cared, and in no small amount, what Charlotte thought of me. I needed her complete absolution, craved her seal of approval. Without those things, I felt lost.

The logic still escaped me. Here was a woman, an adult mother of two, who regularly wore crop tops and skintight leggings to school pickups and had an Instagram shrine to her favored child. A person whose overuse of exclamation points in formal writing bordered on puerile, who was bamboozled by her closest friends. And yet her acceptance of me seemed like the only thing that would make me feel at home in Miami Beach.

I'd made mistakes with her, and that guilt ate me up, too. There's nothing worse than that feeling you get when you know you've done something wrong. That you were at fault. But maybe it was time to let Charlotte go.

I went home, threw on my own cozy heather gray sweatsuit, and slipped into bed with my laptop.

March 18, 2019
From: Melody Howard
To: Sunset Academy Parents
Subject: For Your Consideration

Dear Sunset Academy Parents,
I've never taken the opportunity to properly introduce myself. My name is Melody Howard and, along with my husband and third-grade daughter, Lucy, I am a recent transplant to Miami from Wichita, Kansas.

Over the past six months, I have had the chance to meet many of you and become settled into the Sunset Academy community. First of all, thank you for welcoming me with open arms. I am so impressed with the incredible passion and hard work I have seen from the parents, faculty, and staff of this special school. We feel blessed to be here!

As you may know, I have decided to run for PTA president and hope to earn your vote in June. Gabriela Machado and Charlotte Giordani have done a great job leading the organization and have accomplished exciting initiatives for the school, but I believe that I can add an element of professionalism that will take Sunset Academy to the next level.

My professional background is as a nonprofit consultant, focusing on effective marketing campaigns, branding strategy, communications, and sustainable fundraising. I am well prepared to use these skills to help better many of Sunset Academy's practices. These include, but are not limited to:

- Adhering to all bylaws expressed by the Miami Dade Association of PTAs

- Full financial disclosure for all donations and expenditures

- Creation and management of Sunset Academy PTA social media pages, and other public relations and communications initiatives

- Event strategy and management overhaul for all existing and future Sunset Academy event platforms

I would love to meet more of you in person to share my vision for Sunset Academy. Please do not hesitate to contact me anytime—I will make myself available.

Regards,

Melody Howard

It felt liberating to finally take a stand and state my intentions. When Lucy came home the next morning, courtesy of a Giordani nanny drop-off in lieu of me picking her up, I knew I'd made the right decision. After all, running for PTA president wasn't about me. It was about *her*, and her future.

"How was the sleepover?" I asked, unpacking her overnight bag. It wasn't that I was expecting to find something that shouldn't have been there, another "stolen" item. But after the last incident, I'd resolved to keep a closer eye.

"So fun," Lucy said. "We did rainbow bracelets and blindfold makeup. It's where one friend covers her eyes and does the other friend's makeup." Lucy was watching me transfer her dirty pajamas and bathing suit to the laundry bin. "I literally had lipstick all over my forehead." She laughed. "Maddy's mom took the funniest pictures. Then we jumped in the pool and washed it all off."

My stomach tightened. "That's so great, sweetie." I was glad that Charlotte was treating her well, and that she was comfortable in the Giordani home. I was. But it definitely felt weird, too.

Then I noticed something on Lucy's wrist, an ornate-looking friendship bracelet. I braced myself. It absolutely could have been homemade, but not by a third-grader's hand. The knot was complicated, and the color combination looked professional, like something you'd buy in a fancy local boutique. My nerves couldn't handle another stealing situation.

"Where did you get that?" I asked, picking up her arm, perhaps too roughly.

Lucy snatched it away and immediately changed her tone. "Ax made it. Maddy's brother."

"Oh really?" I asked, not sure if this scenario was preferable to theft.

"Yeah, he was teaching Maddy and me how to make them. He's actually, like, an amazing artist." Lucy fiddled the bracelet between her fingers.

I shuddered, remembering the vacant-looking eyes staring down at me from the Giordani second floor that day at the pool. "Honey," I said, "it is a really beautiful bracelet. But don't you think that Axel should be playing with kids his own age?" It was a little creepy. I mean, he was in middle school and she was in third grade.

Her whole demeanor changed. I could tell that I had lost her on this one. "Mom! Why do you have to be so weird about things?" She stomped over to her bed and slumped onto the mattress. "He was just playing video games and Maddy begged him to teach us some bracelet knot he knows. He's actually so nice."

"I'm sure he is!" I answered, too brightly. "Just do me a favor, please? Try not to spend too much time with Ax when you're over there."

The last thing I needed was *another* Giordani to worry about.

DARCY

Oh, how the mighty had fallen. It was almost biblical. Those who looked down on us, from their golden thrones, with their gilded parking spots, perched inside their pink glass houses, were taken down by their own greed. For them, it had been preferable to live a sham, one that would inevitably be uncovered, than admit mediocrity. Who can stand to be simply average, even if it means averagely rich? So they built the walls so high around them and peered down their noses at the rest of us below, and it must have felt good while it lasted. But what about now?

And all those pawns who had guarded their king and queen, hanging on their every word, ready at a moment's notice to fan the royals' weary brows, to bow deeply in gratitude for all their good service, they had changed their tunes at an obscene speed. The formerly loyal wasted no time with whispers. *You know, I always suspected something fishy with those two.*

The truth is, not one of them cared if the Walkers' power was real or imaginary. The display of it was enough, and only a public reckoning could have turned them away. This was widespread "fake it till you make it" to a criminal degree. And while the Walker name will forever be synonymous with "fraud," by next month another bold-faced Miami name will take a tumble—whether because of sexual indiscretion, money laundering, bribery, spousal murder, or grand larceny—and the conversation will pivot to the new splashy headline.

Do I engage in schadenfreude? I am only human. I went to law school with a naive ideology and passion for justice. As a child, I imagined myself standing before a judge, teal power suit with matching glasses, shouting, "Your Honor, I object!!" I would defend the righteous and prosecute the real villains—the corporate overlords with their twisted smiles and sacks of money, the greedy politicians with bodies buried deep. I believed that the dregs of society would be punished for breaking their social contracts, and that this act alone could save us from ourselves. What child or young adult understands how far gone we already are? That our best efforts at equity are futile? So, on the occasion that some of society's worst parasites are thrust into the spotlight, like the scared cockroaches they are, it feels just. And it feels good.

Now I wonder what comes next. Does the Walker Auditorium become simply the Auditorium? And what about all the other buildings around town with the same disgraced banner? I personally cannot wait to rip down the sign for the Walker parking space (assuming that Charlotte hasn't already resold it). If Sunset Academy is somehow responsible for repaying some of the donations it received with (allegedly) stolen money, the school will be in trouble. They simply do not have the reserves to cover a reparation. By the time a punishment is declared, the Walker scandal fallout will have touched not only the guilty and the investors, but potentially every nonprofit in town. If that doesn't constitute true evil, then I don't know what does.

What about the pretty wife? The adorned, unsmiling Mrs. Walker hasn't been arrested (yet), so we can only assume her role (or lack thereof) in her husband's vices. She certainly benefited from them, with the endless supply of couture gowns, luxury handbags, expensive shoes, lavish vacation homes, and local stardom. She wielded her power with absolute authority, an entitlement that suggested it was earned. But we, the little people, never saw what was beneath the silken veil. She gave us one note: no more, no less. It was, therefore, possible that

Patricia was too empty inside to even carry out such a deception and was living what she believed was her best life.

When Jackson was in first grade with Maddox Walker, I decided to sponsor a Sunset Academy fundraiser on behalf of my private practice: the Spring Fling, I believe it was. For $1,000, Resnick Family Law was printed on all the school banners for the event, and my logo was prominent on the Spring Fling flyer. I didn't expect to drum up any business from the sponsorship. It was just a way to support the school. Of course, Walker Equities was the title sponsor, and their logo took precedence over mine on all sponsorship collateral. The outcome of this was that Donald Walker learned who I was, and what I did, and he took it upon himself to reach out to me shortly after the event. Apparently, he had forgotten me from the awful Halloween incident the year before. *It was nice to meet you at the Spring Fling. I am going to hold on to your information—it's always great to have a good family lawyer on hand.*

Are Donald and Patricia on the way out? I wondered. There's only one reason anyone would ever want to hang on to my card, and that is because there is trouble in paradise. "Family attorney" is really just a euphemism for "divorce lawyer." I never responded to the email, and that was the last time Donald Walker reached out to me.

CHARLOTTE

People are reacting to me in one of two ways right now, and I really can't stand either of them.

There's the accusatory, the *what did she know* assholes, or the pitying, the *what is she going to do now* people.

And then there's one special snowflake who somehow has managed to pull off both. Melody Howard strikes again. I'd like to slap both of her faces, the one that is *so sorry* I'm going through a *hard time,* and the one that sent a fucking PTA presidential campaign email in the middle of said hardship.

My mother always told me, when someone tells you who they are, listen! With some people it's obvious, and then others, like Patricia Walker, wear their costumes so tightly around them that it's hard to see what's real and what's fake. Patricia could keep up appearances with the best of them. Sit over coffee and muse about society gossip—*Did you hear that Barbara Bettencourt is stepping down from the science museum board due to "personal reasons"?*—and all that tedious child talk—*Maddox just can't seem to focus during math. It's not challenging enough for him.* But there was nothing else there. To be fair, that's how they all are. The super privileged class, Miami's "ladies who lunch." Do I consider myself to be one of them? Not *really.* James does well. I mean, I don't have to work, but I'm not on speed dial with the GM at Hermès. God, speed dial is dated, right? I'm not on a first-name basis with the managers at designer boutiques like those other ladies.

Those are your basic rich bitches on steroids, and you can spot them by their uniform: gold Rolex Daytona, Birkin, three-carat studs in each ear, five LOVE bracelets stacked one on top of another. They'll top the list at every charity luncheon's fashion contest, but if you crack them open and look inside, you'll find dust. Only dust. Like cracking open a Fabergé egg and, instead of finding a golden yolk, discovering that the soul of that glossy, enameled masterpiece is just plain concrete.

Was any of it real with Patricia? It's hard to say. How much of anything is real? Aren't we all striving to show our preferred face at all times? The wife who hides purchases from her husband by using extravagant permutations of credit card payments, the husband who browses the internet on "private" mode. We all keep a little something to ourselves.

There was a time, not so long ago, when things were truly private. Now with social media, and cookies, and GPS, and cell phones, it's like we have to share with the world every time we fart. *Today was silent, but indeed deadly.*

So Patricia turned out to be fake, but what does that say about the rest of us? Ugh, I know, I'm getting so existential about it. Don't think for one second that I am comparing myself to a couple that bilked their friends, investors, and community out of millions, because I am not. I'm just saying, we can all stand to look in the mirror. A lot of us are responsible for creating these perfect life narratives, and then we all spin and spin, and cover our faults, cover all the grays it causes, conceal our pasts, conceal the dark circles under our eyes because this shit is exhausting.

Who among us is real? Name one person.

Don't confuse my acceptance for forgiveness; I hope Patricia spends the rest of her days in clearance Old Navy chinos, asking people if they'd *like fries with that*. I'm just saying that she wasn't the only one around here who was playing make-believe. She was just the worst of them, it turns out.

And I'm not giving Don a pass, hell no! I mean, talk about little dick energy. The red Ferrari should have been a dead giveaway. But Don wore his new money like a medal of honor. *Look how far I've come, now I'm giving back to the little folk*. That whole vibe. Everyone is shocked and also not at all surprised when those guys go down. Oh, it *was* too good to be true? Ya don't say. Have to give James credit for this one. He didn't want to call it out, but he smelled something off with the Walkers from the start. I almost feel bad for Don. He wanted to be rich so badly, needed it to feel like a man.

Patricia, on the other hand, tried to appropriate the air of old money. Like she'd watched too many Grace Kelly movies and had to always appear like a golden age of Hollywood starlet. As if the symbols of generational wealth were fine bespoke tailoring and estate jewelry. Have you ever seen how actual billionaires dress? Like Warren Buffett and those guys? They look like destitutes, more often than not, and you never see their wives dripping in diamonds and Hermès. *Rich screams, wealth whispers.*

Now that I think about it, there was something weird about Villa Rosé. (Well, more than one weird thing, they built a goddamn pink glass house.) There were no old photos. Not one single displayed memory from a time before kids. The whole Walker existence began with prosperity, according to their bookshelves and walls. No grandparents, childhood Christmases, or family vacations. No evidence of humbler times.

I first met Patricia years ago at mommy and me—I know, how original. There was this Miami Music Mamba program that was *the* quintessential baby class when Maddy and Maddox were little. Every Wednesday, a dozen smoking-hot Magic City mamas would gyrate to "Wheels on the Bus," our babies shaking noisemakers and shimmying their diapered booties along with the beat.

Patricia was that terrified new mother carrying around her delicate prince like he was an egg, creating a bubble between Maddox and the outside world and guarding that space with the sheer force of her own anxiety. When Ms. Ashley would begin the welcome song and all the little crawlers would scoot, scoot, scoot as we'd sing their names, elegant Patricia would slide on her hands and knees over her precious son, shielding him from every runny nose, crocodile-snapping, crab-pinching baby in their path.

It was a sight. Patricia would have caught her baby's poo in her bare hands if it spared his tushy from touching a toilet seat. I already had five-year-old Axel at home so you know, it wasn't my first rodeo. Maddy was the baby who would crawl over and sit inside the box of instruments to make sure she had the best one. Even then, she was the boss. *No baby is taking my maraca and putting it in his mouth!* Meanwhile, I'd busy myself with the other moms, sharing baby tips and gossip and whatnot.

So this goes on for a couple of months: mommy social hour for me, and nervous Patricia practicing anxiety-reducing breathing techniques. Then, one day, something happened. Patricia had an uncharacteristic lapse in attention as some earth-shattering text comes in. Maybe her mom had a bad fall, or her husband found her secret credit card bill for the month, who knows. So Patricia is glued to her phone, and Maddox must preternaturally sense his momentary freedom, because off he goes! Wiggle, wiggle, wiggling down to the rattan little instrument box, where my Madeline is sucking on a pair of cymbals with furious attention like it was made out of rainbow lollipop.

It was as if the room froze around little Maddox and me: Patricia solving the world's problems on her phone, Madeline coaxing some hidden flavor out of a well-worn instrument, and all the other moms and babies bobbing around, oblivious to the impending doom. I swear, my nose started itching in that moment, a mother's intuition. But before I could even answer the call, it happened. Maddox reached into the instrument box, grabbed a fistful of Madeline's scant hair, pulled her down to him, and bit hard into her apple cheek. The sound that came out of my baby's mouth! Half human, half animal, that scream could have shattered my iPhone screen into a million pieces.

Patricia snapped out of her daze and watched in horror as I plucked her son off my frantic child, his fingers still clutching the tiny white wisps of Maddy's hair. My baby's cheek was streaked with frothy saliva, teeth marks dotted her face in black and blue, and she gasped for air between staccato shrieks. The other moms rushed in to soothe Madeline, all the while stealing disapproving looks at the biter's mother. In mom world, the parent is always guilty of the child's crime. Finally, Patricia came to life and made a show of scolding Maddox: finger in the face, shout whispering *no, no, no . . . gentle hands! Mouths are for smiling. We do not bite our friends!* Now Maddox was wailing, too, and the class had devolved into a cacophony of blood-curdling screams. Even the babies who had no part of the incident were losing it.

"I am so sorry," Patricia mouthed to me, her face a wreck.

"It's fine," I assured her. "Babies do this, especially boys. You should meet my son sometime. If I had a nickel for every kid he bit or scratched, I'd take a private plane to Tahiti."

And that's how it started. The next week, she smiled. The week after that, she brought me a key lime pie from Joe's. Then we exchanged numbers, then playdates. The rest is history.

Interview Transcript with Donald Walker

For profile in *Magic City* magazine, summer issue 2019
By Andres Castano
March 19, 2019, Session 2

INTERVIEWER: Thank you for taking my call, Donald. I'm not here to judge. I just want to get the story straight. First of all, how are you doing?

DONALD: How am I doing? How about, What day is it? I know it's March something. I stopped tracking as soon as the cell door closed, and my world shrank down to four cement walls with a toilet attached to one and a steel door on another. Stolen from my home on bullshit charges and stuck in a room with two sets of bunk beds and three dudes with varying degrees of BO and more tattoos than I can count. They couldn't believe their good luck when I was shoved in with them. Clean-cut guy like me, an easy taunt. *What you in here for? Tax evasion?* And this is just the holding cell. This is where you sit until a judge is ready to see you. The next step, for the bad ones, now that's when the nightmare starts. If these stockade thugs are the guys who get to go home, can you imagine the monsters in actual prison?

INTERVIEWER: Do you think that you are going to prison?

DONALD: Ha! That's where these people want to send me. Listen, I know how it looks and I can explain everything. I really can. But right now, my lawyers need me to keep mum. There are ears everywhere and some very powerful people want to see me taken down. Why? Because there's a goddamn culture war against the rich. God forbid you went to a good school, worked hard, and made something of yourself. People can't stand it. They cannot stand it. And that is what is wrong with our country today, my friend. Some populist senator takes up capital gains as her great evil, and all of a sudden, fund managers are rebranded as domestic terrorists. The lefties get on board and what do they do? Round us up and ship us off, but they haven't built the forced labor camps yet, so for now it's prison. Once we are all hidden away, unroll all the new shining Marxist platforms and come together to salute the Communist States of America.

The truth will come out though, man, just wait. And everyone will get the money back. Right now, it's in the government's hands, everything is frozen. How's that for hypocrisy? They accuse me of stealing investor money, and then they lock all the assets up so my clients can't even get out. They are the criminals!

INTERVIEWER: I'm sure it's all a misunderstanding, as you say. I've read that you are back home now, awaiting trial?

DONALD: That's right. First, the prosecutors tried to label me a flight or security risk, say I shouldn't be eligible for bail. Those bastards would love to see me rot, guilty until proven innocent. This is iron curtain shit. Well, they better get used to losing, because the judge threw that out, set my bail at ten million dollars, and Patricia put up the Aspen home and the Hamptons beach house—they're in her name—as collateral. Let's just say she's not happy, but she knows this whole thing is bullshit. So the court throws this janky ankle bracelet on my leg, and I'm to be monitored at home until trial.

Home sweet home, right? Except the fake news is grifting outside my property at all hours, trying to catch a glimpse of my fall from grace. These people love to see the mighty crumble, must make them feel better about their own shitty lives. *Rich people, they're just like us.*

These reporters are *enjoying* this. That's why I'm talking only to you. I know you see through all that Nancy Pelosi *finance is evil* bullshit.

INTERVIEWER: It is my job to get to the heart of the story. How are Patricia and the boys?

DONALD: Off the record, the boys aren't here. That would be child abuse, man. Patricia sent them to her parents' place in Kentucky. Kids must think they're out there camping. It's traumatizing enough that Maddox and Monrow had to see me hauled off in the middle of the night, like some goombah crime boss. That part stings, when I think about the look on my sons' faces when I got dragged out of our home in handcuffs. Confused, scared, trying not to cry. They were so fucking brave. Tell me, what kind of disgusting sadist wants to put innocent kids through something like that? These FBI jerkoffs get off on it. They were probably smiling the whole time, satisfied with themselves while my boys watched their father reduced to a common bad guy.

No, my kids couldn't be here, living in the shadow of news vans and gawkers, their dad neutered, but instead of a cone on my neck there's a GPS on my ankle. Patricia is here, but she's not happy. Good thing this is a big house. I get it. Put yourself in her shoes: when all this went down, she'd been preparing for the back end of charity season in Miami, the marathon of professional makeup, champagne toasts, and air-kisses. I don't know how she does it. Better her than me, man. That shit is exhausting, I'd rather pull a twelve-hour day at the office. Of course, she loves it. Some women are built for that life. But make no mistake, it is a job. And Patricia has to be out there representing our family brand. And then, *boom,* our world explodes right in the middle of all this shit, and what is Patricia supposed to do? It's not fair.

Our so-called friends are even more vicious than the media. The friends who have reached out—and the silence is deafening for those who haven't—are more like pathetic hyenas, sniffing around our rotten carcasses, than concerned friends. You're the only one I'm talking to. The only one.

Interview Transcript with Patricia Walker

For profile in *Magic City* magazine, summer issue 2019
By Andres Castano
March 20, 2019, Session 5

INTERVIEWER: Patricia, how are you? More than anything, I just wanted to call and check in.

PATRICIA: Oh, thank you, Andres. Honestly, I'm not well. It's terrible. I've just been shut away at home, hiding from society, and can't bring myself to talk to anyone. We are getting *death threats.* It's been . . . just so hard. Unbearable.

I'm sorry. I just need a couple seconds.

INTERVIEWER: Take all the time you need. I'm here to listen.

PATRICIA: Okay. Sorry about that. This isn't me. I'm not some whiny, weak person, some sensitive snowflake. But no one understands me right now. Everyone just assumes this or that, always the worst. My husband and I are criminal masterminds, they say. We preyed on our friends and all our beloved charities. I was somehow complicit; I knew about it all along. It's not true, Andres! One day, I woke up to FBI agents and guns and flashlights. My boys were woken up and watched as their home was turned upside down, their father put in handcuffs. I was just as shocked as they were! It was traumatizing. I still haven't processed it all.

They came before dawn, while the whole family was fast asleep, these *law enforcement officers.* And they didn't knock. They just burst their way in and started shouting. So I was jolted awake and started poking Don. *Is someone breaking in?* To wake up like that, with that fear. It's something I'll never ever forget. Imagine what that felt like for my boys. "Get the gun," I told my husband. I literally thought that we were going to have to defend our lives.

But before he could reach under the bed for it, one of the officers forced open the master bedroom door and pointed a gun right at us. One wrong move, and he could have shot me! I'm sorry, but remembering this is very upsetting.

INTERVIEWER: I cannot imagine how terrifying that must have been.

PATRICIA: I mean, I thought we were going to *die*. But no, they weren't there to kill us. They were there to *arrest* my husband, accusing him of accumulating our wealth *illegally*. Stealing it from investors. Can you imagine? All we've built. All the blood, sweat, and tears. I've dedicated my life to uplifting this community and, in one second, that image is shattered with these ludicrous allegations? I'd almost rather be dead.

Don't worry, that isn't a threat. I'm just saying. Sometimes living can feel worse.

Anyway, when that awful day was over, I really couldn't see or speak to anyone. I had to retreat. Go within. I called my parents, that's how desperate I was, and told them that I was having marital difficulties, which isn't exactly a lie. Said that I needed them to take the boys for a while. They came. Listen, I have my issues with them but that's a conversation for another day. There's quite enough to unpack here already without opening that Pandora's box.

INTERVIEWER: The boys are with your parents? They are well?

PATRICIA: Yes, yes. I sent my parents round-trip tickets. The boys and I met them at the airport, and then they all turned back around and went to Lexington. No questions asked. I told Maddox and Monrow not to mention the FBI, the raid, et cetera. Luckily, my parents don't know how to Google. I doubt they even own a computer.

Saying goodbye was the worst part of the whole thing, Andres. It was like . . . giving birth in reverse. They looked like such little men, fighting back their tears, trying to be brave for me. I must have looked so scary, mascara all the way down my cheeks. Not the Mom they're used to seeing. But it was a relief, too. I really think I needed the space to figure this whole thing out, without distraction. I've been meditating every day, waiting for the universe to give me a sign.

INTERVIEWER: Perhaps we could meet for coffee.

PATRICIA: Yes, I'd like to, but you know there are reporters camped outside my house? All day? Such leeches. I hope you don't take offense to that. I know you're one of the good ones. Anyway, that's why I'm basically in hiding. Wife of the *disgraced businessman*. I feel their eyes burning into me all day, watching like Peeping Toms from the street. I live in a goddamn glass house! They can just look right in.

I wish I could sneak out back and jump on the boat to get out of here. That would deny them the satisfaction of chasing my car down the driveway. The reporters can't access the other side of the house, the side on the water. But, nope! The boat has been *seized*. Who knows what stolen money he used to buy it, according to the feds, and Don *is* a flight risk, after all. Such garbage.

I just don't know, Andres. I have no idea what comes next.

Walker ran massive Ponzi scheme alongside legitimate business, authorities say

March 20, 2019

Disgraced South Florida businessman and philanthropist Donald Walker swindled his investors out of more than $700 million, federal agents and sources close to the investigation say. The alleged fraud, which was originally thought to comprise various illegal and deceitful business practices, was in reality a scheme where new investors' money was used to pay back earlier investors.

"I'm losing everything," Lucca Campos, investor and longtime trainer for Walker, said. "I trusted this man with every cent I've ever saved. He was supposed to be the smartest guy in the room. He made it seem like I was lucky to be 'in.'"

Walker's alleged victims include a diverse group of corporate pensions and endowments, family offices, and also private investors.

"This is one of the worst financial crimes we have ever seen. Not only in scale, but for the complete lack of empathy that Mr. Walker shows for the people and institutions he stole from," said Michael Channing, Miami-Dade County prosecutor.

Aside from investors, many South Florida charities that depended heavily on donations from the Walker Family Foundation are now at risk, following allegations that those contributions were made with ill-gotten gains.

It is unclear what, if any, reparations will be made to the alleged victims, and where those funds will come from.

The legitimate portion of Walker Equities, LLC, was a holding company that owned, among other assets, a construction company, a steel parts manufacturing business, and a cold-pressed juice brand. According to federal agents, the holding companies reported no profit in 2018.

This is an ongoing story.

DARCY

A Ponzi scheme, really? That's straight out of *White Collar Crime for Dummies*. Donald Walker didn't even have the originality to come up with a complicated financial model with which to steal from people. Come on, man! Work for that stolen money! But nope, he just used money from new investors to pay off old investors, and then pocketed the rest. Pathetic.

When things like this happen, which they so often do in Miami, you almost have a pang of amusement for some of the *victims*. Ultrarich people who were lured, despite market conditions and education, into thinking they could reap outsize returns. But this particular bad actor, Donald Walker, he preyed on the rich and working class alike.

Take, for example, his constant companion, Lucca the personal trainer. This poor guy spent five days a week loading barbells for Don, and was expected to be at holidays, birthdays, you name it. Weirdly fifth-wheeling with Don, Patricia, and the Walker boys. He always looked a little uncomfortable and out of place. I mean, why would this guy, a single young man in his late twenties, early thirties max, want to shadow this family all the time he wasn't on the clock?

Apparently, Lucca gave every cent back to Don. Every cent he earned from Don and his other clients went back to Don, to the *fund*. This guy thought he was going to turn his little nest egg into a full-grown chicken. And why would he think otherwise? This rich, larger-than-life benefactor was taking him in. Probably said he was doing it as a *favor*. Now Lucca has nothing to show for it.

I think there's another layer to it, too. The reason Donald Walker never publicly denied an affair with Charlotte Giordani. I don't have proof, but I have a strong suspicion that Lucca was *more* than just Don's personal trainer/friend/small investor. If you know what I mean.

Don was always whispering in his ear at parties, sidling up next to him in a way more intimate than he did even with his wife. With Patricia it was show, like the cameras were always on. With Lucca it felt authentic. At the Halloween party this past year, for example, the Walkers and Lucca showed up in coordinated eighties workout outfits. Like Olivia Newton-John with two backup dancers.

Except Patricia was mostly on her own: taking selfies in front of the smoke machines, talking to Charlotte (probably about how fancy and fabulous she was). Meanwhile, Don and Lucca were slapping backs and carrying on like frat boys. I remember watching them—Lucca telling some anecdote, waving his hands in front of his chiseled abs, and Don bent over in hysterics—and thinking, I never see that natural closeness with Don and his wife.

Maybe it was love, maybe a deep connection, but there was definitely something there. And something that was lacking in the marriage.

In hindsight, maybe they couldn't have been *that* close. Not the way Don completely fucked Lucca in the end. And I don't mean "fucked" in the fun way. Of all the victims, Lucca was one of the few who had nothing to fall back on. No diversified portfolio, no trust fund. Everything he ever earned was invested with Walker Equities, and now it's all gone.

Real peach, that Donald Walker.

But yeah, I don't feel all that bad for the majority of his victims. All those smug faces at Sunset Academy drop-off, avoiding eye contact to mask their shame. If they weren't so spineless, I'd worry about an assassination attempt on Don or Patricia. So no, I don't feel bad for most of them. Lucca, though. I feel terrible for that one.

Elliot thinks they're all idiots. Every last one of them. The Walkers, the investors, the charity development directors who groveled on their hands and knees for Walker donations. "Got what they deserved," he said.

"Carol was certainly right about them," I told him. "As was I, I might add."

"Twenty points for you, darling," Elliot said, referencing our ongoing game of who could predict the news. "Should we wager on Don's sentencing? I'll let you go first."

MELODY

Things must have been dire, because during the first week of April, Charlotte called me.

The conversation was to the effect of *Listen, I hate to do this.* And that was one of the truest things that has ever been said, because I'm sure she'd rather have taken a bath in hydrochloric acid than ask me for help. *I hate to do this, but the PTA is in the middle of a financial shitstorm, and we don't have a treasurer. I'm good at raising the money, but this is over my head.*

Sunset Academy's PTA was conducting an internal audit to discover if all those Walker Family Foundation contributions needed to be recouped and returned to Donald Walker's bilked investors. They were analyzing three years of donations that totaled $485,000. The funds had been spent on a variety of capital improvement projects and educational materials at the school, including installing a new STEM lab, cafeteria improvements, academic software, the list goes on. Great for the school, but only if the donations had been made legally.

I got right to work, and the books were *interesting,* if not nonexistent. In all my years consulting for nonprofits, I'd never seen anything like them. It was shocking that the Sunset Academy PTA qualified for its 501(c)(3) status every year, and also surprising they had the good sense to call for an audit. At least someone on the PTA board had the presence of mind to do the research before the feds came knocking.

Gabriela Machado, it turns out, was more capable than I had thought, and she was not keen on the end of her PTA president tenure being mired in scandal.

"Gabriela *suggested* I call you," Charlotte had said, though I am positive that there was no choice given in the matter. "Bottom line, you have experience in this, I don't. I'll give you everything I have. Every email, invoice, tax donation letter. Heck, I'll give you my Social Security number if it helps protect the school."

I told her that I'm no magician, but that I'd do my best. Financial scandals weren't in my wheelhouse, but I could hire a CPA and sort through the documents.

Greg was hopeful. "This might be a blessing," he said after work that day. "You'll prove your worth. Show the Sunset parents what you can do."

We sat around the kitchen table over baked chicken with lemony potatoes, Lucy's favorite. Our daughter sat entranced with her iPad, watching jerky TikTok dance videos.

"Lucy, no iPad at the table," I reminded her, like I did every night. She put it down with a sigh. "You're right, honey," I told Greg. "I should look at this as an opportunity. But I'm not going to lie, the challenge scares me."

"Nothing you can't figure out," my ever-reassuring husband responded.

A thought came into my head. "Lucy, have you heard anything about this Walker business? Has Maddy mentioned it?" I immediately regretted asking it, trying to get gossip out of my young daughter. Greg gave me a *are you seriously doing this* look. "Because, I mean," I continued, "you never know what the truth is. And we shouldn't judge."

"I know that, Mom," Lucy said, mouth full of thigh meat. "I heard Maddox's dad is in jail. And I heard that Maddy's mom is very *stressed*."

Greg shook his head at me. "Luce, this is adult stuff," he said. "And it will all work out, don't worry."

"I'm not worried." Lucy finished her last bite and reached for her iPad. "I mean, I feel bad for Maddox. That's really sad."

"It is!" I said, a little too emphatically. "It's very sad, and we hope that their family is able to heal and move on from whatever this is."

How do you talk to kids about these things? It had to be mentioned, right?

Greg was clearly uncomfortable about having the conversation with Lucy. "Hey, Luce." He went for a diversion. "*Disney on Ice* is coming to town. I was thinking about getting dad and daughter tickets for us. That is, as long as your mother is okay with it."

Lucy groaned. "No offense, Dad. But I think I'm getting a little old for *Disney on Ice*." She gave him a worried look.

Greg shook his head like it was fine, but I know him. He was bruised. "Yeah, no sweat." He recovered himself. "Maybe a dinner out, the two of us?"

I couldn't suppress the smile. I married a good man. A great father.

Lucy brightened. "Let's do sushi!"

CHARLOTTE

Ax got expelled. Expelled!

Or, as the school put it, *suspended pending a disciplinary hearing.* Which sounds suspiciously like the same thing to me.

You know how if you get so overwhelmed, when thing after thing goes wrong, like your dog dies, and your hair color comes out wrong, and then the grocery bag breaks and all your raw meat and fruits and milk splatter onto the ground and mix together into some grotesque kind of punch, and Lord knows the Botox doesn't let you frown anymore? So you just laugh. Like a crazy bag lady on Ocean Drive who thinks she's Jesus. Just laughing out loud to no one?

That's how bad it got.

Forget the fucking Sunset Academy PTA nightmare. But seriously, what kind of asshole knowingly steals hundreds of millions of dollars and then acts like he's the Bill & Melinda Gates Foundation, and gives a ton of it away to all these *worthy* causes? Everyone gets caught, even wannabe Robin Hood.

Anyway, that's Melody Howard's problem now. She is a supposed expert in nonprofit crises, and oh isn't that *convenient.* Well, let her have it. If she can save us, then Godspeed.

I can't waste my energy on that right now, not when my home life is the *Titanic.* We're sinking, and I'm trying to play "Nearer, My God, to Thee" as the ship goes down.

Axel got expelled. Kicked out of school and asked to not return.

That incompetent Miami Beach Middle principal said that they *feared* my boy was "beyond their abilities to help" and was a "potential danger to himself and others."

He had been making some of those doodles of his, and a classmate stole his notebook and passed it around to the other nasty kids in the cafeteria. This prompted a scene straight out of the Bully 101 handbook, and all these thirteen-year-old boys and girls started pointing and jeering, calling him "Ax murderer." Little shits.

Well, Axel had had enough, who wouldn't have, and he ripped his notebook out of the last kid's hands who had it, and this happened to be a girl. Don't give me the *never hit a girl* BS because we are always talking about equality, and you can't have it both ways. Ax took the notebook with more force than he meant, and the girl stumbled and fell backward on her head.

I'm not proud of that! He shouldn't have reacted that way. But can I understand his frustration? And shame? And hurt? Of course I do. He acted poorly, and I wish he didn't do it. I'm disappointed, but also, it was an accident! And can you blame him after he was tortured by a full room of his peers leading up to that moment? This was the ultimate eighth-grade nightmare.

You can guess what happened next. Ax had an altercation with a girl who was pretty and popular and you know, he is not. So a throng of hormone-pumping jocks had to jump on top of him and beat the living daylights out of him. Until school staff were able to pull them off.

Jesus, he had to get ten stitches in his face, and it's still black and blue. He couldn't even open his left eye. I barely ate while he was recovering, even Maddy was shaken to tears. It's her brother; she loves him.

Ax mostly stayed in his room and didn't discuss it at all.

We were mad! His father and I don't condone fighting at school. The artwork, that's another story. It has become increasingly depressed looking, and it does worry me. We have kept up with therapy, which seems to be going well. Ax actually talks to the therapist—hallelujah!

She can't tell me much—client-patient blah, blah, blah—but she hasn't said that he's a dangerous person, and she hasn't called the police. So we have that!

I'll never forget the phone call. So many phone calls from school with this kid. But this one was the worst. This one tied my intestines into a knot that still hasn't released. When I hung up, I dreaded taking one step forward, closer to the school and into the space where my boy was beaten and bloodied and rejected and cast out. I wished I could press rewind, to walk him to nursery school, play hide-and-seek, bounce him in my arms. What I wouldn't give for the days when a nighttime "accident" was the hardest problem.

I'm sure he expected me to scream. It might have even scared him when I didn't. I just didn't have it in me. It was weird, almost out of body. And in the moment, I was more terrified than mad. I wanted to hold him, heal him, put a Band-Aid on the whole thing. Run away with him! Maybe we could have started over somewhere else, and I would have spent more time trying to understand Ax. I fucking failed him. I realized that, finally.

When I saw his face . . . no mother should have to see that. It was already swollen, bleeding, a compress against the gash on his forehead. His good eye was glassy and wouldn't meet mine, his filthy band shirt was splattered with red. He looked broken. Like a baby bird that fell from the nest.

And to add insult, there's the principal telling him that he's no longer welcome at Beach Middle.

Get out of here, weirdo! You're too unique for our homogenous school.

I wish I would have recognized his talents earlier, how his uniqueness could have been fostered rather than feared. But now here we are, and I must spend the rest of what time we have together making up for that. Yeah, he's different and that has always unsettled me. He gets sullen; he doesn't love company, but he can also be sweet. He loves animals; he loves younger children. But he hates children's parties; he hates getting dressed up. Madeline makes it *easy*.

You know the reason parents are terrified of their kids being different? It's because we are worried that the things we don't understand will lead to all the stupid mistakes we made along the way. All those horrible decisions that could have ended up in any number of unthinkable ways. That's what parents see when our kids show *signs*. We remember how our parents had no clue that we were sucking on pacifiers, not to be cute, but because we were blowing the fuck up in an ecstasy-fueled rager. We laughed at how out of touch our elders were. Now we are petrified of becoming those elders.

But I'm going to do better. I *need* to do better. The world isn't going to do Ax any favors, and I'm going to be an ally.

I keep digging deep into my memory, trying to pinpoint exactly when Ax took a turn. It's so funny, as parents we think we will remember every moment exactly as it happens. Every milestone is so damned important and special. But unless you make a photo book of every second, you just forget. The fog of it is so thick.

There was nothing blatantly abnormal, per se. He was fussy. Okay, babies are fussy. He has always been quiet and tended more toward parallel play as a toddler but again, all the books say that is totally normal. But he also laughed until applesauce came out of his nose when I made funny faces at snack time and shook his booty to "Hot Dog!" every time the *Mickey Mouse Clubhouse* came on.

By elementary school, it was clear that Ax was *different*. He didn't fit into a neat little box, and I'll admit that I hated that. I mean, the kid could have been a catalog model for Janie & Jack. He was gorgeous! But he would have none of that, not interested. Not obsessed with making friends like I always was, and like Maddy still is. Yes, I didn't *understand* him, but he wasn't sad, depressed, destructive. He wasn't throwing off real red flags like hurting kittens or anything like that.

So he was a bit of an introvert and charted his own course. But if I had to choose one moment when it started to get ugly, when a pain started to blossom, or took root and really grew, it would be the sixth-grade holiday show. Miami Beach Middle was already a huge transition for Ax. The kids were older, rougher, meaner, and behind my son's complacent eyes there lies a very sensitive boy. Even moving to middle school with a huge group of familiar faces from Sunset Academy, Ax retreated further and further. After-school conversations turned from one sentence to more of a disinterested grunt.

Then the holiday show came around. It's equal parts endearing and delusional that Beach Middle thinks they can re-create the spirit and sweetness of an elementary school show with prepubescents. But damned if I wasn't excited for it! How naive I was. Getting onstage was never Ax's thing. Lord knows how he came from my womb.

From what I gathered, between the after-school grunts, the sixth-graders were all practicing some nonreligious winter songs, and some brave souls were doing some kind of dance. Most kids were just in the giant chorus, and we were asked to send them to the show in any old holiday costume. Now, if you know me, costumes are always a custom situation. I have my preferred Etsy vendors for Halloween and various theme party and performance occasions, so I was well prepared to make sure Ax had the most professional look on that stage.

I suggested Rudolph the Red-Nosed Reindeer. *No.* Olaf from *Frozen. Hell no.* And finally scored a noncommittal shrug for Will Ferrell's Buddy the elf. So I put in the order for a hunter green pointy elf hat with matching jacket and bright yellow pants (the giant gold belt buckle was my favorite). Honestly, he looked straight out of the movie. It was perfect.

Ax definitely had butterflies the morning of the show. I could tell by the way he stabbed at his chocolate chip pancakes without taking more than a few bites. At eleven years old and growing like the very hungry caterpillar, he could usually take down the whole batch without coming up for air. I thought Axel looked absolutely darling in his costume, though he slumped over all the way to the auditorium as if someone were sitting on his shoulders. But oh my god, how his blond curls poked out of that little green hat.

When we arrived at the backstage entrance for drop-off, my stomach sank. All the other sixth-grade performers were dressed like holiday versions of sluts and thugs. It was like how adults dress for Halloween: sexy Ms. Claus for the girls, ratty white T-shirts with three felt black dots over basketball shorts (the cheapest excuses for snowmen I'd ever seen) for the boys. They stifled laughter as Axel shuffled past them to check in, tearing the green hat off his head.

In the auditorium I found James and Maddy saving me a left-hand side seat in the sixth row—so my husband finally shows up to something and can't be bothered to score the primo spots, but that's another story. The show starts and I'm telling you, I could hear my heartbeat over the merry little opening jingle. But how bad could it be, right? Without the hat, the costume wasn't so ostentatious, and it's not like the kids would torment my son in front of all their parents, right? You'd think that anyway, but middle schoolers are vicious as hell.

The curtain rose and Ax was in the back row of the chorus, apparently fascinated by whatever was on his feet at the moment. The sluts and thugs broke out into a screechy, voice-cracking rendition of "Let it Snow," Ax mouthed along a half beat behind, and all the parents tried to smile and look like the whole thing wasn't actual torture.

By the third song, I was starting to relax. The kids were all equally bad, and Ax didn't even stand out in his awkwardness. But then after an almost bearable sign language performance of "Winter Wonderland," the chorus changed formation and Ax's row moved to the front. Well, straight out of a textbook guide on how to be a bully, some shit-eating snowman thug stuck his leg out and tripped my Axel as he was making his way to the front row. My poor kid ate it and landed square on his face! I gasped from my seat and grabbed Maddy's arm, who already had tears in her eyes. James looked angry, but maybe that was just his face.

The stage roared into unrestrained laughter. Those punks might as well have been pointing in unison. It was so sinister. Even some of the parents were smirking—I worry for their souls. My every instinct compelled me to leap onto the stage and scoop up my baby in my arms, to carry him off like an infant. Tears were stinging my eyes. But I was frozen in place for what felt like minutes. Of course it was only seconds, and some administrator rushed the stage as Ax was picking himself up and sprinting behind the curtains.

An announcement was made. "Students, control yourselves! This is a holiday show for your families. We will conduct ourselves with dignity!"

We didn't stay for the rest. I rushed to meet Ax backstage, where I found him red faced and blotchy. All because I had to buy him that dumb elf costume.

I felt immediately guilty, sure that I had caused the whole thing. Not that he wanted to talk about it at all. Ax was sullen on the car ride home, and that was the first day we experienced the *straight to his room once home* phenomenon we've come to know so well. He started asking to skip school every morning: stomachaches, phantom colds. I wasn't buying it. I offered to buy him new clothes, things that were more hip. Help him fit in a little more with those awful kids. Now I ask myself, why would I want him to be accepted by a bunch of a-holes? I guess it just seemed better than his being rejected. In hindsight, maybe I was projecting *my* biggest fear onto him. Of not fitting in. When he isn't made of the same stuff as me, and perhaps never gave a crap about being accepted in the first place. Maybe I was hurting him instead of helping him, all along.

Anyway, he was having none of it. A week after the holiday show, Ax came downstairs with home-dyed blue hair and a new badass attitude to overshadow his shy demeanor. He returned to school after winter break as a different kid.

Interview Transcript with Lucca Campos

For profile in *Magic City* magazine, summer issue 2019
By Andres Castano
April 20, 2019

INTERVIEWER: Thank you, Lucca, for agreeing to sit with me today. I can't imagine what you have been through. As I mentioned on the phone, *Magic City* had been planning an extensive profile piece on the Walkers for our summer issue. Now we find ourselves at print deadline and, as you can imagine, we cannot publish the story we were planning. We are pivoting the feature into an exposé on the *real* Walkers.

If you don't mind, I'd like to keep everything on record, which is why I record all of my interviews. Is that okay with you?

LUCCA: Yes, sure.

INTERVIEWER: Great, thank you. Let's begin. I understand you were both a close personal friend and an investor in Walker Equities, is that correct?

LUCCA: Well, yeah. I was Don's personal trainer. We met around eight years ago through his wife, when he was training for an ultramarathon. I guess you can say we became close.

INTERVIEWER: And you were invested in the fund?

LUCCA: Right, that is correct. After about two years of working out with Don. He was always talking to me about business, giving me advice. When we met, I was working at Miami Elite Fitness, but he encouraged me to go out on my own, open my own shop. So I did, and he helped with contracts, the lease. It was small potatoes to him, but he did it as a favor. My company ended up taking off, so for the first time in my life I had some extra cash. I looked to him for advice. He agreed to take me on as an investor. The smallest one in the fund, he liked to remind me.

INTERVIEWER: How close would you say you and Donald Walker became?

LUCCA: Extremely close. My family is all scattered, mostly back in Rio, so I spent holidays at the Walker home. Thanksgiving, Christmas at their Aspen house. Honestly, I wasn't always comfortable living that lifestyle with them, but they made me feel like part of the family. I was at all the boys' birthday parties. Don confided in me, things he didn't tell anyone else. Even Patricia. I believed that he thought of me as a brother. Which now, I mean, it sounds ridiculous.

INTERVIEWER: I can see that this is emotional for you. Do you need a minute?

LUCCA: Ugh. Yeah . . . I'm sorry, it's a lot to . . .

INTERVIEWER: Totally understand. Take all the time you need.

LUCCA: [clears throat] Yeah, so we were very close, the Walkers and me.

INTERVIEWER: In all the time you knew Don, would you ever have expected him capable of something like this?

LUCCA: Honestly, no. I just thought he knew more than anyone else. Like, secret knowledge on how to make money that had the potential to change the course of my life. Which it did . . . it did change the course of my life.

INTERVIEWER: How so?

LUCCA: Well, I guess it changed twice. First in my lifestyle: private planes, après ski, Dom Pérignon. Things I hadn't even heard of before Don and Patricia. It was almost embarrassing in the beginning. I felt like such an impostor. But Don was so warm, and he always seemed to want me around. It felt nice. I was important to someone who, himself, was very very important. I mattered to a guy like that, a guy like Don. The way people treated him, like he controlled the sunrise. But then he turned to *me* for advice, to share his thoughts. Even deeply personal things, like his relationship with Patricia. So I guess he made it safe, to trail him in that life. He needed me next to him on the jet. That's how it felt anyway. So I let myself believe that I belonged there.

INTERVIEWER: No one would fault you for that. You are a victim in this thing. You mentioned your life changed twice. What was the second time?

LUCCA: Ha. I lost everything. I gave Don all my savings and then some, thought I was making the smart move. Thought I was securing my future. I took the bait, you know. Flying high, rubbing elbows with CEOs. I knew I'd never be them, not really, but I thought I had a seat at the table. Now I'm . . . I'm at zero. I'm worse off than I was when I met the Walkers. [Clears throat.]

INTERVIEWER: You spent a lot of intimate time with the Walkers, traveling and holidays. Do you think Patricia was in on the alleged Ponzi scheme?

LUCCA: Ah, I don't know. Patricia . . . as close as I got to Don, I never cracked the surface with her. We socialized, of course, but with her I felt like a guest. My relationship was with Don. As for the two of them as a couple . . . they looked great together, in public. Privately, it's hard to say. They weren't that warm with each other. Don . . . he confided in me quite a bit. She seemed like . . . a trophy, maybe? The kind of girl he couldn't get growing up. But their relationship? I wouldn't call them a team. So, who knows what she knew? It's anybody's guess.

INTERVIEWER: Do you think their marriage was just for show?

LUCCA: No, I don't think it was for show. But I wouldn't say they were madly in love, either. I think they loved the idea of what the other represented. Like, they looked damn good in glossy pictures together. I really admired Don on a lot of levels, you know, before . . . but I did suspect that he cared too much about how things *looked*. It was strange to see someone so successful caught up in that. Patricia, she *definitely* cared how things looked.

One Christmas we were in Aspen, and we arrived on the twenty-third. Don was supposed to have a tree delivered and decorated at the house so it would feel, you know, Christmassy when we settled in. So, we get there and it's snowy and freezing, we pull into the driveway, Patricia, Don, the nanny, the boys, and me. We get inside, the heat is pumping. It really felt nice, we were in the spirit you could say. Then Patricia sees the living room and there's no tree. Oh man, she went nuclear, just exploded on Don. *You had one job! Now it's Christmas, we have no tree, the whole holiday is ruined!* Going off.

Don is a defensive guy, very charming, but he does not like to be challenged. He gave it right back to her. They were screaming, getting in each other's faces. I was worried it would come to blows. So I took the boys to the game room and started a round of pool. Not five minutes later, the doorbell rings, and it's Miami social friends . . . some trust fund couple who was also there for the holidays. They were meeting us for drinks before dinner in town. I went to grab the door and Don and Patricia light up brighter than any Christmas tree I've ever seen. Arms around each other, fixing martinis for the guests, Patricia sitting on Don's lap while they clinked glasses. Literally minutes before they had looked like they were going to kill each other. They could mask the situation on a dime. Maybe that was their bond.

INTERVIEWER: Do you think their image is what kept them together? Perhaps it was even a motivation for his crime?

LUCCA: Yeah, I've thought about that a lot. Maybe. I think he hid his demons really really well. I think he's weak. And when you're dealing with weakness like that, a lot of people risk too much to appear invincible, you know? To hide their insecurities.

INTERVIEWER: You almost sound like a therapist.

LUCCA: I've done a lot of thinking. A lot of reading. Trying to figure out how this happened to me. How I let it happen, ha. But no, I can't even afford a therapist.

INTERVIEWER: What can you tell us about what your life is like now?

LUCCA: Shit. I'm working, trying to pay off debt so one day I can start saving again. Right now, I'm focused on the bills . . . on keeping my business. Which is no guarantee at this point. And I'm waiting. There might be some compensation for Don's investors. If they can find the money. *Victims*, they are calling us.

INTERVIEWER: Do you feel like a victim?

LUCCA: Shit. To be honest . . . I feel like a loser.

INTERVIEWER: And why is that?

LUCCA: I fell for a shiny ball, chased it around like a house cat, got snapped up in a trap. So stupid. I blame myself.

INTERVIEWER: You don't blame Don Walker?

LUCCA: I'm angry with him.

INTERVIEWER: If you could talk to him now, what would you say?

LUCCA: I'd say, Why? What was missing in your life that you needed to create one that wasn't yours? Why'd you betray our trust? I mean, what did he think was going to happen?

Interview Transcript with Patricia Walker

For profile in *Magic City* magazine, summer issue 2019
By Andres Castano
April 25, 2019, Session 6

INTERVIEWER: It is so nice to see you in person, Patricia. I have to be honest, I was surprised to receive your phone call.

PATRICIA: It's nice to see you, too, Andres. I . . . didn't know who else to talk to. It had to be in person. I just don't know who is listening these days. Feds. Don.

INTERVIEWER: Patricia. Are you okay? Let me get you some water.

PATRICIA: No, thank you. I don't want water. It's like . . . I can't breathe. This is all too much, and I can't even meditate. I mean, I try! But every time I close my eyes and try to sit still, it feels like I'm drowning. And then on top of it, I try to reach out for support and everyone is ghosting me. Deepak isn't returning my calls. And I'm scared! Right now, I'm just so very scared.

Look at my cuticles. Look at them! I haven't had a manicure in over a month, and I started chewing my fingers again like some . . . some . . . low-class trailer lady.

INTERVIEWER: Breathe, Patricia. Breathe. Did something happen?

PATRICIA: This has to stay off the record for now, okay? I have information.

INTERVIEWER: It stays between us.

PATRICIA: Okay. It was the middle of the night, last night. Don was sleeping in the guest room. It was dark and quiet in there, so I knew he was asleep, and I just couldn't settle down. Call it a feeling, intuition, I don't know. I put on socks and tiptoed around the house. I didn't know what I was looking for but, honestly, maybe this is something I should have done a long time ago. I just always trusted that Don knew better and had everything taken care of. I never questioned it.

Well, now with my life turned upside down, my kids in another state, my reputation destroyed, I wanted to know what was really going on. It's all so confusing. I just kept waiting to wake up and have everything go back to normal. Some terrible misunderstanding. I stayed in town to watch Don clear his name, to stand by his side when he's declared not guilty, but what if I was wrong?

I didn't know what I might find. And honestly, I don't know if I would have been relieved or disappointed to find nothing. I went room by room, starting with my husband's closet: looking under socks, feeling under drawers. Then the office. I unlocked all the cabinets with a paper clip. Oh, I'm not as naive as people think, I've been around the block. Searched every file and paper for . . . something. Some smoking gun. I almost gave up after that, but a little voice inside my head told me to *check the wine cellar.* So I did.

Now, we have more than a million dollars' worth of wine in there. Cases of Chateau Margaux from 1996, 2000, 2004. Screaming Eagle allocations you won't find anywhere else in the world. We even had a coffee table book made about the collection. So, anyway, there's a huge combination lock on the cellar to get in and, of course, I have the digits memorized. I'd always go in there to grab a special bottle to bring as a hostess gift.

So I let myself into the cellar. All the bottles were perfectly lined up and temperature controlled. It smelled like new oak. I walked up and down the aisles running my finger along the perfectly clean bottles. No one else had the combination besides Don; he must have recently dusted. My mind started to wander and I don't think I was fully paying attention, but as I was passing the New World Cabernet section, something caught my eye. One of the Harlan Estate bottles was off-kilter, with its neck off the rack. But why would Don be messing with the bottles? He can't drink on house arrest. He's tested regularly.

I went closer to inspect and something didn't look right. I took the Harlan bottle off the rack and that's when I saw it. A tiny crease in the wall. A fucking secret door. Because of course he had that built in. Betrayal after fucking betrayal. I personally worked with the architects and builders at Villa Rosé on every little detail, and Don goes behind my back and builds a goddamn secret room. It took a little fiddling, but I found the release button on the Murphy door. The wall swung open with the racks still attached and I covered my mouth, bracing myself.

Behind the door was a crawl space big enough for a guy Don's size, but no larger. I half expected to see stacks of dead bodies when it opened, but all I saw were cases of Far Niente, like extras that didn't fit into the racks yet. There were four of them, stacked two high, two long. I open the first one: wine. The second: wine. I felt like a crazy person, in that moment. Like some deranged jilted wife unsuccessfully looking for texts from a mistress. Then I pull those top cases down and start on the bottom ones. The third one: wine. The last one: cash. Bundled in hundreds. My heart started pounding, but okay, maybe it makes sense to stash some cash. Weird place, but fine. I pull the cash off the top and below it, there are documents. Passport with Don's picture and a fake name. There was no passport for me, Andres. Under the documents, gems. A bag of fucking gorgeous glittering precious gems. And then, guns.

INTERVIEWER: Do you think that . . .

PATRICIA: He's going to run, Andres. And he will probably get away with it. I don't know what his plans are, but I can guess. Seaplane to pick him up behind our house in Biscayne Bay? He'd be in international waters within thirty minutes. The lying, cheating bastard. And he's obviously not planning on taking me with.

What do I do? I can't tell anyone, can I? I don't know if I should confront him directly, he is my husband, after all. Or call the police? Or just run away myself? Meet the kids in Kentucky . . .

That's another place I can't go back to. I need to get my boys, but I have enough ghosts here without needing to confront all my childhood traumas.

No, I'm not scared for my life. I'm scared for my future.

You asked me once about my childhood. Where I came from . . . I left that all behind. Some people just aren't raised in the places they should have been and I'm convinced about that. My parents weren't abusive—well, not toward me, anyway. And my dad doesn't drink anymore, but growing up, they struggled. They really struggled, and they probably shouldn't have had kids. My parents were kids themselves, first of all, and they couldn't remotely afford to take care of us.

God, it's such a cliché sob story. My sister, Katy, and I were carted back and forth between relatives, none of whom had the money or desire to raise us. We heard things we shouldn't have, saw things we shouldn't have. I was the lucky one, a little younger. Katy had it worse. Now she's managing a Red Lobster in Louisville. Which is the best she's done in years.

I moved back in with my parents when I was sixteen, in eleventh grade. Dad was sober by then; Mom was working two jobs. It was peaceful but the damage was done. I counted down the days until I could get out of there. Got a full ride to Louisville, interned at a PR firm in New York. Met Don.

He was handsome, and charming, and brilliant. He was going places, building an empire. I thought my life had changed forever, that I had met my prince and that a terrible spell had been broken. Thought I broke some tragic cycle. So stupid.

Late at night, when I'm alone with my thoughts, all I keep wondering is whether I sold my soul. If now it's time to pay up.

INTERVIEWER: Patricia. What would you like me to do with this information?

PATRICIA: I want you to hold on to it. Just in case something happens to me. Can you do that?

CHARLOTTE

Ax went back to school on Monday. How's that for helicoptering? Like hell I was going to let some bimbo principal tell me that *my son wasn't welcomed back*. I took it up to the school board, we have friends there, and Principal Nelson's hands were tied.

That depressing brown building, with its pee-stained-looking hallways and 1980s lockers, was certainly not too good for my kid. Axel moped and complained, the whole *everyone there hates me* teenage thing. How do they throw the "H" word around so lightly? But the Giordanis are not quitters, and you better believe he marched his grumpy self back in there for good this time. And I wasn't going to turn my back anymore; I was ready to stay on top of him.

Principal Nelson met me in her office during drop-off to discuss the *conditions of Axel's reentry*. Basically, we agreed to regular counseling and strict supervision moving forward.

"And what about those kids bullying him?" I asked. "You're going to have to keep an eye on that and discipline those children, too." You can't go around blaming the champagne bottle for exploding when it's been left in a hot car. Ax was being reactive; the school needed to keep an eye on the trigger.

"We have a zero-tolerance policy for bullying," she said.

Really? My son, and his shadow of a black-and-blue facial wound, would beg to differ.

The nerve, like I was some kind of idiot. Umm, half your students' Instagram accounts would also seem to suggest otherwise, lady! #fuckmiamibeachmiddle #sandyjacksonisaho #loseralert.

I know how to find things on social media. If you really want to know what's going on in a teenager's mind, check their online profiles. And Nelson's non-bullying angels were anything but. If Sunset Academy was home to a thousand shining unicorns, Beach Middle was the rainbow poop they left behind.

But that's just middle school; it's the age. All those kids want to do is eat, sleep, and get laid—but they're too young for sex, so they just seethe all day with some mix of crippling insecurity and tedious lust that turns them into shitty little demons who torture their friends. It's a moment.

When Ax came home that Monday afternoon, I made a point to be there. Usually Teresa, our nanny/housekeeper, would be the one to greet him after school, which I assume Ax preferred to having me do it, but changing that up was just one of the alterations that I was committed to making. I spent hours whipping up some of those Nutella muffins he always loved and mini homemade bagel pizzas. Food is his love language. I waited for him in the kitchen. Of course, it was going to have been a difficult first day back for Ax after everything that had happened, and I wanted him to feel *heard*. I'm not going to lie, any interaction with a thirteen-year-old feels awkward and forced, like a bad Tinder date. And I was all nerves waiting for him to get home.

Axel came in with a scowl that would have petrified Medusa. Backpack slung low, shoulders rounded so far they could have touched his toes.

"Hey, sweetie, how was your day?" I asked. I know, original as fuck. Silence.

"How did it go? Your first day back . . ."

When did I become so pathetic? You think you know yourself, and then you become a mother.

He made for the stairs, but I cut him off and grabbed his arm.

"Young man, please answer me when I speak to you." He turned to me and I all but tripped over my feet. I still couldn't get used to the face staring back at me. Hollow eyed, like he hadn't slept in weeks, and that awful gash, the scar still fresh and pink and raw. *Not my baby*.

"It was fine, Mom," he answered, and shrugged himself loose to continue up the stairs.

I watched his back disappear into the bedroom as he closed the door, and then I heard the miserable click of the lock.

In an absurd moment, I yelled, "I made snacks!"

Tell me, how do you reach an eighth-grader? It's a sick riddle. Or an unanswerable question. Please sweet baby Jesus let me keep my Madeline Rose from this awful fate.

I packed up some muffins and bagel pizzas and left them by Ax's door. Two hours later, they were gone. I took it as progress.

PATRICIA

That's it. I'm taking my power back.

No more therapist asking me how my husband's betrayal *makes me feel*, as if that's not completely fucking obvious. No more pointless interviews. I *feel* like clawing Don's eyes out and throwing them into Biscayne Bay. I *feel* like the rest of my life is a black hole of poverty, shame, and loneliness. Oh no. I'm not going down without a fight. It's on me now. And I'm not as helpless as people think.

I set an alarm for five A.M. yesterday morning. Don was snoring in his room, and I packed a weekender with essentials, a couple outfits and toiletries. And a small duffel with my favorite pieces of jewelry, a few of my favorite bags: the Birkins, my new Chanel 19, that kind of thing. I put them in the big car and left the front door open a crack so I could sneak back in as quietly as possible. Then, and here is where I might've been crazy or brilliant or, who knows, probably both, I went into the wine cellar.

I took the whole stash. Gems and cash in my luggage, passport and guns dumped into Biscayne Bay. I figured, at this point, I don't have much left to lose and this asshole is going to sink the whole family, anyway. I mean, this escape plan proved that he's guilty, right? Well, guess what? He's going to face his crimes. I made sure of it. It was the right thing to do for the victims.

Don't get me wrong, I was terrified! Never ever have I been so scared, and I've seen some awful things in my life. I thought I might pass out or throw up transferring everything to the car. By the time I was finished, it was six A.M. and the sun was threatening to rise. Honestly, Don has been taking prescription meds and sleeping until noon since he got released, but still. Every random sound in the house gave me a minor heart attack.

After I packed the car, I got the hell out of there. Can you believe that? No sentimental last look at the dream home I spent years conceptualizing and building. Not even a tear. I'll never live there again. New chapter. That was the last night I'd ever sleep in that bed. The Villa Rosé master bedroom. My marital bed.

Good riddance to all of it.

I checked into the Four Seasons, where I'll stay until the trial is over. Then I'll bring the boys back and move into a new place. Maybe a condo South of Fifth. Maybe Bal Harbour.

Oh, and I called my lawyer. I'm filing for divorce.

MELODY

I sat at the conference table in Principal Garcia's office, where she allowed me to work due to the sensitive nature of the project. So far, no lawyers had come calling, but I suspected we were running out of time on that.

The office was unusually subdued for Miami, which is to say, it was a normal office. Parquet synthetic wood floors were topped with IKEA bookshelves and metal file cabinets. The desk was an Office Depot floor model, the principal's assistant was keen on telling me.

"I can't speak for the PTA," she said, "but the school watches our budget very closely."

The Walker scandal was open gossip at school, which, given the accused's relationship to school fundraising, threw the entire Sunset Academy PTA into suspicion.

I'd been volunteering at the school daily from drop-off to pickup, working on the PTA books and writing bylaws, for weeks. It actually felt great to be "working" again, like the puzzle pieces of my life in Miami were finally clicking into place. There was one notably absent character in the clean-up process . . . Charlotte. Not that I was complaining.

"How not surprising," Darcy had said on one of our update calls. "Shit gets real and Queen Bee is MIA. If there's no photo op, she's not interested."

She was probably right, I mean, not one call to ever check in. You'd think after her *years of selfless service,* Charlotte would want to be kept in the loop. Make sure the empire she built was still standing and, more importantly, that the children would still be able to thrive with well-funded educational platforms. I suppose I could have called her, but I was grateful for the distance.

Gabriela, on the other hand, was a pleasant surprise. She showed up every day, stilettos and all, to lend her support. *Anything I can do.* And she seemed to mean it.

Together, we pored over thousands of emails and restructured all the PTA's spreadsheets to put together an accurate picture of the finances. Gabriela often ordered us acai bowls for lunch. "They're a superfood. Full of antioxidants," she would say. They were like mushy bowls of sour fruit, but I ate them with only a half-forced smile. It was thoughtful, and honestly, if that mush could make me look half as good as her, it would be worth it.

"I think it's time to bring Charlotte in on this," Gabriela said, about three and a half weeks into our recon mission. We had just finished closing the 2018 books over quinoa bowls with mango salmon (another of Gabriela's favorites).

"One of you will be in charge of all this next year," she added, "and we need to protect the school moving forward. We came really close to sinking. Too close."

"Came close? I don't think we are in the clear yet," I responded. I didn't mention that Charlotte was the one who had put us in this situation, however unintentionally, by cultivating and milking the Walkers like Midwest dairy cows.

"All the more reason to get on the same page," Gabriela said. "I'll call Charlotte and set up a meeting at school. How's next Monday after drop-off?"

Peachy.

I don't mean to sound like a jerk, but I hoped Charlotte wouldn't show up. It turned out my life in Miami was so much simpler without her. Palm trees and sandy beaches, cotton candy clouds at sunset. Our only contact now was the drive-by drop-offs when she would deposit her daughter at our house for weekly sleepovers. A half wave with the window up at best. And that was fine!

Despite Charlotte and my repelling each other like the force of two negative ions, Madeline and Lucy acted like lifelong best friends. Classmates began calling them Madeluce, and the nickname stuck so well that they scribbled it onto every backpack and folder the two of them owned.

Embarrassingly, the girls knew about Charlotte's and my falling-out—way to set an example, I know. I'm not blaming either one of us, specifically. It's just hard to hide these things from your kids after a certain age. They just get it. But it didn't seem to affect Lucy and Maddy's relationship. On the contrary, their relationship bloomed fuller every day. That was a relief, at least.

Madeluce had their standing sleepover date at our house the Friday before my dreaded meeting with Charlotte and Gabriela. Maddy arrived at my doorstep, mother in car, with her blush monogrammed overnight bag and a portable ring light to illuminate the duo's TikTok videos. Her hair was pulled back into two perfect Dutch braids, and she wore a cropped sweater over her denim cutoffs. Nine going on nineteen.

As soon as I opened the door, Charlotte pulled out of the driveway and vanished into the night.

"Thank you for having me, Melody," Maddy said, as she skipped past me. She found Lucy on the sofa and pulled her by the arm into Lucy's bedroom. Door closed. When did this happen? It was only recently that I couldn't take my eyes off Lucy and her friends during playdates. Now they were almost free range.

It irked me. So I pulled a classic mom move and knocked on Lucy's door with a tray of homemade banana nut muffins. "Hey girls, I brought a little something to eat before dinner," I said.

"Oh my god, Mom!" responded Lucy. "We were in the *middle* of a TikTok!"

Charming. My first instinct was to kick the door down and confiscate all technology, but I extra-honeyed my voice and let myself in instead.

"I'm so sorry, sweetie. Why don't you stop for a bite and then start again? I know the TikToks usually take time to get right."

Lucy rolled her eyes like a dial meter, turning my fumes to rage. I thought I had a few more years before the mother-daughter bond started to show cracks.

"No big deal, Melody," Maddy said. She had her mother's perfect smile. "You're right, we were still practicing that one."

"I'd love to see," I said, hoping for a rare glimpse into their world. Greg joined me in the doorway.

"What are we watching?" he asked.

"It's the 'Candy' dance. By Doja Cat. I think, like, four million TikTokers have already done it. Lucy, let's show them."

My daughter responded to her friend with the *look*. The same one she gives me when it's time to shut up. At least I was in good company.

"C'mon, it's a good one," Maddy pressed.

"Yeah, I love Dojo Cat," Greg said.

"Dad!" Lucy flushed. "It's Doj-A Cat. She's not like a karate-fighting Dojo Cat."

Greg was neutered, but Maddy won out. She pressed a button on her iPhone and immediately the two girls launched into a synchronized gyration of hips and suggestive hand motions to the lyrics, something about a sweet spot and putting something in someone's mouth.

After the fifteen-second performance, Maddy picked up her phone to analyze their choreography. "Nailed it! Posting," she declared, and then smiled at Greg and me.

"Yeah, that was great!" I said, horrified. Greg left the room. "So when you say you're posting, does that mean . . ."

"Oh, don't worry, Melody." Maddy waved a manicured hand in the air. "I have a private account. My parents are soooo protective."

How responsible of Charlotte.

I met a furious Greg back in the living room.

"Just to be sure we are on the same page," he began. "We are not fucking okay with this, right?"

"No . . . I mean, no. But I don't know. It's a common thing these days, and the account is private, so . . ."

"Are you joking? They are nine fucking years old. I feel like I'm on *To Catch a Predator.* This is sick!" Greg's hands were in his hair.

"Actually, they never used real kids on that show. It was always adults pretending to be kids. Like a catfish situation," I said.

"Really, Mel? Is this cool to you? Our baby girl is twerking to oral sex songs and posting videos of it to the internet?"

"It's more complicated than that," I told him, trying, and failing, to articulate how I really felt about it. "Of course I hate the videos, and the dancing. It's . . . so bad. But this is the norm these days. How are we supposed to tell Lucy she can't do something that she doesn't even realize is dangerous? Especially when she's fitting in so well."

"Okay, so we are prioritizing popularity over safety? Is that what we're doing?" Greg's hands balled into tight fists, his eyes wide and maniacal. "What does this open the door to? 'My friends are doing drugs so I can, too. Everyone is doing it'?"

"Wow, you've never sounded so much like a dad before." It was a low blow. And the worst part of the argument was that he was right. I knew he was right.

"Okay, Mel." Greg swallowed hard. "I think you've been in Miami too long. I can't believe we are even fighting about this. What, are you too afraid to call and talk to Charlotte?"

He'd met my low blow with a lower one. The truth was, I no longer cared what Charlotte thought about me. I was proving my worth while she was rolling around with filth. She was certainly not someone that I needed to impress anymore.

"Fuck you, Greg."

It was the first time I'd ever said that to him.

I braced for the hurt look in Greg's eyes, but what I got was so much worse. Like when your parents caught your adolescent self stealing a $20 bill from one of their wallets, and you bawled uncontrollably and asked, "Are you mad at me?" And they shook their heads no and answered, "Just disappointed."

"I'm sorry—" I started to say, but Greg cut me off.

"Why are you even running for PTA president, Mel? Because you care about the school and starting up your business or because you're turning into one of *them*?"

My breath caught in my chest. How dare he compare me to those women, to question my integrity and my motivations. Greg, my husband, best friend, and number one support.

"You don't mean that," I said, voice shaking.

"I think I do, Mel," he answered. "You're not acting like you. This TikTok thing, this obsession with beating Charlotte, the new clothes and bags. What are you trying to prove?" Greg was walking backward away from me, as if trying to escape a crime scene.

"You don't get it," I answered, because I had no idea what else to say. "I'm doing my best to start a life here. For all of us. You're the one who made us come. If you didn't want me to fit in here, why'd you make us move?" In hindsight, it was a tad dramatic.

Greg just quietly said, "Wow," and closed the door to our bedroom.

PATRICIA

One last time. I would have waited longer, maybe for Don's court date. During my escape, I'd taken valuables, some clothes, some bags. Enough for now, really. But the boys. They're still at my parents' house. Imagine. Seeing them every day for almost a decade and now I haven't held them in so long or felt the weight of their bodies in my arms. And all their things are still at Villa Rosé.

I need something more than the thousands of digital images on my phone. Something tangible. Proof that they exist off a goddamn screen. Something they held and loved, that still smells like them.

The Four Seasons is beautiful, and lord knows I needed distance from this house of cursed memories and this disgusting man. But I had no idea how hard it would be to be alone. At least hating Don within the confines of the house gave me something to focus on. There hasn't been one visitor at the hotel. I FaceTime Maddox and Monrow every night, and I talk to my lawyer, and that's it. Thank god I'm independent, but it's just too much.

The favorite stuffed animals from their beds, that's all I needed. So I waited until three A.M. Set an alarm. By now, I'm sure Don has realized that I made off with his get out of jail card. I've filed for divorce. He can't say anything because we have to assume that his phone is tapped. But I know he's angry. And when Don is angry, he's dangerous. That's why I had to time it perfectly. Don would be in deep,

Ambien-induced twilight by three A.M., and I would be able to sneak in and grab the toys. In and out in less than three minutes.

But now, in Maddox's bedroom, I can't stop going through his drawers and smelling every article of clothing like some absolute psycho. The sweat in the soccer jersey that no detergent could ever eliminate. I never thought I'd be so grateful for his stinky shirts. The chlorine on his bathing suits.

I'll just go through both of their rooms and take whatever I can fit in one roller bag. That way, I'll have some extra things for them in case they come back to town earlier. It really just makes sense.

Pretty soon, the boys and I will start over. A family again, without the rotten apple. We will heal and come back stronger than ever, and then . . . but wait. What was that noise?

DARCY

I saw the email moments after turning off my morning alarm, eyes squinting and foggy with sleep.

4:32 A.M.
From: Donald Walker
Subject: Consultation

Darcy,
We met some time ago at a school function.
My wife has filed for divorce, and I need to retain a family lawyer to represent me. Are you available for a phone consultation in the next couple of days?
Don
Donald Walker, CEO
Walker Equities, LLC
100 Brickell Avenue, 7th Floor
Miami, Florida

File that under "what we could all see coming." But *me*? The man probably has an all-star barrage of attorneys representing him; does that firm not have a family practice? And also, could I even entertain representing this man? Could I not?

I marked the email as unread. No cogent thoughts could be formed about this before coffee.

I shared the email with Elliot, and he thought the matter was simple enough. A high-profile case, good for the firm's reputation, likely a drawn-out process incurring a treasure trove of billable hours. As both my husband and my business partner, he saw the case as an opportunity to elevate my career. Divorce lawyer to infamous fallen men? Like an anti–Gloria Allred?

"It's a no-brainer," he said later that morning, sitting across from me at my desk. We came to work separately that day: I had dropped Jackson off at school, and Elliot had left the house early for a breakfast meeting. "If Walker wants to retain us, we're taking it."

"But he's *such* a sleaze," I countered. The thought of having weekly phone calls or meetings with Don Walker, of having to depose him, dig into and defend his parenting, it made me shudder. There was also the likely possibility that this divorce was merely a play for Donald to shuffle assets to Patricia before a verdict was made on his fraud trial. That was not the kind of client I wanted to be associated with. Everything would have been simpler if I could have just handed the account over to my partner/husband, but he didn't think Don would go for it.

"If you don't take this on, no sex for three months," Elliot teased. It was funny because my husband is funny. Funny as long as it wasn't true.

"Well, that's sexual harassment in the workplace. As your business partner, I have to say that I don't appreciate your speaking to me that way. And as your wife, I have to remind you that you'd be missing that new thing I've been doing. With the blindfold."

Elliot threw a crumpled-up Post-it on my lap. I unfolded it and read "Pretty please? I want to read about our firm in the newspaper."

I agreed to take the consultation.

Two mornings later, I was on the phone with Donald Walker. Sitting in my office with the door closed, I repeated a mantra over and over in my head: *You are a professional. You are a professional.* I strained to keep my voice even, focus drifting between the various images on my desk. It was adorned with the requisite family photos: a wedding portrait, Jackson's third-grade school photo, Elliot and me holding Jackson at the hospital from behind a C-section curtain (I always found that image amusing: proud new smiling parents with their greasy newborn, knowing that behind the curtain was a severed abdomen with partially exposed entrails). I kept the photos there, I think, to remind me that I was unlike my clients. Happy. Content. Steadfast.

Not that I harbor disdain for my clients. It's more like fear. Like the oncologist who dies of cancer. Your brain knows it not to be scientifically true, but you sometimes worry that the work is contagious.

"She served me three days ago . . . Patricia's lawyer did," Don told me.

"Okay, I'm very sorry to hear that," I said. "This is a difficult situation, and—"

"She went to a hotel. I don't know which one. She didn't tell me. After everything I did for her. Plucked her from blue-collar obscurity and made her a damn duchess."

"Okay, and you've been at home. What I mean to say is . . ."

He breathed heavily into the phone. "Yes, I'm on house arrest. In my *masterpiece* of a pink glass house. You know who made me build a pink fucking house? My wife! And now I'm in the fight of my life against these bullshit charges and she walks out like . . ."

"I understand," I said. "Have you and Patricia been speaking, or do you prefer to communicate through the attorneys?"

Don cleared his throat. "We have not spoken since . . . since she went away." He paused. "We have a prenup."

"Ok," I said. "If you do decide to retain me, I will need a copy of that, along with the letter from Patricia's attorney. I will send them a letter letting them know that I will be representing you. My hourly rate is seven hundred dollars . . ."

"She's not taking my fucking kids. I'm going to tell you that right now. Those are *my* kids."

I had to shield my ear from the receiver, lest my eardrum rupture from the volume of his voice. "Is Patricia seeking full custody?"

"Yeah."

So the divorce was real. I almost felt bad for the guy. Almost.

"What are your goals for the divorce and custody proceedings? What is the best-case scenario in your mind?" I asked.

"The best-case scenario is that I get my *fucking* life back, Darcy. How much will that cost?"

I put the phone back to my ear. "I wish I knew."

Despite my reservations (that he was a terrible person, that he was a career criminal, that he made my skin crawl), I took Don on as a client and we made a plan to meet the following week at his house to discuss the divorce proceedings.

The last time I'd been at the pink glass house, it had been full of caterers in white gloves, tasteful uplighting in all the right places, and a sparkle of polish on every surface. The mark of regular and deep housekeeping. But for this meeting with Don Walker, it felt more like I'd stepped into a late-stage Grey Gardens than the glamorous Villa Rosé.

Even as I pulled up to the gate, the impression was markedly different. Overgrown grass spilled wildly onto the walkway, and the once-sparkling pink glass had been covered in a layer of dust and grime, rendering an opaqueness to the entire facade of the house.

With a knot in my stomach—I really didn't want to be there but reminded myself that I was doing a job—I pressed the electronic doorbell. When I couldn't hear a sound on the other end, and a couple minutes had passed, I knocked with vigor.

Don Walker swung the door open and, holy hell, I was not ready for the sight . . . or the smell. Now, remember, this was someone who had fancied himself Miami's most dapper man. Expensive haircut, custom-made shirts, always clean-shaven. But what stood before me was closer to Tom Hanks at the end of *Cast Away*. He was scraggly with salt-and-pepper stubble covering his face and neck, and his sideburns had grown out like a sixties Beatle's. His hair was greasy and fell in all directions just above his eyes, and he wore natty-looking gray sweatpants and a stained "Cody, Wyoming" T-shirt.

"Heyyy, Darcy," he said when he answered the door. "Thanks for coming." And barefoot, he ushered me into the living room. "I appreciate your meeting me here," he continued, and pointed to the ankle bracelet on his right leg. "They've got me on LoJack."

It took all my self-control not to gasp as I sat down on the sofa opposite Don, pressing the folders and papers I had brought hard into my lap for something to occupy my hands. Dirty laundry was splayed over all the fine living room furniture, draped over the dramatic pink velvet sofa, and piled on top of the black marble coffee table. It was clear that all household staff had long been dismissed.

Dirty dishes that had begun to grow spores littered the side tables, and coffee-stained papers were strewn on the floor. This man had clearly never cleaned up after himself. Or he had reached a stage where he didn't care to. I'd be surprised if at that point he had showered once in the past week. I was grateful when he didn't offer me anything to eat or drink before we sat down.

"Well, first of all, how are you doing?" I asked, trying not to show any emotion on my face.

"Never better," Don answered, and then laughed maniacally. I winced. "Listen, Darcy, it hasn't been great." He straightened up. "What am I supposed to say? The government set me up, and my wife sent my kids away and ditched me like I'm nothing. Fucking takedown stole my life! I'm not okay . . . I'm very not okay."

Don ran his tongue across his top teeth, as if that were a way to brush them without toothpaste.

Listen, I've seen a lot in my career. Let's just say people aren't calling me when they're having their best day. Once, I watched a wife throw herself on the floor in front of a judge and beg him not to grant her husband's divorce. I'm talking screaming, kicking, having to be restrained. In Florida, only one spouse has to file for a divorce for it to go through, so it didn't exactly go her way. Then there are the people who stay together for the kids and show up at my door the day after their youngest graduates from high school. Except by then they hate each other so much that the only ones who win are the lawyers. But what I saw at the pink glass house that morning made me uncomfortable in ways no client had before.

Don was agitated, fiddling with something incessantly in his hands. Something sparkly. Patricia's obscenely large engagement ring.

"Has Patricia been back here?" I asked.

Don looked startled and pocketed the ring. "Just to pack some more shit. We didn't speak."

The man was unhinged, a sliver of his former self. And he was probably guilty. I mean, he was almost definitely guilty of the white-collar crime. This shouldn't have been a sympathetic man, but in that moment, I did feel for him. His fall from grace was so epic that it made me look at my life and wonder how I'd react if I lost everything I held dear. Patricia hadn't even pretended to stand by him. His kids were gone. The sexy trainer best friend who might have been a lover was speaking out against him. Don appeared to be utterly alone.

Then things took a turn. "Let's talk about possible outcomes," I said.

Don nodded, then looked me in the eyes. "Okay," he responded. Then he smiled and said, "God, I love an educated, independent woman."

I immediately regretted coming to see him alone and attempted a pivot. "I took a look at your prenuptial agreement, and it's very solid."

"You know Patricia was always cold, a very cold person." He leaned in closer and put his hand on my knee. "I haven't felt the comfort of a beautiful woman in such a long time."

I don't think I've ever physically recoiled from someone so fast. My first instinct was to slap him across the face (it was such a punchable face), but instead I jumped to my feet. "That is completely inappropriate, and this meeting is now over," I said.

As I turned to leave the living room, Don grabbed my arm. "Wait! I'm sorry!" His eyes were bloodshot. "Please don't go. I'm just lonely."

"I'm sorry to hear that," I said, in my firmest tone. "But I cannot represent you."

I continued to the front door, and Don started crying behind me. "Darcy, stop! Don't go. I just fucked up!"

Don't turn around. Don't turn around, I told myself, not wanting to see him cry. Not able to witness the meltdown. But also, afraid that he might do something . . . violent. He seemed like a man with nothing to lose. My heart pounded all the way to the door, down the driveway, and into my car. Then I pulled away and put Don Walker behind me forever.

CHARLOTTE

Ax had been back in school for one week. I still believed that the ex-pulsion was a terrible idea, and that I'd done the right thing by forcing his way back into Miami Beach Middle.

But the week had been hard, and at a minimum I saw that there was no quick fix, no Band-Aid big enough to make things all better.

I had driven Ax to school every day after his return. Partly to make sure he was actually entering the building, and partly so he didn't have to ride the bus with those assholes who called him Ax Murderer.

With my eight-minute daily window, I pulled every trick out of my hat to try to get him talking. "Hey, any new favorite SoundCloud artists I should check out?" Or "How about meatball parm for dinner? It used to be your favorite!" It didn't matter what I said, it was always met with a muffled, "I don't know." His lean body slumped against the passenger-side door. I'd try to squeeze in an awkward side hug as he got out in carline, which Ax would basically shove off. I get it. I was trying too hard and looked pathetic.

After school, he got a ride home with my friend Tina—her daughter is a sixth-grader at Beach Middle—so I could take Maddy to her ex-tracurriculars. I wish that Teresa could drive, but a nanny/housekeeper who also drives is a fucking unicorn. Anyway, by the time Maddy and I made it back home every evening, Ax was already upstairs with the door closed, blasting noise music so loud on his headphones that we could still hear it through the door.

James's take was to give him space and let him come around. "Exerting his independence," he said. Meanwhile, every fiber of my body rebelled against that.

I called Principal Nelson on Wednesday to check on how Ax was settling back in. I might as well have been talking to a goddamn banana. *He's fine. He's been very quiet. No incidents to report.* Yes, there're no *incidents*, you moron, but is my child comfortable? I'm not naive enough to expect him to be happy right away, but is he *miserable?* Well, I straight up asked Nelson that, and the bitch said, "Why don't you ask him yourself?" Oh, how profound a thought! Genius! Like I hadn't fucking thought about that and tried. How does a middle school educator with a Cracker Jack PhD not know that angsty teens aren't exactly likely to bare all for their mothers?

"I'm asking *you*, to tell me what *you* have observed," I said.

"We have observed a troubled young man who has been forced to return to school and is probably doing his best to survive it. And you can count on the fact that we are *observing* him, given his history."

There aren't enough expletives in the English language for what I wanted to say.

Instead, I said thank you, but you better believe my tone was saying "choke on a hairy ballsack."

It was a huge relief when the weekend finally came around. The Monday to Friday stress-induced diarrhea was making me weak and jumpy. Why didn't I hide a tiny GoPro in Ax's blue bird's nest of a hairstyle to keep tabs on him at school? I could have avoided so much anxiety. Or exacerbated it, I guess.

At tennis, the other moms kept asking me *What's wrong?* and saying *You seem down* in that awful *I don't actually care I'm just nosy* way. Those girls are as transparent as Patricia Walker's eight-carat oval. Wherever that is now, probably an evidence room.

So the weekend came around, and Maddy as usual slept over at her BFF Lucy's. And that was *it*, my opportunity to devote all my attention to my firstborn, whether he liked it or not. Of course, he did not.

But Ax agreed to have dinner with me, sushi at our favorite place. I think he even showered. Threw on his favorite anime hoodie and skinny jeans and actually got in a car to go out in public with me. I let him connect his iPhone in my car and blare some SoundCloud noise on the drive. He was more animated than usual, nodding along, his oceanic blue eyes fixed on the horizon. I tried to find the rhythm and shoulder shimmy but kept losing the beat. It was so painfully obvious, my desperation, but for once he let it slide.

At the restaurant, I talked too much and drank my whole glass of water before the waiter took our order, like I'd never talked to a boy before. It was all incoherent babble—PTA drama, how Maddy did less than stellar on her third-grade SATs, and what are we even paying these test preppers for anyway? Basically, all topics that Ax couldn't give two flying you know whats about, but I knew he wasn't going to open up before edamame, and I just kept saying weird, desperate things to avoid silence.

I must have worn him down by the time I launched into a story about how incompetent Instacart shoppers can be because he cut me off and said, "Mom, I really don't want to go back to school."

He looked me in the eye, like really made contact. His bruises had faded to yellow. And the look wasn't blank, or hateful, or accusatory like it had been lately. He was pleading. Soft. I saw in his face, for the first time in ages, the shadow of the gorgeous towheaded boy. The one who fell asleep on my chest as a baby and snuck into my bedroom until second grade. My Axel was still in there. And he needed me.

"Well," I said, "we only have a few weeks left, and then I'm going to look into a lot of different options for you over the summer. Have you heard of ASH? The Arts and Science High School? I think you'd be perfect—"

"I can't wait a few weeks. You don't understand . . ." His whole body tensed, like a toddler on the verge of a tantrum.

What was the big deal? Yes, Beach Middle was a cesspool, and not the best place for Ax, but why not just slog it out and end the year on a high note? Don't let the disgusting bullies win. They'd be so happy to see Ax run and hide.

"Anyone can wait three weeks, honey. You just have to decide that—"

"Mom! I'm not going back there. You can't make me. I won't go back there!" Ax smacked the table. "Why won't you listen to me?"

"You're making a scene," I whispered, trying to dial the tone back down. We'd already traveled so far from that softer moment, just seconds earlier.

"I don't fucking care! This is my life. I'm dying over there, Mom!" His eyes were wild.

Now we were in the spotlight, center stage. Like we were the stars of an improv show, and the whole restaurant was our audience.

"One week," I said. A ridiculous concession. In hindsight, I was just trying to *win*. "You can take exams early."

I had to turn away from Ax's gaze, which possessed so much unbridled rage, it seemed like it would burn me alive.

"Fuck you, Mom! All you care about is yourself!" he shouted. And in one swift movement, he stood up and hip-checked the table, which launched a bowl of steaming hot gyoza into my lap. I yelped. And he was gone.

A busboy rushed over to me with clean towels, and a whole restaurant of sympathetic eyes met mine. As if I were the victim instead of the offender.

"Nothing to see here, people!" I shouted. "Go back to your own miseries!"

I drove around in the dark, up and down every block between Sushi Haven and home, looking for Ax, shouting his name like I was searching for a lost dog. After twenty or thirty minutes I gave up and went home. Defeated. Cried into my pillow until minutes after midnight, when I heard the alarm beep. He was home. Safe.

And with the absence of any rationality, I forgot my sadness and absolutely raged at my teenage son. Throwing open my bedroom door, I met Ax in the hallway, mascara smeared like bruises around my eyes.

"How dare you speak to me like you did tonight!" I started in.

"I am *not* going to school on Monday, Mother! I will run away and never come back!" He was sweaty and smelled terrible, from whatever walkabout he'd just taken.

"The hell you will!" I responded and lunged forward to confiscate his phone. It slid easily out of his hand, a slight jerk at the last second, too late. "You're not going anywhere without this! And guess what, I'm taking away your computer and video games, too. Unless, that is, you get your shit together and go to school on Monday!"

Ax took a step, opened his mouth, closed it. His eyes welled up; mine did, too.

"I hate you," he said, barely above a whisper. And turned back to his room, slammed the door, clicked the lock.

Every fight I've ever had with Ax has started with a measured response, followed by an eruption, ending with immediate regret. I tiptoed to his room and slid the phone under the door for him. Went back to my room, washed my face.

I'm sorry, I texted him.

The next morning, I saw his response. *I'll go to school on Monday.* What an idiot I was to think I'd won.

MELODY

That Monday morning, the day of the meeting at Sunset Academy, felt ominous. I woke up to charcoal skies and a steady downpour of fat, sloppy rain, like a save the date announcing that hurricane season was around the corner. It was mid-May, and the glorious Miami spring breeze was quickly giving way to our first full summer in the subtropics.

I pulled my hair back into a messy ponytail and threw a cardigan over my khaki jumpsuit. The outside air was already hot and sticky, but I knew the inside of the cafeteria would be an icebox.

My sleep had been fitful, at best. This would be my first real conversation with Charlotte since trying, and failing, to reconcile following the Walkers' downfall, and the thought sent my brain into a hamster wheel. What catastrophic word vomit would I unleash this time?

I dropped Lucy off at her classroom. The two of us had huddled on the way under a pathetic umbrella that was probably designed for one, and then I rushed to the cafeteria for the meeting.

By the time I sat down at the designated lunch table, dingy rainwater stained my white canvas sneakers and my jumpsuit was peppered with splotches of raindrops.

Charlotte was already there. Her hair looked freshly blown out, glossy brown locks framing her face in delicate waves. She wore fitted jeans and an immaculate white button-down shirt. The blouse was tucked in to reveal a red leather belt with a large letter *H* as the clasp.

Her polish was irritating . . . and intimidating.

"Hi, Charlotte," I said as I sat. She smiled a tight-lipped grin without looking up from her phone.

Principal Garcia and Gabriela joined us before things could get more awkward, and after a little back-and-forth about the weather—*that's Miami for you; five minutes later and it's sunny and gorgeous*—and complimenting one another's children, we got to work.

"The purpose of this meeting," Gabriela began, "is to come up with a plan to protect the PTA from any issues of malfeasance moving forward. Since one of you will be leading the organization next year"—she looked between Charlotte and me—"and hopefully whoever is not elected president will remain an active participant, we thought it necessary to bring you both in to brainstorm and get on the same page."

There was one month left in the school year, and the PTA board positions would be put to vote in just a couple weeks.

"I want you both to know how much Sunset Academy appreciates your commitment to our kids," Principal Garcia said, sitting tall in her power suit. "But no matter who wins, we need to make sure that all actions of the PTA are beyond reproach. Again, we so appreciate everything you do . . ."

"Thank you, Principal Garcia." Charlotte put her phone down. "I want the very same, I assure you. The potential smear on the PTA that a former donor caused is inexcusable, and I guarantee you that I will work tirelessly to make sure nothing like that ever happens again."

"Yes, I agree," I added, worried that Charlotte would try to dominate the conversation. Her PTA status was vulnerable after all that had happened with the Walkers under her watch, and I was ready to seize the opportunity. "We need to put a structure of checks and balances in place for the board and to ratify a new set of bylaws before the next school year."

Charlotte's eye roll was almost audible.

I fumbled with my fingers under the table, a childhood habit I couldn't break. Principal Garcia gently interjected herself with a speech about researching best practices from well-run PTAs and *borrowing* good ideas, when her walkie-talkie started beeping. *Garcia, come in. Code Red.*

"Just one moment," the principal said, stepping aside and bringing the walkie-talkie up to her ear.

I watched Garcia's eyes register something shocking, unmasked alarm. Was it panic? She retreated to a corner and gave orders, her free hand pressed to her forehead. "Make the announcement," she said into the device as she hastened her steps back toward us. "Get me on a line with Miami Beach Police."

The rest of us were on high alert by now. "What happened?" Charlotte asked, gripping the edge of the cafeteria table. Her shiny red nails made an ironic counterpoint to the cheap wood laminate surface.

Principal Garcia put her hands up in a *don't shoot* gesture, still gripping the walkie-talkie with her right index finger and thumb.

"We are on lockdown. There has been an *incident* at Miami Beach Middle School. I don't have much more information than that."

Charlotte looked like she was facing down a rabid tiger. "Is it a student? Is anyone hurt?"

"I don't know," Garcia answered. She started to turn away, and then must have changed her mind. "There is at least one casualty. I'm not sure of all the details. Please, don't panic—"

"Oh my god! Is there a shooter? Has anyone been apprehended?" Gabriela stood up, her voice shaking.

I could barely hear the words over my own heartbeat.

An alarm blared from the school intercom. "Attention, faculty and students. We are under a Code Red. Please lock your classroom doors and make sure all of your students are accounted for. Do not open the doors until we have made the all-call. Repeat, this is a Code Red. Lock your classroom doors. No one may enter or exit. Follow all Code Red protocols."

"Oh my god!" Gabriela repeated, spinning her head to make eye contact with each of us in turn.

Our school in Wichita had never been locked down, at least not while Lucy was enrolled. A *casualty*? I couldn't, didn't, want to think about what that could mean. Miami Beach Middle was only one block from Sunset Academy. Could a dangerous person have left Beach Middle to continue a shooting spree at the elementary school?

"Ladies, I know this is a stressful situation, but I don't have that information yet, and I won't until I get to my office and speak with the police. For now, I believe that Sunset Academy students are safe." Garcia straightened her jacket, not making eye contact with any of us.

"You're saying there's a chance they might be at risk?" Gabriela was close enough to kiss Principal Garcia. "I'm going to my daughter's class," she said, making for the door.

"Gabriela, stop!" Garcia broke her measured facade. "Lockdown means nobody moves until the police and I make the call. Now, if you'll excuse me, I need to deal with this with the proper authorities. In the meantime, please *stay put*."

"Charlotte, what is happening?" Gabriela pleaded, her eyes watery. "What do you think is happening?" As though Charlotte possessed a magic ball that could grant her omniscience.

Charlotte hadn't moved since we first heard the news. Her face was blank, eyes unseeing.

"Charlotte!" Gabriela shouted.

It broke the spell.

"I have to go," Charlotte whispered and launched herself from the cafeteria table with cheetah-like athleticism.

Gabriela tried to block her from the door. "You can't go out there, we're on Code R—"

Too late. The whoosh of Charlotte's exit sent a breeze in its wake. The flash of her was incongruous with her constricting clothes and high heels. Her purse was left on the table.

"What on earth is she thinking!" Gabriela turned to me with pleading eyes. "It's dangerous out there! There could be a shooter!"

"Maybe she's worried about Maddy. Or her son over at Beach Middle," I said, feeling an urgency to provide answers. "Just like you were about your daughter. I think we need to stay here until we get the all-call."

Dear Lord, what about my Lucy?

CHARLOTTE

I should have said no to that cursed meeting at Sunset Academy. I should have prioritized my family over being sucked dry by my philanthropic commitments, but that would have meant giving up on my bid for PTA president. Something I'd worked toward for four thankless years, and now that it was my turn, it was in jeopardy because Sally Come Lately had decided to give it a whirl.

The afternoon carpool had agreed to take Axel to Beach Middle on Monday so I could be on time to the Sunset meeting. It feels monstrous now, but I was relieved to not be the one to send him off to school after the weekend's blowout. I could barely look him in the eye on our rare encounters the day before.

"Text me when you walk in," I messaged Ax when I sat down in the Sunset cafeteria, waiting for the others to arrive.

No response. I kept checking my phone through Principal Garcia's painful preaching. "We need to make sure the Sunset Academy PTA is protected against any future inconsistencies."

Oh my god! The fucking euphemisms. *Inconsistencies.* Do you mean white-collar fraudsters? Let's just spit it out!

Checked my phone again. It was 9:07. That's seven minutes after the last morning bell at Beach Middle. *Why didn't I cancel the meeting and take him myself?*

Then Principal Garcia received an urgent page.

An emergency, Code Red at Beach Middle down the block, both schools locked down.

Melody flushed like a nun getting fingered. Clearly never heard of a Code Red back in quaint old Kansas. Gabriela spiraled. Asking absurd questions that Garcia obviously didn't have answers to.

One casualty we know about, the principal said. Gabriela demanded to know if there was an active shooter. A *casualty*? Lockdowns were common, but usually because some homeless man made weird eyes at a kid through a fence, once because there was a robbery at the CVS down the road. But never because of actual violence at school. *Casualty?*

This was no ordinary Code Red, and like a cold shower I was jolted to an unthinkable chill. *I have two children who are potentially in danger.*

No response from Axel. *Oh my god*, I wondered, *could he have run into the shooter?*

Then, a darker thought. No. It was impossible.

Melody and Gabriela kept clucking like two hens in the roost, and my ears stopped registering words. Just clucks.

An announcement on the intercom buzzed like white noise. Something about the Code Red. *Stay in place.*

Stay in place? How much time had I already wasted?

I have to go.

I'm not even sure if I said it out loud, or if it was the voice of God appearing to me saying *GO*. But something lifted me out of the cheap chair and threw me out the door, away from the cafeteria, running. Past the front office, shouts behind me: *Stop! Get inside!*

Feet slipping in four-inch stilettos, but my legs were faithful, automatic. The security guard, Derek, was posted at the gate, walkie-talkie in hand.

"Mrs. Giordani, I have to ask you to get back . . ."

I flung my body into the gate, opening the door. It was locked only from the outside. Who on earth would be trying to leave in a Code Red? Derek made a half-hearted attempt to grab my arm, but quickly recoiled.

"Mrs. Giordani!" he said once more, but all I could hear was the white noise in my head. A throbbing, whooshing noise.

My legs hadn't stopped. I rounded the south side of Sunset Academy and sprinted across the street toward the fenced-in PE field at Beach Middle. I was vaguely aware of a sharp pain in my right ankle, but a single thought broke through the noise and wrapped my guts in a vise. *What if it's too late? My baby.*

It was my fault. I had been warned, more than once. I had thought, if I just willed him better, maybe Ax would be okay. *Please fucking God, let Ax be okay.*

I could hear the sirens multiplying, red and blue flashes approaching as I neared the corner and pivoted east. Police cars and ambulances lined the street, but no crime scene.

The officers didn't seem to notice as I flew by the first line of cars, rounding the next corner and sprinting to the front gate. The ambulances and police sirens were now deafening, drowning out even the white noise in my brain.

Then I saw the lines of caution tape in front of the Walker Auditorium. Huddles of officers, a gurney being erected, Principal Nelson walking back and forth, phone attached to her ear.

"Ma'am!" an officer called to me from the street. I realized that they would never let me through the gate. But they couldn't keep me out.

I stopped short and made a beeline to the fence, which was my only opportunity. I scaled the chain-link in leaps. Finally kicking off my murderous heels. In four or five pulls, I was over the top and jumped straight down to the waiting grass. I was on campus grounds.

Shouts came from all around, but my body didn't hesitate. Barefoot, I was more agile than before. I pumped my legs extra hard and within moments had pushed through to the tape, elbowing two officers to throw my body onto the crime scene in front of me.

And there it was. The body. Don Walker.

DARCY

The Walker Auditorium at Miami Beach Middle was a multimillion-dollar project and had been primarily funded by Donald and Patricia's Walker Family Foundation. Naming rights don't come cheap in Miami, and a legacy building at one of the largest public schools in the "right" part of town is a great way to prove your value. Especially if you don't actually have any.

On that fateful day in May, no doubt burdened with the collapse of his empire, marriage, and public standing, Don Walker had joined the throes of backpacked middle schoolers entering the campus grounds, perhaps blending in like a teacher or administrator. According to security footage, he had headed straight for the Walker Auditorium, let himself inside, climbed the inner staircase to the fourth floor, and let himself outside to the patio. From there, he climbed onto the roof and stood at the edge.

How long did it take for someone to notice, five seconds or five minutes? Eventually one student spotted him, and the word spread until it became a spectacle of points and gasps. Is that what he wanted? No doubt, the police were already on the way since he broke his house arrest.

Principal Nelson was radioed, and she locked down the campus without hesitation. All students were shuffled inside and the gates were secured. With the innocent eyes averted, Miami Beach PD sent up their best negotiator, and that person made it one step onto the roof before Donald Walker took a swan dive to his death on the cold concrete below.

Could I have guessed from our meeting the week before that he was a man on the edge? No pun intended. I can't get the thought out of my head. That perhaps I had intuited something and *ignored* it. Unhinged, yes. In dire straits, absolutely. But he seemed to still be grasping very tight to the belief that somehow, someway, someone would snap their fingers and he'd be back in the sparkling pink glass house with the gorgeous wife and the adoring community.

It's a sordid tale that was all too "made for Miami." Fake it till you make it, till you break it, and disappear.

And it was sad. Sad, because he had been a man proven so fragile that he couldn't stand to even look in the mirror. And sadder still because he left behind two innocent sons, with the added gift of deepest childhood trauma.

I heard that Charlotte Giordani had a complete meltdown when she heard and stormed the Beach Middle gates, barefoot and with her top unbuttoned, to glimpse her alleged lover's lifeless body. And when she saw him? They say she started laughing uncontrollably. I always said she was a sociopath.

Sunset Academy also went into lockdown. Every classroom barred its door: no one in; no one out, for a full ninety minutes. I heard that one kindergartner wet himself while waiting. I wonder what that child's parent said to him or her that night at home, after he/she probably spent the rest of the day in some crusty lost-and-found pair of pants from the front office.

How many people have had their days, their weeks, their lives, blown over by the Don Walker tsunami? Of course, he won't be there to watch everyone try to pick up the pieces. Or answer some questions for his boys when they're grown and the therapy leads them to have an open conversation about the father who so spectacularly let them down.

I've seen more than my share of deadbeat dads, but wow. Walker puts Darth Vader to shame.

No one has heard from Patricia, or at least no one is admitting to it. She's probably changed her name to Phoebe Williams and taken up residence in California. As far from familiar faces as she can get. She'll swear off plastic straws once and for all, and buy her groceries only at Erewhon. She'll marry a tech guy instead of a finance guy and have two more children and live in an eco-friendly home.

The hottest debate in town is: Did she know? Of course she fucking knew. That's my humble opinion anyway. How could she not? Patricia never struck me as particularly ignorant, or particularly anything, as she so rarely spoke (to me at least). But she doesn't just have air between her ears, and in hindsight the whole charade is just so plainly obvious.

Irritatingly, just about everyone is now claiming that they *always knew something was off* with the Walkers' fortune. Well, if everyone knew, why didn't anyone *say it*? Why didn't I?

MELODY

We stayed locked down in the cafeteria for about an hour and a half, Gabriela and me. Just long enough to go nose blind to the stale peas and carrots.

The ever-dutiful lunch ladies were there the whole time, seemingly unfazed, chatting with one another while clinking chafing dishes into place and arranging neat lines of apple juice and milk boxes.

Gabriela worked the phone, texting and calling contacts at the police, city hall, her husband. Finally, an off-duty detective told her that the situation had been *contained*, and no students had been injured. Beyond that, he couldn't comment.

It was enough to settle our nerves though, and we slid into easy conversation, sharing our life stories like two girlfriends having coffee.

Gabriela's parents were small children when they came to the United States, part of the first wave of Cuban immigrants in the early sixties. These "golden exiles," I learned, were wealthy and highly educated. And they were terrified of the new leader Fidel Castro, and everything he had already taken from them.

Her grandparents had been doctors in their home country and were not willing to see their private practice seized by the Cuban government. So they gave up everything they had, every cent, to come to the United States in search of a better future for their children. At first, Gabriela's grandmother had to clean houses and her grandfather worked for a landscaper. Eventually, they saved up enough money to open a restaurant, and then a pharmacy. Today, that pharmacy is the third largest in all of South Florida, behind CVS and Walmart. Fascinating. Her family truly embodies the American dream.

When the all-call was announced, the two of us raced into Principal Garcia's office for a download. I would have been hesitant to impose myself, knowing Garcia must have a lot to do following the dramatic incident, but Gabriela marched on in and I followed. That's when we learned about the suicide at Miami Beach Middle. So very tragic. Don Walker had jumped from the top of the brand-new performing arts center, the one he'd spent all that stolen money on to name. Garcia delivered the news with the stoic resolve of a monk. As if it was something that happened all the time.

It was chilling. I'd met the man and, though I had no special fondness for him, it was hard to imagine him *dead*. Ceasing to exist. Staging his own public execution, and at a school no less. What kind of place was this? It was sickening, difficult to reconcile.

I later learned that when Charlotte bolted from us in the cafeteria, she was racing to Beach Middle, probably to check on her son. But I have no idea. Did she also know something about Don? Everyone wanted to know if it was a lovers' quarrel, on top of the fraud allegations, that sent him over the edge. I had started to believe that the affair rumors were false, after I had made the terrible mistake of repeating them. But now . . .

The next week I received an email from Charlotte.

May 31, 2019
From: Charlotte Giordani
To: Melody Howard, Gabriela Machado
CC: Ileana Garcia
Subject: Sunset Academy PTA

Principal Garcia, Gabriela, Melody:
I hope you are all well and beginning to settle after the tragic event that occurred at Miami Beach Middle.

Serving on the Sunset Academy PTA has been a privilege and an honor, and not one that I take lightly. That is why I must respectfully rescind my candidacy for PTA president.

Recent developments have shown me that I need to spend more time on personal affairs, and I will not have the emotional or physical availability to meet the demands of the presidential role. I will remain involved in my daughter's classroom and would love to volunteer for events as needed.

Good luck to you all in your future PTA endeavors, and I am sure we will be in touch. Go Sunset Seagulls.

Best regards,

Charlotte

Picking up the pieces after her lover's death, perhaps? I mean, that's what some people thought and maybe that's partly my fault. I wasn't even so sure anymore if the affair thing was true. But obviously something was fishy there, right? It was sad, and I felt more sympathy for her than maybe I should have. But I didn't send banana bread this time, I didn't even respond to the email. The whole thing just felt so dirty, and I didn't want to touch it.

Greg said something along the lines of "Congratulations, but please promise me that this role isn't going to change you." I told him he definitely had nothing to worry about there. I was nothing like those people and thank god for that.

I told Lucy that we might have to take a little break from the Madeluce sleepovers, just until the dust settled a little bit. The fire in her eyes when I said it could have set the whole house ablaze, but it had to be done. No more enabling parenting; I had to put my foot down. *We're not in Kansas, anymore.* If we are going to make it in Miami, unscathed, we are going to have to be more selective about with whom we socialize.

CHARLOTTE

I pushed through the line of officers and threw my body beyond the police tape like I was sliding into home base. Not breathing, I braced for the unthinkable.

Metallic tang on my tongue, vomit rising in the back of my throat; my ears were buzzing.

Then I saw the body, the tangled mess of it, the blood and the brains. But not my boy.

And I gasped so loud it was like scaring myself awake. The worst thing I've ever seen, the wrongness of it. It was gruesome and terrible, but it wasn't *my* boy. It wasn't Axel.

It was a grown man, who had made his own adult decisions that had brought him to that place on the concrete. Splattered. A tragic end to a deliberate life. It wasn't a child. It wasn't my boy.

I can't begin to describe the relief to you, but it felt like a second chance at life. It was like a gift, a puppy for your tenth birthday! It felt like joy. The kind I hadn't felt since . . . since they were born?

And it couldn't have been more inappropriate if I had stripped naked and sang "It's Raining Men," but I started laughing hysterically. Through snotty tears, I belly laughed so hard, I gasped for breath. You should have seen the look on their faces! The officers, the paramedics, Principal Nelson.

But they can all suck a fat one for all I care, because it wasn't my boy. He's still flesh and blood, and he might be hurting, but he's still *here* on this Earth. Breathing. And I've been given what I definitely don't deserve. Now I'm awake, and he's just a teenager, and I have *time*.

And what better gift is there in the world but time?

The first thing I did when I got back home was officially unenroll Axel from Miami Beach Middle.

JUDGE CAROL LAWSON

What is justice?

I couldn't describe it for you after years of law school, more than a decade of private practice, and four years on the bench. If you had asked me in my twenties, I'd probably have had an answer. But now, like Supreme Court Justice Stewart's infamous quote regarding obscenity, I can't define it, but *I know it when I see it.*

Was justice done in Miami in the case of Donald Walker? Miami and justice are too often at odds. This town is a haven where people come to avoid justice and taxes, to rebrand themselves.

We are the antithesis of justice.

Certainly, Walker's victims deserved reparations and that could happen only after exposing his crimes. So if those who had been swindled were repaid, and the criminal was punished, it would be just. No doubt, there were some invested who suspected a fix but were seduced by the returns. What would justice be for them?

Now Donald Walker is dead, and it could take years for the forensic accountants to untangle his sins. Maybe Patricia will be of some assistance, but probably not. And nobody can find her, anyway.

He needed to be exposed.

I made the phone call based on a hunch, called an old friend who prosecutes white-collar crimes and said, *Just look into it. Could be nothing*. But it was something. Donald Walker was found to be a fraud.

He was a narcissist and a bigot, and he stole money from friends and family, collapsed within himself, and now there are two children, in pain, without their father. Who should they blame for the apocalyptic fall from grace they've experienced in their young lives? Their own dad? Me? I can only hope that, in the long run, I did those kids a favor. Perhaps their wealth is gone (was it ever really theirs?), but at least they won't be raised by a criminal.

And Miami is exactly where it has always been. Once again, we witness the rise and fall of a corrupt benefactor. But don't worry. There will be another one right behind him, more generous and more corrupt. Everyone will forget about Don and Patricia Walker. The city will move on to the shiny new glamorous person. And on and on the wheel will spin.

There's one question I may never be able to answer for myself. Do I have blood on my hands? I might. But if so, I can live with that. And maybe Miami will be a little bit of a better place because of it.

MELODY

THE DAY OF THE PTA ELECTION

From: Melody Howard
June 5, 2019
To: Sunset Academy Parents, Sunset Academy Staff
CC: Ileana Garcia
Subject: Your new PTA President

Dear Sunset Academy families and staff,
It is an honor to introduce myself as your new PTA president for the 2019–2020 and 2020–2021 school years!

Over the past year, my family and I have been fortunate enough to become a part of the Sunset community and I can tell you firsthand that the experience has been wonderful. The parents and staff at our school are so warm and welcoming and are all invested in providing the best education and environment for our precious children.

My daughter, Lucy, will be entering the fourth grade this year, and she and I both hope to get to meet you all around campus.

I have lots of exciting things in store for our kiddos, and a little fun for us adults, too. Keep an eye out for updates—we will be kicking up our family mixers and fundraising parties to a new level this year!

Please feel free to drop me a note to say hi. In the meantime, have a great summer, and Go Sunset Seagulls!

Warm regards,
Melody Howard
PTA President

CHARLOTTE

FIVE MONTHS AFTER THE PTA ELECTION

Did you hear that they're trying to sell Villa Rosé for $28 million? You can't make this stuff up. Rumor has it that the real estate agents found quite a mess in the wine cellar.

Whatever. I don't have time for that business anymore. Tonight is Ax's first group show at ASH, the Arts & Science High School. He's the only freshman showing a painting! Of course, I offered to plan the event. One must always be willing to use one's talents for good!

*** HOT NEW LISTING***

1800 Peacock Drive - Villa Rosé
Bayfront Masterpiece on highly sought-after Peacock Island
10,000 Square Feet of living space/300 feet of open bay

Expertly built in 2019, no detail has been spared in this modern masterpiece. This exquisite home features eight bedrooms and twelve bathrooms, a brand-new luxury kitchen, hidden catering kitchen, separate guesthouse, and Olympic-size outdoor pool. Enjoy breathtaking sunsets from the bay in the comfort of your own backyard. Constructed in all hurricane-proof floor-to-ceiling rose-colored glass, this home is one of a kind and priced to sell.

Asking $28 million
For More Information, contact: Karly Weber, The Weber Group
1-800-WEBERGP
KWeber@thewebergroup.com
WWW.TheWeberGroup.com

ACKNOWLEDGMENTS

This book was a ton of fun to write, and while many of the themes here are representations of how I see Miami, I must take a moment to praise the dedicated and talented teachers, administrators, and PTA at my children's Miami-Dade County public school. I can't think of a more difficult or important job, and I salute you. Thank you for all you do.

If anyone reading this is an aspiring novelist, I highly suggest that you seek out an opportunity to workshop with Jennifer Close. I've done it multiple times, continue to do it, and can honestly say that this book would never have been published without her guidance. Thank you, Jennifer. Times a million.

Thank you to my dream agent, Helen Heller, whom I was almost too intimidated to query. I'm so glad I did. You immediately saw potential in this manuscript and had a clear vision for how to make it better. To my editor, Rachel Kahan, I'm still pinching myself at the opportunity to work with you. Thank you for understanding what I was trying to do with this book, and for helping me make it better. Reading your editorial note was one of the most exciting moments of this process.

The team at William Morrow is world class and I am in awe of what they do. Ariana Sinclair, thank you for holding my hand and making this process (at which I am a total newbie) painless and fun. I am also grateful to Rita Madrigal, Stephanie Vallejo, Olivia Lo Sardo, Kelly Cronin, and Jen McQuire for bringing this book to life.

Isabelle Felix, your sensitivity read was thoughtful and brilliant and helped me improve this manuscript in a way I never could have done on my own. And I still smile thinking about your flair for memes as line edits.

It takes a writing village to put a story out into the world, and I am fortunate to have a wonderful one. Thank you to my "OG" workshop crew: Brigid Hogan, Kari Pilgrim, Valli Porter, and Alison Williams. You are all better writers than I, and I am so lucky to share work with you. To the brilliant Catie Stewart, thank you for reading every half-baked idea I come up with and for answering my panicked text messages. May we forever stress over our manuscripts together. I am also immensely grateful to the other writers I workshopped *Pink Glass Houses* with, including: Mayuri Chandra, Eileen Connors, Kati Eisenhuth, Cliff Jacobs, Michael Mayer, Kim Parker, and Monica Villavicencio.

Thank you (and RIP) to the Catapult writing classes, which were invaluable to my drafting process for this book. Moriel Rothman-Zecher and Blair Hurley, you were both incredibly helpful in guiding me to the right voice and tone for this manuscript, and also your classes were so much fun.

A real friend is always there for you. A superhuman friend will read your three-hundred-page early draft and provide feedback. Thank you to my ride-or-die friends and early readers: Kirsten Vogel, Amy Stojanovic, Jessica Lurie, Kiki Sheets, Tracy Slavens, Alejandra Pimienta, David Anderson (love you, Dad), Batsheva Levy, Divi Greisman, Kristen Scorza, Leslie Wiener, and Robert Starke.

If you're lucky, the owner of the best independent bookshop in town will also read your first draft, cheer you on, and celebrate with you when your manuscript sells. Mitchell Kaplan, thank you for your friendship, mentorship, and for giving South Floridians a space to read, sip very good coffee, and think freely for more than forty years. Books & Books is an institution. You are a legend.

And finally, to my family, thank you for your unconditional love, support, and stubborn belief in me. India and JJ, my two amazing children, have declared this "the best book in the world." Unfortunately, they won't be writing the reviews. Jamie Elias, you were my devoted husband while I wrote this manuscript and have become the world's best ex-husband by the time of publication. Thank you for encouraging me, even when it was difficult. Thank you for deciding that we get to make the rules, together.

ABOUT THE AUTHOR

ASHA ELIAS lives in Miami Beach with her two children, two dogs, and two rabbits. She studied journalism at the University of Miami. *Pink Glass Houses* is her debut novel.